The Other Side

of

Impact

A Novel

by

David Thomas Dozier

2015 © David Thomas Dozier

ISBN0692511245
ISBN-13: 978-0692511244

FIC039000 FICTION/Visionary & Metaphysical

Published by
Dozier Web Publishing

Printed in the United States of America
by
CreateSpace, An Amazon.com Company

for all the characters who have chosen me to tell their stories

and especially

for Marie and Bryan

Author's Note

This book is a work of fiction. All characters and events are imaginings of the author. Any similarity to real people or events is coincidental. While geographic locations may be real, fictional events occurring in those venues did not take place as depicted.

Quoted material used as sectional headings belong to their authors.

Meetings of the FAA and NTSB as depicted in the story did not occur. Any references to transcripts, dialog and reports of agencies mentioned are fictional.

Airplane disasters, although disturbing, have always fascinated me. Beginning with United 93 during 911 and its horrific impact in a field near Shanksville, Pennsylvania and many ensuing air disasters, including the recent Germanwings flight that was consumed by a mountain in the Alps, catastrophes of this kind always lead to more questions than answers. Through months and in some cases years of investigation we are left with plausible causes pointing to mechanic failures, pilot error or intent, but of course we will never know precisely all of the contributing factors that coalesce to bring a plane down.

The idea for the book began when I was watching news coverage of heart-stricken survivors striving for explanations from airline officials during a recent air disaster. Their fear, anguish, anger and search for hope had a profound effect on me. I think as many of us do following fatal accidents, I began to entertain those *what if* questions. *What if that passenger hadn't boarded the plane? What if the pilots had reacted differently? What if one change in circumstance could have affected the course of a doomed flight?*

And more profoundly, *what happens to the collective energy of a hundred souls when sudden death occurs* upon catastrophic impact? *What is on the other side?*

It is to the survivors, those who are left behind, that this work is dedicated.

D.T.D
July 16 2015

Introduction

Golden Airways flight 100 with one hundred passengers and five crew members aboard, flying from San Francisco to Denver, nose-dives into a Colorado mountainside at 500 mph, obliterating all but a few small pieces of wreckage. No human remains are discovered.

The Other Side of Impact is a story of many personal lives: the passengers aboard the doomed flight, crew members, air traffic controllers, recovery teams, members of the FAA and the NTSB and the many loved ones left behind, emotionally stranded by this horrific accident.

What happens during instant death? Does the energy of consciousness simply evaporate or does it transform and continue on to some other level of presence? Is death an instant finality as most atheists and agnostics proclaim or is the vitality of life inextinguishable, more than just one consciousness, extending beyond what most minds can comprehend?

Ethan Andrews, an ex-priest, and his flying companion Jessica Gibson take us into their lives and the many *consequential* lives affected by the air disaster. The experiences are real and seem grounded in reality; other times the mystery of metaphysical awareness suspends that sense of realness and forces us to see beyond, into a universe of alternate possibilities.

The Other Side of Impact is a fast-paced narrative, a thriller at times, a mystery, a spiritual adventure and a drama of human suffering, hope and love. The possibilities it raises are both inspiring and surreal, and grounded in the causality of human drama and irony.

Prologue

Boy and horse were one, from a distance where Billy stood, a slowly-receding form against the dazzling landscape of deep snow and carved morning shadows.

They were half a mile away and making slow progress due to the overnight snowfall, the chestnut Buffalo mare trudging precariously on the narrow trail leading north through the Gunnison National Forest.

This was the boy's first solo excursion to Uncompahgre Peak, the highest elevation in the national forest.

Billy figured it would take the boy three hours to reach the base of the summit and then another two to ascend three quarters way up the peak. He expected the boy to return by evening if the snow let up, which it was predicted to do by early afternoon. Even if the snow continued, he knew that his young son would be fine. He had taught him everything he knew about horses and trail-walking and how to survive in the worst kinds of weather.

At ten years of age, the boy felt fearless atop the chestnut mare, a horse he'd named *Noohkweet*, which meant *river* in the Ute dialect, because of its flowing mane and glistening flanks.

He'd looked back only one time to wave to his father and now, an hour into the trek, he felt truly on his own, released like an eagle from his father's perch.

While he knew that he was making his father proud, the boy had his own reason for making this trip to Uncompahgre Peak.

It had come to him in a dream. He was to serve as witness to a spectacular event, a revelation that would bring him great wisdom and maturity. He didn't know what it meant specifically but felt privileged that he among all others in the reservation had been chosen for the mission.

The boy knew the national forest was closed because of the heavy snow and the uncleared trails, but he plodded on, carefully watching the mare's footing as it tested each step in the deep snow. Sometimes he was forced to dismount and trudge ahead through the deep sections, stomping a trail for the horse. He had known of many cases where horses had fractured their forelegs when twisting knee-deep in snow and ice.

An hour later the boy was forced to take a break. His horse was sweating heavily, its flanks warm beneath the steamy coat of melting snow.

The snow was blowing wildly, sometimes from all sides as sudden gusts of wind swept up over the canyon ridge. Where banks of crusted snow lay on the edge of the trail, sloped like pigmy mountains, the boy knew a sudden slip in that direction would prove fatal for both horse and rider.

They took cover beneath a spreading ponderosa pine, its laden branches providing some shelter from the swirling snow. The boy wiped down the horse, its flanks now quivering from both exhaustion and the cold wind. He poured his canteen into a small trough cup and encouraged the horse to drink. The boy himself was neither thirsty nor hungry but he forced himself to drink from the canteen.

They rested for twenty minutes and then the boy mounted the horse again, proceeded north along the narrow trail. They came upon clearings where the wind had sculptured shallow valleys and mesas in the snow, some where the pine trail was visible, others where rocky plateaus emerged from the snow.

The horse shook his mane and, sensing the firm ground beneath, attempted to trot, but the boy held firm on the reins.

"Not now, Noohkweet. You must keep your pace," the boy spoke to the horse. And the horse seemed to understand, bowing its head until his rider let up on the reins.

In two hours they reached the base of Uncompahgre Peak, where lakes of snow blown by the wind lay like patchwork across the broken trail. The mountain rose above them, jagged and black and mottled with vast capes of crusted snow.

The wind was unremitting and probably worse at the crest. The boy's face stung as if whipped with pine needles, and his hands deep inside his bearskin gloves ached from the cold.

He looked up at the crest of the mountain. Driven by icy gusts, the snow blurred against the granite sky.

The boy looked at his watch. Despite the harsh weather, they had made good time since leaving the reservation. They would rest here at the base until they'd warmed up and then begin the ascent, which would only take them to the narrow plateau halfway up the mountain. From there the boy would follow the gorge between the peaks to a spot where he could imagine the great plains stretching through Colorado to Kansas and beyond, eventually spreading to the Appalachian Mountains in the east.

Ancient tradition held that the great Ute creator *Senawahv* would rest at the crest of Uncompahgre Peak and survey the land he had created for all animals and plants and foods of his kingdom. It had lost its sacred meaning through the centuries, although the boy felt that the creator's spirit still rested there.

They began their ascent, the boy in the mare's saddle with a firm grip on the reins. Both the rocks and the snow were slippery, and it was important that they moved in a zigzag fashion, several steps up and then stopping horizontal to the mountain to pause. A direct ascent was impossible, and though for the horse this approach was instinctual, it was essential that it follow the boy's lead.

The method was time-consuming and at times made the horse restless, causing it to snort and shake its mane with impatience. The boy leaned forward in his saddle and continue to speak with the mare, raking his fingers through its thick mane and rubbing gently at its neck. Slowly but surely, boy and horse edged up the mountain.

Against the turbulence of gray clouds, the summit looked like a towering monument, an edifice left by the gods. It did not scare the boy but unnerved the mare, which tossed its head and neighed in protest.

When they reached the canyon gorge the wind changed direction and swept around through the pass in sudden erratic gusts. The mare stumbled and then froze, moments later jockeying for safe footing as the boy let out the reins.

Not wanting to have the mare risk a fall, the boy dismounted and led the animal up the steep, snow-filled incline. Slowly, step by step, they reached a point where the ascent became unnavigable because of the steep incline and the ice-coated rock.

"Noohkweet, you must stay here," the boy spoke to the horse. It shook its head and whinnied as if understanding the boy's command.

Climbing up one side of the rocky crevasse, the boy glanced down at the horse and then leaned back against the rising black wall supporting his body.

He closed his eyes and could hear only the scream of the wind and the sound of pelting snow against the hood of his bear-skin jacket. He felt this to be the place. It was here that the truth would be revealed to him. He was to bear witness to this truth. And he felt proud.

The belly of the beast cast a frightening shadow as it advanced and swept over the boy and horse, soundless, incomprehensible, a dragon's colossal imprint.

The boy dropped to his knees. He saw its huge silver wings and its long belly and then followed the descent of the beast until, in a furious implosion and a nearly instant consumption of all sound and image, it was gone, swallowed by the cold granite wall of the nearby mountain.

PART ONE

"In three words I can sum up everything I've learned about life: it goes on."
— Robert Frost

Chapter One

Upon disembarking Golden Airways flight 100 from San Francisco to Denver, all passengers and crew aboard the flight were led to a waiting lounge at the airport, where they were asked to remain until airport officials released them.

Some were in varying states of impatience and confusion about the summary delay. People had connecting flights to make, others were waiting to return to their families and loved ones. There were three weeks left until Christmas and many had decided to take advantage of early season plane fares.

In the chairs in the front of the room members of a rowdy group of businessmen on their way to a conference were clearly impatient and effectively making it known to others in the room.

Ethan Andrews had it figured out. At least he thought so. He had experienced delays many times during his tours in Africa. In light of the recent Ebola crisis and its appearance in the US, airport officials and the TSA were on edge and being especially vigilant.

It seemed a plausible explanation. One of the young passengers aboard the plane had been sick with a high temperature for most of the flight and had been whisked away by a waiting ambulance on the tarmac as soon as the plane landed.

Ethan reasoned that the delay was based on a temporary quarantine. Perhaps they were waiting for the results of the girl's blood tests at the hospital before letting anyone leave the room.

Even more convincing was the fact that they'd all been asked to seat themselves in numbered chairs according to their exact seating positions aboard the plane. They obviously wanted to know each passenger's proximity to the infected girl.

They had been waiting in the lounge for over half an hour now. Coffee and donuts had been made available on a long conference table covered with a white plastic tablecloth.

Ethan expected nurses to arrive and test the temperatures of passengers, along with TSA individuals who would check on the primary origin of passenger travel. He had built a tolerance for such delays. His missionary work had taken him in and out of foreign airports where protracted layovers were common. He had missed connecting flights on many occasions in frenzied African airports that made punctual travel more a matter of luck than custom.

The flight had been an uneventful save for the young passenger's illness. Moderate turbulence had caused the Boeing 737 pilots to adjust their flight plan to a more southerly route across the San Juan Mountains before descending into a holding pattern over Denver International Airport.

Ethan turned to his flying companion and explained his reasoning for the unusual delay. She appeared a little less tolerant about the holdover. She had been trying to contact someone on her cell but was unsuccessful, probably due to the poor coverage in the airport.

"If that's the case," Jessica Gibson said, "then they should announce the reason and not leave us all in the dark."

"You're right," Ethan began but was interrupted by two Benedictine nuns who approached from behind.

"Father," said one of the nuns, peering out of her white coif, her face a convivial oval. "Do you know why we're being delayed?"

"Oh, I'm sorry. I'm not a member of the clergy anymore," Ethan explained and then shared his theory with the sisters.

One of the nuns looked offended. "Then why do you wear your clerical collar?"

Ethan quickly removed the collar and shoved it in his jacket pocket. He took their hands. "Remember that patience, sisters, is a virtue and sometimes a harbinger of better things to come."

The elderly nun looked puzzled by the ex-priest's statement. She might have queried him further but instead squeezed his hand. "In God's kingdom there is a reason for everything," she finally said.

As soon as the nuns returned to their seats, Ethan gave Jessica a mischievous grin and quickly replaced the collar.

"There's something sacrilegious about that," Jessica said. "Why do you still wear it?"

"It gives me certain privileges," Ethan said.

"Like what?"

"Well, in one way it's like a handicap parking permit. I get doors opened for me and cashiers asking me if I need help with grocery bags. People are always bowing their heads. Sometimes, if I'm lucky, I get free movie tickets and discounts at stores."

"Good grief."

"To be honest with you," Ethan said, "it's just hard to part with it...my last vestige of priesthood. I know I shouldn't have boarded the plane with it on. Most of the time I really don't wear it."

A brief sound of static filled the room coming from the two large ceiling speakers in the front section of the lounge. It alerted everyone that an announcement was about to be made. People perked up and seemed eager to find out when they would be allowed to leave the room.

They were all disappointed.

◆

Jessica tried to relax in the hard-backed folding chair, the kind used at card tables, but found it very uncomfortable. She repositioned herself several times before turning and looking out the long paneled window. She remembered how snow seemed so exciting when she was a kid, how she looked forward to days off from school, sledding all day, her mother's hot chocolate and that wonderful sense at the end of the day that all of it had been a special adventure.

Sometimes, usually from a hotel window, she could look down upon and reconnect with the more sublime aspects of a freshly-fallen snow, the cottony silence, the smooth sculptures of trees, sign posts, and amorphous mounds that only hinted at the shapes of their frozen captives. Snow back then had a cleansing effect.

Now as a business woman working for an international advertising firm, nearing the coveted status of frequent flyer, Jessica viewed snow as a true four letter word. It meant delays, and sometimes missing connecting flights. Snow storms meant long waits for cabs, rude drivers and trudging through icy slush to check into a hotel.

This time there were no connecting flights to worry about, no hotels to scramble for, no meetings, no urgency other than to find her car in the long-term parking area and drive home to her house in the Lakewood area of Denver.

It was a Thursday, well after noon now since the half hour delay began. The false alert from the speakers seemed to have a deflating effect on just about everyone in the lounge. Young people scooted down in the seats, their legs stretched out to the side or under the seats of chairs in front of them. Some threw their head backs, their ear pod cords dangling, trying to make use of the delay by catching a nap, or a faraway adventure.

Jessica's thoughts were racing. Free time was not something she was accustomed to, at least not extemporaneous ones.

Earlier that morning in San Francisco she had almost missed the flight. She had slept through her alarm at the hotel, was held up checking out of the room and then had to wait twenty minutes for the taxi to arrive. The driver, a garrulous expatriate from Jamaica more accustomed to showing tourists around, drove with his head turned sideways, engaged in unremitting monologue. He obviously loved the *City by the Bay*.

She had made it to the airport with only fifteen minutes to spare. But the airlines had overbooked and she was placed on standby. As she was leaving the gate to await the next departure, an agent informed her of available seats.

Her lucky day.

The business trip, a western conference of the Executive Advertising Association, was largely a social event and hadn't been the most stimulating conference Jessica had ever attended. The downtime had given her time to dwell on her failed marriage and the impending divorce. She and Allen had been separated for over a year, her ex taking his damn time to finalize the divorce papers.

The money divide wouldn't be a problem: they both had investments and prosperous bank accounts. She didn't want the main house, satisfied with the large downtown condo for the time being. Their daughter Macy was still in college back east. Jessica liked to think that her daughter too had come to terms with her father's estrangement. He certainly wouldn't have won *Father of the Year* during her childhood.

Like Jessica, Macy had matured during those many years her father chose not to be around. She had tough skin and a strong will of her own. Like her mother.

Jessica just wanted the divorce to be final. She was tired of meeting with attorneys and settlement accountants and signing court petitions for this and that. Allen was wearing her down, and he and his attorneys probably knew that.

Christmas was only two weeks away. Macy would be arriving soon, and she just wanted to spend a cozy holiday with her. Just the two of them, although Jessica held a suspicion that Macy might ask if her boyfriend could come along. In fact, she was surprised that her daughter hadn't mentioned it yet.

Jessica, too, had invited an unexpected guest.

◆

Ethan watched Jessica, her face looking forward, a narrow, contemplative look in her eyes, her expression that of a student working out a complicated formula.

Until their meeting aboard the flight, Ethan had only shared his personal choice with one other person. His decision to leave the Church was not for lack of faith in God but for deeply-held feelings that papal infallibility and the concept of church divinity were doctrines he could no longer accept. His work with refugees had spoken to him otherwise. Working with people whose needs were far more urgent than papal dogma and clerical teachings seemed to be aligned with his own beliefs and practices.

He did not find himself alone. The hidden exodus of priests from the church was, no doubt, alarming to the Vatican, but it had been going on for decades now. It didn't bode well for the many parishes throughout the world that lacked priests altogether, many led by the laity themselves.

One of the most controversial and influential reasons for some priests was the issue of celibacy. For Ethan there seemed no practical and convincing reason for not allowing marriage among priests. He also believed that female priests should be allowed by the Vatican, finally shedding the thousands year-old prohibitive doctrine.

Ethan saw no reason, save for antiquated dogma, that he should not be allowed to marry. He thought it the more selfish of his rationales for transitioning from the priesthood, but nonetheless viewed female companionship as a personal decision, not one to be deprived by the Church.

Mainly through correspondence, he had developed a romantic friendship with a person who lived just west of Boulder. They had met in Zaire while working with local missionaries. Kathryn was a divorcee, a Catholic, and someone who shared the same values about faith and working with the underprivileged. She had a residential cabin south of the Rocky Mountain National Park, a hand-forged log structure made of stripped pine and cut stone sitting a mile from the nearest neighbor. She adored the privacy and isolation, and sharing her life with her large Belgian shepherd.

Kathryn had invited Ethan to spend several weeks at Christmas in the cabin, away from city life, the refugee front lines and the hassles of schedules and obligations. While he had visited several times before, he was especially looking forward to this visit in order to share with Kathryn his final decision. He was also anticipating the environmental solitude and long morning walks on the quiet mountain trails.

Ethan was going to miss his traveling companion. They had developed a relationship, somewhat more than casual, through conversation by sharing some of their personal lives with one another.

In the old days of commercial flights this was not uncommon. People dressed up and were courteous, as if flying back then was a privilege. Not so these times when passengers' conversations were usurped by private movie screens, laptops, smartphones and headsets, not to mention the ambient rudeness that seemed now an inevitable part of air travel.

Ethan Andrews watched the long window in the lounge clot with snow. Flakes coagulated at an alarming rate, soon forming huge amebic-like formations, elongating and joining others that moved across the fogged windowpane like ghostly creatures. The heavy-falling snow beyond could be seen as a cascade of whiteness against the blurry gunmetal sky.

He was interrupted by the static of the intercom and finally a voice.

"Ladies and gentlemen, thank you for your patience," the woman began. "In just a few short minutes someone will be joining you to explain what all this is about."

Chapter Two

C aptain Scott Anderson had boarded the Boeing 737-300 half an hour earlier than was his custom. There had been a maintenance hold for a front brake problem and he wanted to check the repairs out for himself.

The 300 was an older and highly dependable version of the highly successful 737 series, and had entered operation in the mid sixties. Over the years it had been refitted with new GE high bypass engines, a sophisticated Electronic Flight Instrumentation System, among other structural design improvements.

Scott loved the plane and had been flying the model for almost ten years. He had joined Golden Jet when the company had reorganized in the early 2000s. Every time he sat down in the captain's chair he marveled at the relative simplicity of the instrumentation panel and the cockpit's almost cozy feel. It was very different from the larger 747 and 757 planes he'd flown in earlier days.

It was a bright, clear morning in San Francisco but was already snowing moderately at the Denver airport, their intended destination. No adverse weather was predicted on the flight path, although he would be coming in high due to the slow-moving snow storm now choking the airport in the mile-high city.

Denver International wasn't the easiest airport to land at, although Scott had seen worse. Crosswinds there, one coming from the plains of eastern Colorado, Nebraska and Kansas, the other shooting off the Rocky Mountains to the west, could make approaches treacherous. When it was snowing, the challenge was even greater. But Scott was no stranger to the airport, having landed there more than fifty times just in the last three years.

He would be flying with a young first officer he had never flown with but who seemed to have a good reputation. All he knew of Ted Granger was that he had almost 700 hours of flight time and that he had been co-piloting Boeing 737s for two years. He was an ex-Air Force pilot who received his commercial license five years ago.

"Check...check," Scott repeated to the ground maintenance crew who was on an extension ladder and huddled inside the front landing gear compartment.

"Sticky deployment," the maintenance man said, his voice cracking through the captain's headset.

"Huh?"

"On the last flight the captain reported a jerking noise as the gear deployed."

"Fix it?"

"Debris on the cylinder. I think it's okay now."

"Thank you, *Doctor*," Scott said and signed off with the man.

He began the pre-flight checklist, calling out the instructions on the clipboard, this despite the fact that he would be repeating the procedure once the co-pilot arrived. Scott was a stickler for details and a purest when it came to aircraft safety.

The passengers would be boarding in twenty minutes. Save for the co-pilot, most members of the flight crew were already aboard. He imagined Stacy, his favorite flight attendant, in the galley preparing some hot coffee. More often than not, they found themselves sharing flights on these short-distant runs. As he did, her voice came over the intercom.

"Permission to come aboard," she said in the best Lauren Bacall voice she could muster.

Scott pushed one of the three buttons to unlock the reinforced cockpit door.

"Thank God I have one friend aboard," he said as the svelte flight attendant handed him a fresh-brewed cup of coffee.

Stacy leaned over and gave him a loose hug. "I think," she said, wiggling into the co-pilot's seat, "that a flight attendant should be assigned to the cockpit at all times, coffee brewer and all. It seems a bit silly to have to announce myself whenever you or your co-pilot needs my service."

"I agree. Back and neck rubs, along with the coffee, would be most welcomed even during these short flights." Scott laughed. "Cost would be prohibitive, and I'm sure the FAA would have something to say about lively behavior in the cockpit."

Pursuing her point, Stacy said, "Then there would be no need to open the cockpit door during the flight. I mean, it's a legitimate safety suggestion."

"Good luck. And by the way, how do you expect us to pee in a closed door scenario like that?"

"That's easy. Build a small restroom inside the cockpit."

"Good grief," Scott said, sighing. "I'm glad you don't run an airline. Were that to be happen, there would be no money left to pay the crew."

Stacy quickly exited her seat as the co-pilot opened the door and came inside.

"Ted Granger," the man said in a deep southern drawl, leaning over to shake Scott's hand as he wedged himself into his seat.

He appeared preoccupied for a few moments. He scribbled something on a notepad paper and then put it in his vest pocket.

"I hope that wasn't the cockpit code sequence," Scott said jokingly.

Granger smiled. "Just Lotto numbers. I play weekly."

He seemed oblivious of Stacy, who now was backing up to the door

"Play one for me," Scott laughed as he watched the co-pilot unlock the door for Stacy to exit.

Ted said, "I've heard they're socked in at Denver. I'm glad I brought a heavy jacket. Enough fuel for a long holding pattern?"

"Should be," Scott said.

They went through the formal checklist, this time the co-pilot reading from the clipboard.

"Check fuel/refuel."

"18,000 liters. Check."

"Set nav and com frequencies."

"Check."

"Controls and calibrate joystick."

"Check."

"Fuel systems."

"On."

When they got to the landing gear position check, Scott filled in the co-pilot on the maintenance fix and the problem reported by the previous crew.

By the time they reached the final items on the checklist, a male flight attendant announced to the pilots that passengers would be boarding, all one hundred and fifteen souls, including an infant, two children and a law enforcement officer and his prisoner on their way to the Englewood Federal Detention Facility.

"Almost a full house," Ted said, signing off on the checklist page. He handed it to Scott, who then meticulously reviewed it before signing it.

The muffled sounds of boarding passengers could be heard even through the thick door. Scott heard the baby crying and some lively-sounding voices as the frequent flyers took their seats in premium class.

Fifteen minutes later, Stacy's voice came over their headsets. "Crotch watch completed," she said, referring to the checking of passenger seatbelts. "Do I need to perform one up there, guys?"

"No, but check your own," Scott said banteringly. "Tower says we're good to roll in five minutes. We're number one in line."

As the pushback tractor slowly eased the 737 away from the gate, Scott Anderson assumed a relaxed but deeply serious demeanor. That appearance hadn't varied in the decades he had been flying commercial aircraft. He'd logged many thousands of flight hours and was considered by colleagues and many in the aviation industry to be a flawless pilot. He was aware that there was always the potential for failures, both mechanical and those due to pilot error. He also knew that few accidents were the result of one isolated cause but rather a series of mounting failures. His attention to even the most benign irregularities during flight would draw a concern in his mind. While Crew Resource Management was the standard in commercial aviation these days, a policy encouraging input from all crew members aboard, Scott flew his own plane. He utilized input wisely and scrupulously. This was especially true when it came to young and relatively-inexperienced copilots.

The early morning sun exploded into view as they turned out of the shadow of the terminal and headed on their own power towards takeoff runway 1R. As they turned into position on the runway, the brilliant sunlight poured through the co-pilot's window, casting the first officer's profile in hard silhouette.

It was one of the few times Captain Anderson had flown out of San Francisco Airport with little traffic and a clear from the tower for immediate takeoff.

It was going to be a good, short flight.

Frist Officer Granger called out the takeoff checklist, testing and setting the flaps and ailerons.

"Set for takeoff," he said, looking over at the captain. He wore a pair of aviation sun glasses probably left over from his days in the Air Force, the large gold-rimmed kind that reflected like mirrors. He took his hands off the stick and sat back in his chair.

The engines roared to life and began to accelerate the plane down the runway.

"V1," the co-pilot called out, seconds later adding, "V2," watching the captain deftly pull back on the yolk as the plane lifted from the runway.

The morning was bright, the sky a rarified blue, and there was nothing ahead but an easy four-hour flight, with only a snow storm to weather before landing at Denver.

◆

Ethan Andrews had taken his seat in 24F but not before offering his assigned window seat to the passenger in the aisle seat. She took him up on his offer and thanked him. Thankfully, no one occupied the center seat.

Now, feeling the thrust of the engines lift the plane off the runway, Ethan, former parish priest, now returning from his last aid mission to the massing refugees on the Syrian and Turkish borders, bore a temperament of both satisfaction with his life's work and a nagging uncertainty of what lay ahead. He had already made his decision about the priesthood but knew that an affair of the heart was next on his list.

When the plane leveled off he closed his eyes, hoping flight slumber would ease the many hours of sleeplessness during the past several days. He adjusted the seatback and attempted to fully relax. He heard the message from the flight attendant that seatbelts could be unfastened, but he took no effort to do so.

Ethan opened his eyes to the sound of a serving cart being shuttled down the main aisle. He was asked by the flight attendant if he wished to purchase a snack or drink. He smiled at the attractive middle-aged woman and then asked for ginger ale. She said that she would have to check in the back to see if they had any and would return as soon as she finished serving the passengers in her section.

"May I have a ginger ale too?" the young woman seated to his right said and then smiled politely, if not reverently, at Ethan.

"Father, I haven't had a ginger ale since I was a child," she said. "When I heard you ask for it, the full taste came to my mouth, you know, the tiny popping sensations and that wonderful ginger taste."

"Ethan Andrews," he said warmly.

"Shouldn't I call you Father Andrews?"

"You know, I haven't been addressed that way since I worked as a parish priest. "I forgot that I was wearing this," he added, unsnapping the white plastic neck collar and placing it in his pocket.

"You just defrocked yourself," the young woman laughed. "I'm sorry," she added quickly, thinking her comment might be out of order. "My name is Jessica Gibson."

"Good to meet you, Jessica Gibson. You look like a business woman who doesn't wish to be seated in business class."

"Ah, a clairvoyant priest."

"Am I right?"

"Mainly so," Jessica said. "It's not worth the extra money and, to be truthful, I can't put up with all that business chatter, most of it from men."

Ethan was going to ask her if she had upcoming business in Denver but checked himself in time. The question would have been a little too personal after only a five-minute acquaintanceship.

The flight attendant returned and apologized for not having found the ginger ale. She offered them Diet Sprite instead. Ethan said that would be fine.

Jessica looked over at Ethan with a slightly deflated look on her face and said to the flight attendant, "My taste buds are already primed for ginger ale...but Sprite will be fine. Thank you."

Just after being served their drinks, the captain spoke over the intercom. He introduced himself and his co-pilot and reported the altitude and speed of the plane. He explained that there might be a holding delay at Denver due to the weather, ending cleverly by asking if everyone had brought along their skis.

Ethan noticed that his flying companion had opened a book and appeared seriously engrossed in her reading. He found the copy of *The Guardian* attached with other papers in the folder on his lap. The title of the article was *The Momentum of Faith*, an interesting piece written by a well-known Jesuit priest at Fordham. He had started the article in the boarding lounge and was eager to follow the intellectual treatise.

Captain Anderson looked out his port window and, as they banked towards an easterly course, saw the lush Sacramento valley populated by colorful patches of vineyards and vegetable farms stretching out towards the base of the Sacramento Mountains.

They were flying at 22,000 feet, just cleared for that altitude by the Stockton tower. They would gradually ascend to their maximum cruising altitude of 37,000 feet as they flew towards their next checkpoint at Salt Lake City.

The outside temperature was a minus fourteen degrees Fahrenheit and would fall to minus 67 degrees at cruising altitude. Inside the cockpit and the passenger compartments it was a comfortable 68 degrees.

Both the captain and co-pilot had taken off their jackets. Captain Anderson had been forced to put on his sunglasses due to the blinding sun. He didn't like them because he often had to remove them to get a clear view the instrument panels. He didn't wear eyeglasses but he knew the inevitable was coming at his next medical review. Even if they weren't required at that testing, he planned to purchase a set. Impaired vision had a way of encroaching, often with merely subtle changes. Anderson was not one to let anything affect his flying abilities. Better to be safe than not.

He was looking forward to a 48 hour layover in Denver, compulsory rest required by the FAA because he'd been forced to exceed his flying time during the last twenty four hours. He hoped to relax, as well as get in some badly need exercise. The hotel near the airport had an indoor swimming pool and an expansive workout room.

Scott's wife and two young daughters were back in Santa Monica. He also had children from his former marriage. They both had graduated from Pepperdine University and were well on their ways towards successful careers, one in law, the other in IT.

Scott made it a point to schedule phone calls home at least twice a day, sometimes in flight when his co-pilot took over the controls.

They would talk about the girls and hearsay about the famous folks living in Santa Monica, the Hollywood escapees, the millionaires and the truly wealthy, CEOs of large corporations, all who had built lavish homes on the Pacific coastline.

They also talked about his retirement in three years and their dream of selling the home and moving out to the thousand-acre ranch in Kansas they had purchased years ago. The stone ranch house sat next to an acre-size lake, against the rolling landscape of a sandsage prairie. It was a perfect place to retire and to devote himself to conscientious parenthood. He had been too busy flying during his first marriage and felt because of it he had let both his ex-wife and the children down.

Even the girls were excited, already thinking about horseback riding, haystacks and meeting new friends in school. They were mostly looking forward to having a live-at-home dad.

Anderson planned to continue to fly, not commercially, but in the twin-prop Cessna he was saving to purchase. He would build a small runway on the land, and he planned to teach all in the family to fly.

Ted Granger looked over at Scott and said, "It's amazing how these birds can fly themselves. I wouldn't fly anything but a 737. I mean, these things are as safe as they come."

"No argument there."

Granger was probably in his late twenties and had the laidback personality of a southerner and an accent to match. He seemed eager to gain more flying hours in the 737 and no doubt one day would earn the title of captain. He appeared conscientious enough."

"Where are you from?" Scott asked.

"Lubbock. Texas, that is."

Scott laughed. "Well, I knew you weren't from the Bronx."

Granger glanced sideways. "Now, them's fighting words for a Texan. I was born in Lubbock but spent most of my childhood living with my uncle near Corpus Christi."

"You joined the Air Force?"

"Fighter pilot for three of the four years enlisted. Then went straight to a commercial license and starting flying freights out of Chicago. Some were props until the company bought its first two 737-200s, really antique birds, some pretty battered-up. A whole lot of difference between them and the 300s."

As Granger engaged the Automatic Flight System or autopilot, Scott asked the co-pilot to take over controls, that he had to take a pee break.

The cockpit door opened as Scott got there. The pilot went straight for the restroom to his right at the head of the first class section. Fortunately, no one was using it.

Exiting it a few minutes later, Scott waited for Stacy finish serving one of the first class passengers. She came to the door.

"All souls served and happy," she said.

Scott hated referring to passengers as *souls*, even though it was common ATC language throughout the industry. It made it sound like his passengers were already doomed. But then it did reaffirm the huge responsibility all pilots bore when others' lives were in their hands.

The first class curtain was open and Scott could make out some of the passengers in the mid section of the plane. Two nuns were looking at him, smiling. They beamed like cherubim from their tight coifs.

A little girl was opening the aft restroom door. Although she was too far away for him to see her face, Scott noticed her pause and look at him for a few seconds.

"Mr. Texas at the helm?" Stacy said.

Scott nodded. "Intuition. He's a good pilot, believe me. Hey, any hot coffee for the flight crew?"

"How does he take it?"

"Black."

"You know that for certain?"

"He's a Texan. How else would he take it...with beer?"

Stacy rolled her eyes and told Scott that she would be back in three minutes.

Back at the cockpit door, Scott entered his code on the keypad. The door failed to unlock. He repeated the process. The door remained locked. He looked up at the small camera in the ceiling above the door and waved his hand. He entered the emergency code, a newly-installed override sequence known only to the captain. The door finally unlocked.

Scott sat down and took over the controls. He told Ted that coffee was on its way.

"Why did you override the panel entry?"

"Just to check that it worked," the co-pilot said. "You know, it should be part of the checklist."

"Then we'll add it to the preflight list, not when we're in flight. Do you understand?"

"Yessir, Captain."

Scott was thinking of the recent Germanwings disaster where a co-pilot had barricaded himself in the cockpit, not allowing the captain to enter from a break, and eventually flying the A320 straight into the side of a mountain in the Alps. He wondered whether any of the passengers had noticed his delayed entry. The air disaster was still on the minds of some fliers and certainly many commercial pilots. While some of the larger carriers had installed workarounds for such a scenario, most secondary carriers had not. Golden had placed increased scrutiny on background checks of all of its pilots, vetting would-be pilots for psychiatric and emotional events of all kinds. They had also installed high-definition CCTV cameras directly above both sides of the cockpit door. The pilot's override function had just been installed last month.

Scott decided that he would enter the minor incident in his flight report. He didn't want to ruin the co-pilot's record but felt it was something to be noted by the airlines.

Salt Lake City control broke in to provide an updated set of weather conditions flying into Denver. The ground temperature was 27 degrees Fahrenheit, winds at 35 knots with gusts up to 40, and strong crosswinds. Visibility was two miles and closing and cloud elevation to 20,000 feet. The storm had just passed over the eastern Rockies.

It was going to be a fairly smooth ride until they encountered the western edge of the storm.

Chapter Three

Jessica Gibson was startled awake by the sound of something crashing to the floor. The book she'd been reading when she fell asleep slid to the floor. She sat straight forward in her seat.

The serving cart must have collided with something in the galley. A flight attendant with an embarrassed expression emerged with the cart and proceeded down the aisle, apologizing for the noise to those nearest the galley.

"It gets a bit bumpy back there," she said to Ethan as she passed by. Sorry. I know you two were sleeping."

Jessica smiled at Ethan.

"Very minor turbulence," she said. "Once we reach the mountains it may be a little worse. So prepare yourself for more turbulence as we hit the Rockies."

"You don't mean that literally, I hope," Ethan said, smiling.

Jessica said, "I was once on a flight headed to the east coast where the turbulence was so bad, we fell ten thousand feet in one minute. Everyone was buckled in, but laptops and phones and some stomach contents went flying. Now *that* was a terrifying experience."

Their conversation felt easy, almost as if they had shared flights together before. Jessica found herself talking about her personal life, the troubled state of her marriage and the impending divorce. There was something comforting about opening up to someone she would never see again after the flight ended. It was like calling a hotline and sharing all of your intimate problems, knowing that once you hung up the relationship with the listener was over.

She had done just that once when in a vulnerable mood the first time Allen had mentioned that perhaps they should get a divorce. It was two years ago when she had caused him to be late for his flight.

He had said it while slamming the door when the taxi arrived. She'd felt it was all her fault, had taken a few drinks and, emotionally desperate, she'd called the local crisis hotline. Following that experience, Jessica had forged an emotional wall, buttressed by a sense of infallible independence. She had vowed to never allow herself to be hurt in that way again or to use booze to anesthetize her emotions.

She told Ethan that she knew Allen had been cheating on her for years. There had never been any direct evidence. But the intuition she'd felt was strong. She had been able to see it in the way he treated her when she returned from her business trips, a nauseous politeness and willingness to please that were clearly fabricated and used to quell his own guilt.

Jessica said she had decided that she would never marry again. She would never allow herself to be locked in that kind of relationship. Macy, her daughter, was her only focus now, and Allen was even interfering with that.

"Well, you're still young, Jessica," Ethan said. "And the future bears untold secrets, even for the heart-stricken."

"You don't know me," Jessica said, ending the conversation.

◆

Ethan Andrews, an exiting Catholic priest, a dedicated volunteer helping refugees, a man now struggling with the edicts of the church, and someone who was considering a long term relationship with woman, was a person who was as complex as the relation he had with God.

One could easily reason that he was of the Jesuit order, part philosopher, analyst and given to theological notions. But he was hardly that. He just had an issue with the Vatican.

Jessica must have been reading his mind when she looked over at him and said, "Do you mind," she said, "if I ask you a question?"

He nodded okay.

"Why do priests accept the vow of celibacy?"

"Are you sure you want to hear my opinion on the subject? You could be opening a can of worms."

"Go ahead," Jessica said, "I'm really interested."

"Lifelong celibacy," he said, "lacks rationality, except in the archaic minds of the Vatican. Clerical marriage is allowed by many religions, including Protestantism, Anglicanism, Independent Catholic churches, Judaism, Islam and the Japanese sects of Buddhism.

"Celibacy has served a strict purpose in religious history and that has been to shun priests and other clerics from worldliness. It has facilitated the notion that the Catholic church has control over the lives of both his worshipers and its priests. Historically, it may have held a pragmatic reason, but now in modern times, it seems to me, to have no religious justification whatsoever."

Jessica said, "I think it's particularly cruel for nuns."

"Absolutely."

"Did you ever consider the repercussions of celibacy when you first entered the priesthood?"

Ethan laughed. "Heavens no. I would have even considered castration if that were part of the conditions for priesthood. Novitiates, at least in the Catholic church, are blinded by their absolute faith in Vatican doctrine."

"I don't mean to sound condescending," Jessica said, "but when I was younger I always felt...sorry, a sort pity for nuns. But as I've matured, although I am not of any particular faith, I have learned to admire their silent but fervent faith."

"Well you should," Ethan said seriously, "for they are the true shepherds of the flock."

The conversation stopped abruptly when they glimpsed a view of the captain standing outside the forward restroom.

"Always a disconcerting sight...when you see the captain outside the cockpit door," Ethan said.

"I guess that's why we have co-pilots."

"And strict security regulations. I don't think the flight crew is allowed to venture beyond the restroom. It was customary in the old days, but not now in this new age of terrorism."

A few minutes later when the captain was heading back to the cockpit, they watched him pause for what seemed like an extended time at the cockpit door. He seemed to be having difficulty punching in his entry code. When he finally opened the door, they both shared a look of relief.

It was just too reminiscent of the recent air disaster caused by a crazed co-pilot who had prevented the captain from gaining access to the cockpit, and who eventually crashed the plane into the side of a mountain.

Ethan wondered whether any of the other passengers had noticed. It happened so quickly, he gathered that they hadn't. But Jessica had.

"I've heard that safeguards have been put in place to prevent such a scenario from ever occurring again. A manual override of some kind," she said.

Just then the captain spoke, advising the passengers of a weather update. He spoke in a calm, matter-of-fact voice. He said that due to a change in the weather front and the expanding snow storm they could expect perhaps moderate turbulence ahead. He asked all passengers to fasten their seatbelts and to listen to the instructions of the flight crew.

"I told you so," Jessica said.

"Oh, great," Ethan said, pulling firmly on his seatbelt strap. He noticed that Jessica had already done so and was now looking out the window.

◆

Scott Anderson was looking at the small radar scope but failed to see significant storm indications ahead. Before they climbed to 37,000 feet, Salt Lake ATC had informed them of the possible turbulence just below their altitude. Once they began their descent approaching Denver the possibility of turbulence would be far greater.

Most likely due to a consistent 40 mph tailwind, they were twenty minutes ahead of schedule. That time would no doubt be nullified by the expected hold pattern over Denver. They had enough fuel for up to a two-hour hold, but long before then the pilot would probably choose to divert to a nearby airport. Excessive holding patterns not only involved time delays but more importantly to the airline industry, time in the air meant exorbitant fuel costs.

Scott asked Ted Granger to take over, saying that he wanted to try a cell call to his wife. He was surprised when the call went through.

"Laura?"

Relieved to hear his wife's voice, Scott updated her on his ETA at Denver and said he was hoping to be home after his 48 hour layover there. He asked about the girls, listened to what they were up to and then told Laura that he loved her.

"Must be nice," Ted Granger said as the pilot clicked off the phone. "I mean having a big family to go home to."

"I miss them. It's been almost two weeks since I've been home. This is going to be a special Christmas. I've managed to squeeze in a short vacation."

Ted released controls to Scott and then said he needed to use the boy's room. He used his code to exit. At the door he bumped into Stacy, who was carrying two steaming cups of coffee, one black and the other with cream and sugar.

"Excuse me, Ma'am, he said, tipping his hat.

When the door locked behind her, Stacy said, "Never trust anyone who calls you *Ma'am*."

"You bet I won't." Scott said, laughing.

"I've heard he's quite the womanizer with his charming southern style. You know, he tried to hit on Norma when he boarded."

"Just so he doesn't hit on me," Scott laughed again.

Just then there was a jarring bump, and then another. Stacy braced herself against the bulkhead and then made her way back to the door.

"Here we go."

"Let us know when we need to buckle," she said as Scott unlocked the door.

Scott got on the intercom and advised passengers that they were entering an unstable air pattern and to prepare for some rough weather. He said that crew members would be asking them to secure loose items in the overhead cabinets. He reassured them that this was not unusual when approaching mountain weather and that the turbulence would be short-lived.

When Ted re-entered the cockpit he checked the navigational panel, dialing in coordinates, and then buckled up in his seat. He appeared pale, almost gaunt, and Scott asked him if everything was okay.

He said the chicken salad sandwich he'd grabbed at the airport was probably bad, that he'd felt sick to his stomach.

"Okay to fly?"

"Of course," Granger said, starring blankly through the main cockpit window, looking a bit like a kid forced to ride a rollercoaster.

"Believe me, I can handle this," Scott added. "If you need to take a break, just go."

Ted Granger said nothing.

◆

The girl in the back was obviously sick. Flight attendants were trying to cool her down. She had a very high temperature.

Jessica stood up and moved past Ethan into the aisle. A flight attendant stopped her, reminding her of the seatbelt sign.

"I would like to help. How much ice have you got?"

The attendant hesitated and then nodded for Jessica to follow her. "We've been using towels soaked with cool water but her temperature is over the top. Almost 104 degrees."

"She's flying alone?"

The flight attendant nodded.

In the galley they collected as many buckets of ice as they could carry. Jessica found the extra linen compartment and grabbed an armful of towels.

When they reached the girl, who was crumpled up, her knees drawn to her chest in her seat, Jessica suggested that they lay her across two of the pull-down seats in the back. One of the flight attendants began removing her shoes and socks. She was wearing jeans, and Jessica suggested that they remove those too. The girl protested, flinging her legs and arms and crying, "Leave me alone!"

They finally got her positioned properly. Bundles of wrapped ice were placed around her head, neck and chest.

The pilot must have been notified for shortly he asked if there were any medical staff among the passengers. No one stood up.

The girl was now trembling, making incoherent sounds. Her eyes suddenly opened wide and she grabbed at Jessica's arm, squeezing it with such force Jessica had to pry her fingers off.

"It's okay, sweetheart, you're going to be fine," she tried to calm the girl.

They checked her temperature again. It hadn't budged.

"More ice," Jessica said. "That's the only way to break it."

As she said this, the girl looked up at Jessica with a glaring stare. It was the look of someone who'd just had a frightening revelation.

Her eyes began to flutter and then her arms went stiff. Her mouth clamped shut. She began shaking violently.

The seizure lasted for over a minute and then the girl's body went limp. She appeared to be in a deep post-seizure sleep. For the time being she was out of danger.

Back in her seat, Jessica said nothing to her companion.

After a few moments he asked about the girl's condition and told her that he had said a prayer for her. It irked Jessica because he seemed so blasé about it. She had expected for him to come over and give a hand.

"High temperature. She went into a status seizure."

The plane hit more turbulence and several passengers began to show alarm. A child started crying. The pilot must have instructed the flight crew to buckle-up. Jessica turned around and saw one of them do so in a jump seat next to the ill girl.

"I'm sorry to hear that," Ethan said.

Chapter Four

Reverend Joshua Gunter ran a strict household. He and his wife Belinda were the pride of the small river community of Arrow Point in South Dakota.

He considered all 700 citizens a part of his extended family. While he treated all of them with respect and love, he possessed an uncanny sense whenever a parishioner had fallen from grace. He called them *laggards* and would have no mercy when he singled them out for their sins.

Arrow Point had formed as a dwelling place during the desperate years of the Depression, inhabited back then by a handful of settlers who had given up on their hopes of striking it rich in the goldmines of California. It started with a single *speakeasy*, attracting through those destitute years many souls who had fallen to drinking bootleg liquor, the kind imported from Appalachian moonshine distillers as well as clear brandies produced locally from a variety of fruits.

It wasn't until the mid-fifties when Arrow Point could genuinely claim its first teetotalers. The postwar atmosphere attracted an eagerness for permanence even among those seeking travel and adventure in western escapes. Most were attracted to the community because of Reverend Gunter and the solidarity of the church members, which included just about everyone in Arrow Point.

Sundays in Arrow Point were full of celebration, prayer and the oratories of Reverend Gunter. His sermons were referred to, not by just a few, as filibusters, and could last for two hours or more. The first hour was filled with vociferous fire and brimstone rants, causing morbid fear among most of the listeners. Some were cruelly exposed for various transgressions, mostly based on hearsay and sheriff reports the reverend would receive. In rare cases, those improprieties approaching sexual infidelity or worse would result in public excommunication from the church. Members would rant along with Reverend Gunter against the sinner, female parishioners often mocking a flogging by hurling their shawls and scarves at the sinner.

What everyone waited for on those Sundays were the celebrations of joy, time given to rewarding the good members of the church, those who had donated large amounts to church coffers, the silent heroes of volunteerism and philanthropy and the saints, those who attended church seven days per week. Most of these were elderly members whose constant presence, at least to Joshua Gunter, meant the church was truly a home of permanence.

Sunday sermons at the Arrow Point Baptist Church always resulted in an air of celebration, with joyful sharing of prepared foods and often elaborate BBQ cookouts. An old calliope played lively sounds. They said that the odor of barbecued chicken could be detected well outside the community limits and sometimes, if the wind was right, miles south on the Missouri River. For this reason, the population of Arrow Point often increased on Sundays, mostly because of an influx of hungry loggers.

One Sunday in May of 1967, Reverend Gunter rose before the congregation just before he was about to give his sermon and asked his wife Belinda to stand before the parishioners. A small woman with a congenial face and sturdy bones, not exceptionally attractive but with a wholesome, if not puritanical look, Belinda rose somewhat uncomfortably from the front left pew and waited for her husband's announcement.

"Members of the Arrow Point Baptist Church, we want you to bear witness to some wonderful news." The reverend stopped and looked directly at his wife.

All you had to do is look at Belinda and know the obvious announcement to follow. In fact, many women in the church had suspected it for many weeks.

"Belinda, my wife," he continued proudly, "is with child. God bless, God bless."

"Amen," parishioners responded in perfect unison. One elderly man in the back pew stood up and bellowed, "God bless, Belinda! God bless, Belinda!"

Seeing her very swollen belly, some in the crowd doubted that the pregnancy would survive the day's sermon. Reverend Gunter probably feared that too and had arranged several midwives to be seated adjacent to his wife.

Belinda's due date was less than a month away and her size suggested that she may be carrying twins or even triplets. Her husband wanted a boy. On the night he knew he had impregnated his wife, he told her, as if ordering a specific meal, that she had to bear him his first son. He'd said that in a preaching tone as if Belinda herself could simply dial-in the gender. As the pregnancy progressed, she became concerned about an outcome over which she knew she had no control. She feared that her husband might even divorce her should the baby be female.

The midwifery group consoled Belinda by saying that the gender of the child was in God's hands, not her husband's or her own. She had to accept the work of God.

Belinda had read that cod liver oil improved the chances of begetting a male and made it a routine every morning to consume at least three tablespoons of the foul-tasting solution. Over the months it made her bowels irregular and often caused her to belch unexpectedly. She would have consumed vermin excrement if that were suggested, so determined was she to produce the reverend his first son.

On the third Sunday following the announcement, Reverend Joshua Gunter stood before his congregation, looking pale and sweating heavily. Everyone then knew that his wife was in labor, several members attempting to comfort him before he launched into his sermon. Some exhorted him to go home to be with his wife and the midwives.

"My place is here in this wonderful church in front of my beloved congregation and in the presence of the most holy God," he'd told them.

The reverend's angst about his wife not bearing him a son made his sermon even more fiery, telling the churchgoers that they all belonged in hell, save for the mercy of God. He told them that God had revealed to him His plan, that suffering and punishment were the twin causeways to redemption and that there were Satan's angels among them. He led the congregation in strange dirges, some modified excerpts from the bible, others inexplicable references to devil exorcism.

"Tear out the liver of Beelzebub and grind it to shreds in your teeth and then cast it from your mouths!" he cried out, his hand shaking as he wiped his forehead with his soaked handkerchief.

It was as if he knew already and that knowledge justified casting aspersions among the worshippers. Many saw through the anger and surmised that it was fear. They looked among each other, shaking their heads, reaching to hold hands, their grave faces portending the terrible truth.

The preacher's wife had surely borne him a daughter.

◆

The boy was born to a teenage couple about ten miles south of Arrow Point, in an impoverished logging settlement along the Missouri River.

"Baby" took his first breath inside a rotting sawmill during the region's worst drought. The river had dropped eighteen feet in sections. Dust storms blew in from the plains, and on that day the dusty light sluiced through the slats of the dilapidated mill, causing the boy's parents to cough sporadically as the child was being born. The boy's mother covered her son's mouth with a handkerchief in hopes of protecting his lungs.

The mother's aunt had helped birth the child, using the precious little drinking water available, packs of cotton pads and a good pair of chicken scissors. She had tied the umbilical cord with a section from a spool of string and suctioned the infant with a metal turkey baster.

The decision had been made by the aunt during the first trimester of the pregnancy. The child would have no hope for survival in such destitute surroundings, especially because the young couple had no jobs and no opportunities for education and improvement in living standards.

"Don't you call that infant anything but *Baby*," the mother's aunt had warned her niece. "It ain't yours to keep and shelter with love. You understand, girl?"

She had told the young teenager that a rich couple from Rapid City was on a waiting list to adopt the child as soon as it was born. She called it a blessing.

In truth the aunt was planning to offer the child for sale to a good couple who would proffer the highest amount. It would be a secret deal with no records or any way to trace the child to its parents. The aunt wanted no less than a thousand dollars for the child if it were a boy.

A deal was made in July, 1967, when the infant boy was only a month old. It was made in the middle of the night by a tall man with chopstick sideburns and stern penetrating eyes. With his wife at his side, the couple seemed of good means. They wore good clothes, especially the man, whose polished black boots and pleated pants reminded the aunt of fashion wear she had seen in advertisements from California. They paid in hundred dollar bills and asked for no receipt, but did request a brief meeting with the child's mother.

Reluctantly, the teenager agreed. They met in the abandoned church across the street, the girl sitting stiffly on one of the dusty pews.

"Child," the man said, lowering his head, his piercing eyes causing the teenager to squirm slightly. "In the name of God, I shall have your word that you alone bore this child and that under His will you will make no effort to establish a relationship with him, now and for as long as you shall live."

"Yessir," the girl said, her hands clasped deeply in her lap.

"And that if you should," the man continued, raising his voice, "the devil will take your soul and those of your loved ones!"

And so ended the encounter and transaction. The aunt watched the couple, now with the child, drive off in an old black Packard sedan, a cloud of dark dust enveloping the car as it disappeared into the midnight darkness.

◆

When Lydia turned twenty, now long abandoned by her boyfriend, the child's father, she decided that, against the harsh warnings of the tall dark stranger, she would indeed discover who had adopted her son. She'd found out about the sale and had cursed at her aunt for being so selfish and deceitful. She told her that she would find the boy and return him to his blood mother, even if it took the rest of her life.

The guilt she'd endured over the years had tormented the young woman. If not for her aunt's deception, she would have kept the baby and raised it on her own. She knew now that she could have provided for her son with proper shelter and food. Three months after *Baby's* birth, her boyfriend and father of the child had secured a job as a junior logger and earned a good enough wage to provide for his son and soon-to-be bride.

She often cried herself to sleep, imagining the quick glimpse of the infant's face before her aunt had covered it and rushed from the room, remembering only its deep blue eyes. She should have stood up for her child and never have agreed to an adoption. Courage came to her and she soon found herself incensed by the stranger with his threatening words.

She moved to Southern Shadows, a town just south of Arrow Point. She found a good job at *The Pointer*, a weekly newspaper firm whose editor/publisher was a hard-working journalist who had trained at a Sioux Falls daily and had started *The Pointer* by using all of his savings.

Sam Gudmundson came from a long line of journalists. When he was a boy and visiting his father's printing press, he'd inadvertently placed his hand on the ink of a printing press. It took weeks for the stain to eventually disappear, this following weeks of scrubbing with rough lard soap. His father had proclaimed that Sam would be the fourth generation of newspapermen. The ink stain had sealed the boy's future.

Lydia, Sam's only employee, worked as a reporter, researcher, printer's aide and general gofer in the business. The newspaper operated out of the old post office on Darcy Street, a sweet deal Sam had made when the new post office was being built in the new business section of Arrow Point.

Sam thought Lydia was a natural and was constantly chiding her about getting ink on her hands. She was intelligent and inquisitive and had a knack for the written word, although she never finished high school.

Lydia had been honest with Sam on the day she was hired. She'd told him about her son and how she'd committed her life to finding him. It was not by coincidence that she'd landed the job at the newspaper, where she knew she could easily access the old microfiched articles, police reports and most public records.

She had long since moved out of her aunt's place and was renting a cheap motel room until Sam insisted that she move in with him on the top floor of the old post office. He built her a small room with its own window and desk. He'd lugged up the stairs an old Royal typewriter and had set it with paper on the flat metal desk. He wired a telephone line up the side of the house and installed a receiver next to the desk. It wasn't a private line, but he said she was free to use it whenever he wasn't conducting business.

Lydia's efforts to locate the adoptive parents of her son were met with dead ends, although she'd come across some leads. It had been obvious to her since that day she'd given up rights to her infant that the *procurer* (as she referred to him) was a preacher. Her gut instinct told her that he was from a large city, perhaps Sioux Falls or even from out of state. She'd interrogated her aunt for weeks, but the stubborn woman, afraid she would have to return the money, simply puckered up her mouth and squinted her eyes shut as if she were ready and willing to endure the inquisition of her niece at any cost or physical torture.

There were no records of birth pertaining to her son, and she hadn't expected to find any. No adoption notices. But there were several birth announcements around the time of *Baby's* birth. Public records revealed that there were 18 births in the state around that time, six of which indicated that the parents were listed as *Reverend and wife*. All six were from either Rapid City or Sioux Falls.

Lydia spent weeks tracking down those promising leads and was disheartened to discover that five were girls. The only boy born to a preacher around that time, a couple from Sioux Falls, had died from chickenpox at the age of two.

It was a dead end met with a chilled feeling of disillusionment and fate. Lydia told Sam that it was never meant to be, that her son was probably better off not knowing his birth mother. Sam gave her a day off to console herself and to make a decision to move on with her life and her promising career.

Everything changed the day the carnival moved into town.

◆

When Abraham Gunter was seven years old, a tall but thin boy for his age, he faced his father's rage at the pulpit of the famous church in Arrow Point. He wasn't sure what he had done or what sin he had committed to so enrage his father, but nonetheless felt justly accused because his father was a true man of God.

He had been commanded to stand up at his pew and face the congregation. He was more stunned than scared because he had never seen this side of his father outside of his customary sermonic thunder. He turned to look down at his mother sitting by his side, but she bowed her head, apparently indifferent to her son's predicament.

Gracie, the boy's sister, reached over and placed her hand over his.

"It has come to my attention that my own son has stolen from our church's donation jar," Preacher Gunter said, his icy stare boring a hole through the boy's heart.

"I didn't, Father," Abraham said.

"Will you call a witness of this fine congregation a liar?"

"Please, father, I didn't..."

"That's forty dollars into the purse of Satan!" ranted the preacher.

The boy was crying, attempting to grab his mother's arm for support. He collapsed in the seat and put his hands to his face.

"Stand up, boy, and face your accuser!"

So upset was Abraham that he couldn't muster the energy to stand. The preacher repeated his command, slamming his fist on top of the pulpit.

But the boy's legs were feeble and he was not sturdy enough to stand. He lay crumpled over in his seat, his face buried between his knees, tears, snot and shame sealing his face to his palms.

Reverend Gunter eventually gave up on his rant and allowed the boy to sit through the sermon and the more congenial events of the morning. He did, though, tell the boy that he would not be allowed to attend the grand BBQ.

Gracie, who was Abraham's age, was a thin, shy girl who customarily stayed by her mother's side. She was close to her brother and often stood up for him during bouts of their father's unpredictable temper.

This wasn't the first time Abraham had been the subject of the Reverend's ire. Whether he was being castigated for not washing his face and ears properly or for speaking out of turn, Abraham just couldn't do right by his father. Over the past year the boy had decided that his father just didn't like him, and for this reason felt shunned, even by his mother, who always took sides with the Reverend.

The father did not spare the rod with his son. Just about every transgression was met with a lashing from a horse whip the Reverend kept next to the stove in the kitchen. He never whipped his son in front his mother and sister but took him to the basement, where the boy's screams couldn't be heard.

While Gracie was allowed to attend the small public school in town, Abraham was expected to learn the Bible and memorize words of the Old Testament. His father's strictness often terrified the boy, who found it difficult to read, much less memorize long passages.

In an effort to explain her father's treatment of her brother, one day Gracie told Abraham what he already suspected, that he had been adopted a month or so after she had been born. The boy had never been able to explain why he was the only member of the family with blue eyes and blondish hair. Even when he was five, he felt he didn't share his family's blood, so different were their features from his.

"I can't live like this anymore," he told Gracie one late spring morning as they were sitting on a stone bench to the side of the church.

Gracie looked over at her brother's sullen face and then inched closer to him on the seat.

"I have to leave."

Gracie looked alarmed. "Where would you go, Abe?"

"I could join the army."

"Silly," Gracie said. "You're too young."

"I'll find someone who'll take me. I know I can't stay here anymore."

"Take me with you," Gracie said, now beginning to cry.

"It's me they don't want. You have a good home and a chance to get properly schooled. You must stay, Gracie."

"Where will I find you?"

"I promise one day to return and see you."

Abe made his escape very early one morning when his father was attending a preacher's conference in Rapid City for a few days. It was four in the morning and neither his mother nor his sister was up at that time. He left Gracie a note under her pillow, telling her that he loved her and that he was heading south along the river.

It was a cool pre-dawn Wednesday in the month of July and as he neared the great Missouri River, a chilly breeze blew in from the west. He imagined that the day would be as warm as yesterday, which meant he probably wouldn't need the wool jacket and hat he was now wearing. He'd brought a small canteen of water and a bag of beef jerky, sustenance, he thought, for at least a few days of travel. He had no real plans, only to put safe distance between him and his father. He could only imagine what catastrophic consequence would befall him should the preacher catch up with him.

On the third day of travel, a mile north of Southern Shadows, he heard in the distance a wonderful commotion of voices, animal sounds and the lively whistling notes from a calliope.

He came to a large open field where huge tents were erected, along with wood cages on wheels and colorful trailers. The pungent odor of animal dung assaulted him. Here the calliope sounds were almost deafening. Enormous men on walking stilts, with hats and painted faces were awkwardly ambling about. Beautiful women clad in flowing costumes and headdresses were emerging from trailers. Midgets and obese figures walked side-by-side, along with the jugglers and the tightrope walkers.

Abe's heart jumped a beat when he saw the huge canvas-painted sign that hung above between two telephone poles: *Ringling Bros. and Barnum & Bailey Circus*.

He didn't know how or when it would happen, but felt that something momentous lay in his future.

◆

Sam Gudmundson had casually asked if Lydia would be interested in writing a short article about the visiting circus. It was the first article Sam had assigned her, and she was ecstatic, not to mention that this was the first time she would be attending a circus. With notebook and an old Kodak 35mm camera in hand, she took off for the nearby circus grounds. She wanted to angle her article, to give it uniqueness by focusing on an interesting aspect of circus life. She would, of course, take the standard photos inside the main tent with her press card and permission from the managers, but then wanted to include in her article photos of the carnies themselves.

Lydia decided that her angle would be the strange life of the midgets, a tribe of individuals she had never witnessed before. There were ten of them working for the circus and they lived in two large caravans next to where the elephants were chained to long metal spikes in the ground.

Most of the little people shunned the public attention Lydia was promising them, telling her that they were proud folks who rarely shared their personal lives with others outside of the circus. They would let her take pictures but made it clear that she would not be allowed entry into their homes.

But Lydia was determined to get her story and made it a point to return to their caravans during each day of the circus.

Her breakthrough came when she befriended Fred Clooney, a four foot tall long-time employee who worked as the only midget on the tightrope. His job was to check the safety of the ropes and lanyards before the tightrope walkers arrived but ostensibly was there to entertain circus viewers by feigning falls from the ropes. He was attached to a bungee-like lanyard and when he plummeted to the screams of onlookers, he would be yanked upward just before hitting the ground. The crowds loved it, some even more than the main walking event.

Clooney was very intelligent and had led a colorful life on the road, and in no time was regaling Lydia with personal vignettes of his travels. He was seventy-five but didn't look a day over forty. He was intrigued by her job as a journalist and seemed amazed by the fact that they allowed female reporters.

He had been born in Illinois and had joined the circus at ten when it premiered in Chicago in the early forties. He said it was the only home available to short people which treated them with dignity and a sense of worthiness. The circus became his family and the only venue where he was able to meet others of his stature.

He eventually allowed Lydia to interview him formally, Clooney sharing aspects of his personal life story. He permitted her to take as many photos as she wished as long as they didn't show any of the other midgets.

One afternoon during the last week of the circus he asked Lydia if she would like to come into his caravan while the other little people were off at the carnival eateries.

Clooney was dressed in a purple long-tailed suit that shimmered with tiny rhinestones, with a black bowtie and matching cummerbund.

He removed his black top-hat and bowed for Lydia to enter the caravan.

She was immediately stunned by the fancy embroideries that hung in bountiful tapestries from the ceiling and by the fine-tufted divans and elegant Persian carpets.

"It's like a small palace," she said, admiringly.

"Folks think that carnies are poor and live in traveling shanties, but that's not true. They pay us good, feed us mostly free and encourage us to make our homes as comfortable as we can."

"Fred, did you design this?" Lydia asked as she began snapping away with the camera.

"With the finest tapestry and drapes from India and the Far East, the best that money can buy. They say that Mr. Ringling used to travel to far-fetched places in the world just to purchase items for the his circus."

Lydia said, "This is wonderful."

Afterwards, Clooney asked Lydia if she would like to take pictures of the elephants bathing in the river. He said the animals went down to the riverbank after the shows were shut down just after nine. He told her where they could be found, just south of Thompson Park on the nearest bank. He said he would be there, along with the elephant boys, those who got the giant animals to kneel in the water and then climbed atop and scrubbed the dust and mud from their backs.

Lydia finished writing her article, editing it and positioning the photos that Sam had developed and printed in his darkroom where she thought they would draw the reader right to the opening paragraphs in the article. She left them for the managing editor for final approval. He had told her that if the article was printable he would allow her her own byline.

That evening, a little before nine, Lydia slipped into her jeans and rubber boots and headed off for the river. She had borrowed Sam's new electronic flash. There was a gibbous moon and the light cast a soft, silvery haze through the passing clouds, laying sketches of nervous shadows on the ground.

Approaching the silhouettes of the huge creatures and hearing the sound of snorting and the spraying of water, Lydia crouched down about a dozen yards before the riverbank. She held her camera and waited.

There were three pachyderms standing like behemoth creatures in the river, occasionally splashing with their prodding forelegs and drawing in the cool river water with their trunks and then spraying their backs. There were odd snorting sounds, followed by windy, trumpeting bleats, and other strange grunting sounds Lydia had never heard before.

Several dark-skinned boys sat atop the elephants, holding coarse brushes with which they scrubbed the animals' backs, some leaning so far back on the rumps they looked at any moment they would slide off into the river. Noticing Lydia, one of them mounted the elephant's trunk and was gently lowered onto the dry bank of the river.

"Lydia!" he called, approaching the young woman.

It was Fred Clooney dressed in red shorts that came to his shins and a sleeveless tee shirt, bearing muscular tattooed biceps and white hairy forearms. He was drenched head to foot, water dripping from the cleft of his square chin. His bald head shone in the moonlight.

He grabbed her hand and began leading the way down to the water.

"Aren't you afraid of them?" she asked.

"These animals are as gentle as turtles. Ain't nothing to fear. They treat these boys like they were kin."

Clooney urged Lydia to wade into the water so that she could mount one of the elephants. At first she declined and then just knew she had to experience it, not for herself but for her readers. How many people had ridden a pachyderm? She had to share the feeling with the public. It was a journalist's duty to describe unusual experiences like this.

She put her camera down and followed Clooney to the elephant. The animal wobbled to its knees. Clooney told her to take a seat at the very base of the trunk, facing its head. She stared into the huge caramel eyes, her legs dangling in the water.

At Clooney's command, the elephant raised itself, throwing its head back and ejecting the young woman onto its back, where she sat, dizzy and awed.

There was a black boy behind her who appeared to be the animal's handler. He made a series of clicking noises to which the elephant raised and dangled a foreleg, lowered to its knees and then, drinking in the cool water, curled its trunk backward and blasted all aboard with water.

Drenched, Lydia let out a muffled scream to which the boy laughed and then had the animal repeat the process. Her hair plastered over her face, she caught sight of Clooney laughing himself silly on the bank.

"I want to get off now!" she demanded, sweeping her blonde hair back over her head.

The boy obeyed her wish and had the gentle beast lower her to the riverbank.

Clooney was laughing so hard he had to sit down and there pounded his palms against the sandy embankment.

"I...I don't see any humor in this," Lydia sputtered. She looked down at her soaked jeans and the crumpled lace blouse she was wearing, horrified to see that her bra showed through. Almost immediately, Clooney offered her his dry jacket.

They talked for a while sitting together higher on the riverbank, Clooney sharing carnival stories and his own first attempts at riding the elephants. Soon Lydia was describing how her own experience felt and how she would describe it to her readers. In no time she was laughing at Clooney's account of what she looked like falling back as the first blast of water hit her and then coming up with an expression like she had just been shot.

Watching Clooney jog back to the elephants, Lydia retrieved her camera and adjusted the lens and the flash. She knew she had to get closer to the animals to get a good shot. She already had in mind exactly how she wanted the animal posed, with water splashing from its trunk, its mouth open, its half-tusks exposed, all gleaming in the moonlight.

She stood up and, with equipment in hand, slowly edged her way down to the riverbank and the waiting animals.

◆

Abe had snuck down to where the giant elephants were swimming in the shallows of the river. He was awestruck by their size and by their brutal strength when he had seen one carrying a thick pole to one of the tents on the fairgrounds. Now in the darkness of night with a high moon casting a dazzling trail across the wide river, he knew he had to get closer to the elephants. He had witnessed how the other boys clambered up onto the backs of the huge animals. While he could not imagine himself sitting at that height, he wanted to at least touch the hide an elephant. He had no idea what it would feel like but imagined it would feel rough to the touch.

He was only fifty feet or so this side of the animals. The closest elephant did not have a rider and had finished its stomping and spraying of water. It stood almost motionless, a dark prehistoric form against the dazzling ripples of moonlight. He began his advance by scooting slowly down the riverbank and then carefully approaching the animal. He was upwind and knew the elephant had scented his presence, for it had turned a lazy eye at the boy several times. It seemed friendly enough.

Abe was hot, the back of his neck burned slightly by the day's long walk. Besides wanting to touch the hide of the animal, he imagined what it would feel like lowering himself into the cool river and then floating free under the moonlight.

He entered the water about ten feet from the animal and began wading out until the water reached just below his chest. He lay back and dunked his head and then came up sputtering.

The elephant wagged its spindly tail and then dropped the mouth of his trunk into the water, producing a slight spray that spread out and made shivering circles of moonlight.

Abe swept his hair from his forehead and rubbed at his eyes. Slowly, he sidled closer to the animal, feeling the river's current against legs. When he was close enough to reach over, he began talking to the elephant in soft whispers.

"Good boy...good boy," he murmured, not exactly sure he was addressing the animal by its proper gender.

The elephant slowly swung its enormous head and then lowered it as if to meet its visitor eye-to-eye.

Abe made contact, his small palm flat against the trunk of the animal. He was startled to feel thick, prickly hair and underneath the scaly skin that felt like hardened leather. He couldn't get over the feel of the hair and quickly moved his hand to its flank. Soon he was patting the elephants hide, reaching up to the top of its leg and stroking the underbelly.

He felt like David in the midst of Goliath. But this Goliath was gentle and full of such grace, he couldn't imagine how it could bring anyone harm.

Soon he was pressing his cheek against the leathery hide of the animal and running his hands up and down its massive hind leg. At one point the elephant swept his gargantuan head to the side, now almost face-to-face with his small visitor.

"I know I can do it," he whispered to himself, and then moved around to the front of the animal.

Instinctively, the elephant dropped to its knees, its long trunk laid out in front.

"It's praying," Abe said, and fully trusting the animal's intentions, he approached and sat down at the crotch of the extended trunk. Instantly, he was lifted and then tumbled onto the elephant's back, sprawled there like a small vulnerable creature. When the elephant rose up to its feet and began shaking its cavernous head, Abe slid back, catching himself by digging his fingers into the rough folds of the hide.

"Goliath!" he cried out in a state of exuberance.

Whether it was his loud exclamation or the sudden explosion of light coming from the other side that caused the animal to dart wildly ashore, Abe knew in a second that he was in trouble. He slid forward onto the head just as the animal bucked and found himself sailing through the air.

He landed sideways, a great burst of lighting igniting behind his eyes as his head hit the edge of a log buttressing the riverbank.

An explosion of colors, a receding whiteness and soundlessness. And then all consciousness was gone.

Chapter Five

L ydia Andrews raised her son with such affection and devotion that if the boy had been traumatized at the hands of the reverend, he soon found himself happily estranged from and forgetful of that cruel upbringing.

Feeling so guilty by what she had caused at the circus, she had stayed at his side during each day of his confinement to the hospital. With no doubt in her mind that he was her son, she took him home to live in the attic of Sam Gudmundson's newspaper establishment. Sam had given extra money to pay for his medical expenses and for a new set of clothing for the boy.

The truth had come out one day following a terrible nightmare about his father. Lydia had known all along in her heart but, sitting by her son on his bed that morning, she'd explained what her aunt had done. They both decided that he would officially divorce his false parents and assume Lydia's maiden name. They'd looked at a long list of boy's names in a book from the library, and the boy had decided on the name *Ethan*. Afterwards they petitioned the court for a legal name change, submitting all necessary forms and appearing before the court. The day Ethan received his official Social Security card he was ecstatic.

In 1980, when Ethan was thirteen, Lydia was offered a job as assistant editor at a newspaper in Watertown, not far from the Minnesota state line. It paid a handsome salary and would allow her even more freedom to offer the news to a far greater readership.

Sam had died suddenly the year before from a massive heart attack and soon, with his death, came the demise of *The Arrow*. Lydia had taken over as editor for a while but realizing the effect television news was having on her dwindling circulation, she decided to take advantage of the offer in Watertown. Her decision was based in part on putting more distance between her son and the crazy preacher.

She rented a small cape cod house in the center of the small town within walking distance of the high school and the newspaper. The house had two small bedrooms, a wall-papered kitchen and living room, along with old heating radiators that clinked during the winter months like small prisoners banging on the bars of their jail doors.

The memory of the accident with the elephant came to Ethan slowly, becoming more clear as he grew into his teens. He'd been told that he'd nearly died from his head wound, that it was truly a miracle. The memory of that incident and his miraculous survival anchored itself in his heart as a sign of divine intervention. Although he knew that he couldn't rejoin the Baptist church, in later years the incident at the river had enriched a strong devotion to God and the need to help others.

There was a small Catholic church in town which Ethan and his mother began attending. Father Danny, an Irish expatriate, whose thick brogue was often hard to understand, took special interest in Ethan. With the approval of his mother, the priest reviewed the Catechism with the boy and soon prepared him to become an alter boy and serve Sunday mass.

But first he had to be baptized and officially converted to Catholicism. Ethan and his mother were baptized together in a simple church service with only a handful of witnesses. Soon they received First Communion. Father Danny told the boy that he had been cleansed of all his sins and that God would grant him any wish he asked for.

Ethan was intrigued by that message and decided to test the priest's words. He told no one, but what he wanted most in life was a red Schwinn bike. When that wish came true on a snowy Christmas morning, as he stood there gazing at the shiny red-and-chrome bicycle in the living room, there was no doubt in Ethan's mind that God had answered his wish.

Lydia and Ethan began inviting Father Danny over for Sunday dinners. The priest was a rotund jovial man with a nearly bald head, save for a flap that rose from above his right ear and thusly carpeted his glabrous dome.

He shared fascinated details of his years in Dublin, where he called himself a hoodlum before entering the priesthood. He had fought in the Irish-Protestant conflict with no ideological or religious commitment other than to be with his friends in the conflict. He joined the priesthood for vocational reasons, not, he described, "as a result from a grand calling from God."

Father Danny liked to imbibe, customarily a good Irish whiskey, and would always arrive at the house with his own libation. He never got drunk, but his cheeks would enrich with color as he regaled the Andrews with his traveling tales.

One evening, following a delicious meatloaf dinner, the priest sat down with Ethan on the swing bench on the front porch.

"I know it's in you, lad," he addressed the teenager.

Ethan laughed. "Meatloaf and potatoes?"

"Aye that, but something more serious," Father Danny said. "A true calling to the priesthood. I can see it in the way you serve mass and, mostly importantly, in the deep faith in your eyes."

"You think?" Ethan said.

"I know that for a fact, lad."

Though Ethan kept it to himself, he felt the truth in the priest's words. Mostly he felt it during the mass each Sunday, a warm attraction when he recited the Latin refrains and saw the hardened faith in the parishioners' eyes when they genuflected as he sounded the bells. He liked serving others. He believed in God, liked the solemnity of Church ritual and was inspired by a lifelong service to Christ.

Catholic Formation began with Ethan's studies under Father Danny. Following the Church's guidelines, the priest laid out the long process leading to the priesthood and what Ethan could look forward to in his novitiate studies, seminary college and eventual acceptance by the Church as a priest.

"It takes years," Father Danny said, "testing your faith and devotion and your willingness to conform to the rules of the Church. You will have many opportunities to re-examine your conscience and the ways of abstinence. You will know by the end of your studies if you are truly committed to serving God in this manner."

While he felt the calling already, Ethan found himself doubting his capabilities. He knew nothing of the priesthood except for what Father Danny had shared. It seemed an enormous decision for a teenager to make.

His mother was supportive but wanted Ethan to be sure he was following his heart and was willing to commit to such an important decision.

It was the most exciting time in Ethan's young life.

Lydia Andrews began receiving anonymous threats about a year following her son's final decision to begin the journey to priesthood.

Threats of various nature were not unusual in Lydia's professional life as an assistant editor of a newspaper of moderate circulation. These occurred usually following a controversial article or a political piece that tended toward the liberal side in such a conservative region of the country. Some of these topics she addressed in op-ed pieces; other times she toned down the threats, focusing on common issues and published these in the Reader Comments section of the paper, just above the obituaries.

These new threats were of evangelical nature, biblical scripture from the Old Testament. Having referred to a piece in a Catholic magazine in one of her op-eds, Lydia assumed that they were reactions to that piece. The story had been picked up by regional papers.

The second letter was not addressed to the newspaper in Watertown, but to Lydia Andrews herself with the following Biblical quote:

The rod and reproof give wisdom: but a child left [to himself] bringeth his mother to shame.

She shared the letter with Ethan. He knew immediately who had authored it. Lydia tried to downplay the notice, but Ethan quickly feared for his mother.

"The preacher has found us," he said with enough caution in his voice to raise concern in his mother.

"Ethan, it's been too many years. Surely the old preacher has forgotten."

"He must have found out that I converted to Catholicism. And then there's the matter of the money your aunt took from him."

Even though it had been seven years since Ethan's escape from Reverend Gunter, an icy image of the callous leader stuck in Ethan's mind.

"I'll not pay for my aunt's indiscretion, nor her selfishness," Lydia told her son. What they both did was illegal."

"He's not going to stop. I know that. We don't need him in our lives right now. I could borrow the money from Father Danny..."

"You won't!" Lydia raised her voice.

"Then I'll go back to him if that's what he wants. I'm not scared anymore."

"And give up your priesthood? Ethan, I'm not going to consider any other notions you have. You're my blood son. I love you. I would rather die than have you face that horrible man again."

Ethan was scared for his mother. He knew what the old preacher was capable of. Although he wouldn't mention it to her, he possessed a will to confront his abuser again, this time as a young man with the strength and the will to stand his ground. He'd also been thinking about Gracie a lot and wanted to make contact with his half-sister. He had been planning to do that before heading off to the seminary.

One quiet evening about two weeks after the first threat had been made, Ethan and Lydia were sitting at the dinner table, having just finished the evening meal, when something crashed through the bay window in the living room. Shattered glass rained over the window seat and the hardwood floor, the heavy object thrown now rolling in front of the dining room.

Ethan scrambled out his chair and picked up the baseball-sized rock. It was spray-painted in bright red and had written on it the numbers *666* in black. He dropped it as if it were a piece of burning lava rock and turned back to his mother.

"I'll call the police," Lydia said, a mixture of fear and anger flushing her face.

"Mom, this is enough! The preacher is crazy. I must put a stop to all of this and make sure Gracie is safe."

They argued about it for the better part of that evening, Lydia saying she would not allow him to go and Ethan replying that he was now old enough to make his own decisions. Soon she was pleading with her son to stay at home.

"Trust me, Mom. I will do the right thing."

"What? Kill the man?"

Ethan held his mother and could feel her trembling in his arms. "Do you really think I am capable of such a thing. I could no more endanger a man's life than take my own. My words are my sword, and I plan to speak my mind and put an end to this madness."

Early the next morning there was a loud knock at the front door. Ethan was up already packing his suitcase for the trip to Arrow Point. By the time he came down the stairs, he saw his mother sitting with Father Danny in the kitchen alcove.

Ethan was annoyed that his mother had contacted the priest. It showed that she didn't have faith in her son, that he was still an adolescent and couldn't be trusted in making his own decisions.

"You're not going to sway my decision!" Ethan said, without even greeting the priest.

"Actually," Father Danny said, "I thoroughly support it. You need to confront this preacher and seek closure to your painful past."

Ethan looked at his mother. She had tears in her eyes but nodded slowly with her consent.

Father Danny began, "You know, in a way you are half a priest already at least in your heart. One and a half is better than just a half."

Ethan looked puzzled.

"We are going to confront this man together, Ethan. You're not quite old enough to drive, and a hitchhike would be dangerous. I'll drive and we can be there in just a few hours. We can leave now if you want."

"But it is not safe for you," Ethan weakly argued with the priest.

Father Danny laughed. "Look at me, lad. I'm a tad over fifteen stone, that's more than 200 pounds. I stand near six feet. And I wear a shield."

"It must be invisible," Ethan remarked, just beginning to consider the offer.

"The priestly cloth is not to be underestimated, lad. If I can remain safe from the devil I'll surely stand my ground against an immoral preacher."

Now realizing that his mother would be left alone in the house and that those who had cast the stone were probably still in town, Ethan told her that she wouldn't be safe in the house, that it would be better for her to come along.

"I've already called the police and they've promised to keep an eye on the house. If it happens again, I can always stay at the newspaper."

"Or at the church," Father Danny said. "The nuns there will let you use one of the bedrooms."

"I'll be just fine," Lydia said.

◆

They took the new Route 212 south of Lake Kampeska and headed westward through a patchwork of farmland and small lakes and towering rows of unharvested cornfields. The sky was blue with just a few streaks of clouds.

By the time they reached Arrow Point, where Route 34 crossed the large bend in the Missouri River, familiar landmarks began to appear. Ethan wasn't sure exactly where Arrow Point Baptist Church was located in the growing city limits, but he knew if they followed the old Arrow Point Road they would surely find it.

It was mid afternoon and the overhead sun unseasonably hot. The air conditioning in the priest's car was not working and they had survived the heat by having the air blow through the open windows. Now, driving at the conservative speed limit, Father Danny and Ethan were dripping in sweat, more so the priest who had chosen not to remove his collar and black jacket.

When they passed the old 7-Eleven on Maine Street, Ethan rose in his seat and said, "It's down a way on this street, maybe a mile. I remember now. The preacher used to make me walk there and back to buy him his chaws."

"A tobacco-chewing man of God," Father Danny said sardonically. "He probably had someone else buy him his whiskey."

When they were just a quarter of a mile away from the church, there were signs staked in the lawns and two banners between the telephone polls on each side of the street. One of them read *GOD HATES SINNERS*, another *HOMOSEXUALITY IS AN ACT OF THE DEVIL*, and one even more hateful *GOD HATES CATHOLICS!*

Smaller signs, some on white sheets, hung from the windows of neighbors. The most repulsive was a reference to black people, words accompanied by a hanging noose.

They got to the second overhead banner which read, *DO NOT ENTER UNLESS YOU HAVE REPENTED YOUR SINS!*

Before placing both hands on the wheel, Father Danny removed his collar and asked Ethan to roll up the windows. "It's not just the church, lad. It's a whole brainwashed community. We have more than the preacher to fear."

"We'll never get in," Ethan said dispiritingly.

A black picket fence rose six feet around the church compound, a swinging gate at the front flanked by church officials or devoted neighbors. The church and steeple had been repainted with a hideous shade of gray, making it appear like a granite structure, a fortress not to be entered. Or escaped from.

They drove around once and then approached the black gate. "I think it's the devil they worship," the priest whispered as he rolled down his window. A man stuck his head halfway into the window and looked at Ethan and then seemed startled by the priest's presence. He withdrew his head quickly with a slight gasp, as if he had just been contaminated.

"Don't worry," Father Danny said. "I've been excommunicated and now I wish to repent and join your church." He turned toward Ethan. "And the boy too."

The priest was dressed in his black shirt and pants, which ironically appeared to be the required attire for male churchgoers. Ethan was dressed in similar shirt and pants, an outfit he had dressed in right after he decided to allow Father Danny to make the drive.

The man planted his palm atop the roof of the car and held it in a fashion that suggested he had the power to hold the vehicle from entering the compound.

"You'll first have to be baptized in the river," he said.

"Yes, of course," the priest said and then asked the man how they could arrange that.

"Reverend Gunter must determine that."

"Is he in?"

The man looked sternly at Father Danny. "The Reverend is always in his church."

"May we enter then?"

The man lifted his hand from the roof and directed them to where they could park the car.

They waited inside the church for over an hour. It was half-full of parishioners who were murmuring in prayer, several raising their voices above the others, often repeating the same prayer. There appeared to be a lot of anger in the room as some of the older men were slamming their fists on the pews in wailing dirges of repentance.

Father Danny felt as though he was in the confines of the Satan's lair. He was not scared but upset by all the anger he felt in the room. He'd read about fringe churches like this one but never imagined such a pitch of hatred lay in the hearts of the churchgoers. He could only imagine how the Reverend would behave.

Finally Reverend Joshua Gunter appeared at the pulpit. He had grown a full beard and wore a black medieval-looking cloak with a flattened hood, his pale hands poking through scalloped sleeves. He took a firm hold of the edges of the lectern.

He immediately addressed the priest and the adolescent, his eyes finding them as if they were gems in the rough or foul-smelling sinners who were beyond redemption. The repugnancy twisted his face.

While never taking his eyes off the intruders, the reverend began asking church-goers if they approved of an ex-priest joining the congregation. Most shouted *No!* calling them plants of the devil. One woman with an infant in her arms rose and hissed, "*Wolves in sheep's clothing!*

The reverend was only beginning. "If I have them repent and then cut out their tongues?"

No...no...no! the congregation replied in unison.

"And if I pluck out their eyes for the birds to feast upon...?"

No...no...no! the congregation repeated.

"And if I cut out their hearts...?"

The congregation swelled in waves of *no's* until they had reached such a feverish pitch the preacher's invocations were drowned out by the noise.

Ethan was sick to his stomach. The preacher's wretched look and tone had brought back boyhood memories. He was sweating heavily and began feeling a mounting rage in his throat. Suddenly, he stood up and pointed a long finger at the preacher.

"You stole me and called me Abraham," he yelled, "and tried to raise me as your son. But you are evil to the heart. Look what you've done to these good people. You have filled them with such hatred and anger and fear. You have robbed them of their souls, you, the devil at heart!"

Ethan would have lunged at the preacher but Father Danny held firm his arm. Then the priest stood up, placing the white collar around his neck. He'd taken a small bottle of holy water from his pocket and began blessing the congregation with sprinkles of the sacred liquid.

The reverend looked like he had been struck by acid. His eyebrows were arched over seething eyes, his mouth open and his hands trembling and seeking sturdy support on the lectern.

Parishioners flung themselves from their seats, farther rows leaning sideways as if a great flood had caved in on them. A horrible moaning rose from the crowd, half-plaintive, almost inhuman like creatures in horrible suffering.

Father Danny pushed Ethan out of the pew and was holding the holy water up in one hand with the other making the sign of cross, blessing the wretched church and the mislead church-goers. He stopped short of blessing the preacher and instead raised his crucifix as if sheltering himself from the devil.

In his thick Irish brogue he said, "The grace and peace of God our Father and the Lord Jesus Christ be with you."

Ethan dutifully answered, "Blessed be God, the Father of our Lord Jesus Christ."

He saw Gracie sitting with her mother in one of the pews and leaned over. He recognized her by her eyes and the bright innocence on her face.

"Gracie, come with us," he implored but her mother held her firmly.

He would never know if his half-sister would have left her parents and the church, but it took him no time to see that she was still concerned for him. She spoke his new name and smiled, now a young woman herself, auburn curls and a bonnet adorning her head. He leaned over and whispered that he loved her.

Father Danny looked like he was leading a parade, Ethan behind him, holy water and a brass crucifix in the other. They heard the preacher ranting on behind them, no doubt incredulous at what had just happened in his church.

Finally in the car and backing out of the parking space, the priest and the boy then made haste out of town.

"It was Father Danny who said, "Ethan, my boy, that's the first exorcism I've ever had the privilege to perform."

◆

Lydia was fed up by the time she'd received the sixth telephone threat at her office. After that she had Molly, her assistant, screen the calls. Whoever was calling was trying to scare her. One woman threatened that she would be kidnapped. That message had ended with the words, *You are being watched!*

The police met her at the newspaper. She didn't want to go into any background details but did suggest that the threats were religious in nature.

"The fringe," the detective who introduced himself as Lieutenant Blake said. He seemed to know a lot about these religious groups, saying they were really cults, extensions of radical views stemming from Manson's *Helter Skelter* days in California. "You know, that's where all this radical stuff originated."

"So you think Manson's cults are threatening me?" Lydia said with a bit of humor in her voice.

"No, Ma'am. I think they've got them all locked up," Blake said all too seriously. "It's the notion that's still alive and kicking. Could be someone your paper wrote about or...well, a jilted acquaintance."

"No jilted lovers, no ex-husband or boyfriend," Lydia said. "The last threat referred to kidnapping me. I don't believe a word of it. It just pisses me off that I have to contend with such garbage."

"Yes, Ma'am," the accompanying female detective said.

"Now you're talking about a whole new ballgame," Blake said, shifting his feet on the squeaky floorboards of the small office. "Kidnapping can be a federal offense. I want you to know that the police take this matter very seriously, Ms. Andrews."

They took all the information they needed, listened to several unanswered calls that had resulting in threatening messages on the answering machine and then told Lydia that it would be best that she not go home until her son and the priest returned.

Ethan, with Father Danny in the background, had called Lydia from a payphone just outside of Arrow Point. Each had spoken with her, assuring her that everything was just fine, except for the Arrow Point Baptist Church. Ethan had said something about a mass exorcism. They planned to be back before eleven that evening.

The newspaper office was oddly quiet after the police left. The latest edition had been put to bed hours earlier, the printing press had finished printing the 3,000 copies that had been cut and stocked, ready for the delivery boys to begin delivery to customers at around 4:30 am the next morning. All the staff but Lydia had left. The newspaper business was customarily a frenetic and noisy affair, with typewriters clacking, people talking over each other, the ringing of phones and the ever-present grind of the presses.

Now, Lydia could have heard a pin drop. She dimmed the light in the front office, made sure the doors were locked, especially the one to the loading dock where the papers were stacked for delivery.

Soon she became irritated by her own imposed seclusion. She knew that hiding like this was necessary, but it reminded her of her childhood with her aunt, who had instilled a general fear in her niece.

Close to eleven and probably only minutes away from being picked up by Father Danny and Ethan, Lydia grabbed a cigarette from her desk drawer (a recent vice brought on by the pressures of work) and opened the front door and stood outside.

Even at this hour she could hear the double header baseball game winding down at the local high school, a haze of light in that direction from the newly-installed sodium-vapor lamps. Several car horns sounded in a celebratory overlap. Obviously, the Watertown *Arrows* remained undefeated.

She lit her cigarette and inhaled deeply. It was not unusual to see the less fortunate souls of society, now properly referred to as the *homeless*, poking around garbage cans and the large bins lodged behind restaurants and other business establishments. She watched sadly as an old woman overdressed in dangling sweaters and a shaggy overcoat leaned over the garbage bin on a side street adjacent to the newspaper. If Ethan were there he would have given the woman his last dime and probably offered to walk her to the nearest shelter. He was always trying to help people, mostly the unfortunate.

Reminded of her son's magnanimous ways, Lydia dug into her purse and found a dollar.

She turned toward the destitute woman and began approaching, smiling, buoyed not by her own decision to provide assistance but by the remembered good-heartedness of her son.

She stopped suddenly.

The cigarette fell from her fingers and lay on the edge of the concrete curb, smoke twirling up from the dying red glow of its core and shivering as a warm breeze engaged it in a gentle tango.

Chapter Six

Jessica Lowery Gibson met her husband when she was twenty during a fund-raising event in Denver. He was the son of a congressman but had relinquished any ambition to follow in his father's political steps when he found his talent as a shrewd and very successful business leader.

The marriage was a Denver social event attended by state congressmen and women, the sitting mayor and some of the most affluent denizens of the mile-high city.

With a recently-earned MBA, a new handsome husband and an enormous chalet-type house tucked in the eastern slopes of the Rockies, Jessica felt at the top of the world.

The first two years of their marriage were a page right out of Camelot. Allen was earning a high six digit income, and Jessica was considering several offers from major corporations, including an executive accounting position at Xerox.

Macy was an unexpected and certainly unplanned pregnancy. Jessica had been on the pill since their wedding day and eventually changed to an IUD due to the medication's side effects. She was a slim woman who exercised regularly. The first sign of her pregnancy had been severe bouts of morning sickness. Within two weeks she was showing.

At nearly twenty-one inches and weighing in at nine and three-quarter pounds, Macy Lindsey Gibson was a child to contend with. By her fifth birthday she was not only rambunctious but precociously talkative. She was already reading children's books, including *Alice In Wonderland* and the *Nancy Drew* series. She was a gorgeous girl with fluffy brunette hair and sparkling hazel eyes, coquettish and full of prodding curiosity.

Jessica kept her daughter stimulated by enriching the girl's library. She was an exceptionally-fast reader and was soon reading at least a book a day. Her teachers reported that she was reading at an adult level when she was just seven years-old. She also had a talent for writing, often completing challenging writing assignments that impressed her teachers.

She attended the best private school for girls, was an exceptional athlete and by the time she was fifteen already had her eyes set on Wellesley College, hopefully with an athletic scholarship.

Just before dinner one evening Allen confessed to an overnight affair while at a conference in Hawaii, alluding to it as if it were an event on a business schedule and obviously not expecting to be forgiven for the transgression. Unable to eat, Jessica left the dinner table and went to her room.

It was the second time he'd so casually admitted to an affair, and Jessica had felt the pain but had also let it go, this time no longer willing to see herself as a smitten wife who had no choice but to react to her husband's behavior. She was startled that evening when she let go of the anger and suddenly felt empowered in a way she had never before.

There was a knock at the bedroom door. Macy sat down next to her mother and said, "He's such a shit sometimes."

"He may be a shit but he's still your father, for better or worse."

"You should divorce him. I'll be okay."

"It's not exactly that easy. I mean, my heart still has feelings for your father. I still love him but I know that we can't live together anymore. It's complicated and a process that takes time."

Macy rolled over in the bed onto her stomach, cupping her chin in her hands, her long legs crossed behind her. Her shoulder-length hair became a tent for her face and those gorgeous sixteen year-old eyes.

"I love you, Mom."

"I know. I love you too. We'll get through this."

"You're so spiritual about this," Macy said. "You've always been that way when bad things happen."

Jessica ran her hand through her daughter's silken hair. "What do you mean, honey?"

"It's like you have this weird faith that things will always work out."

"I've just learned to accept events in my life I really don't want to put any energy into fighting. Most of them don't mean anything in the long run. Letting go of things is an innate process. All children naturally do it. Well, maybe not all, but certainly those who have proper support and love. I've just practiced a lot and I think I am a better person for it."

"Mom, you work too hard and deserve better."

"Like what?"

Macy draped one hand over her head, spreading her fingers. "Like a castle and a real prince."

"I've been through Camelot."

"And?"

"It's not what it's hyped up to be. You have to have some conflict in a relationship, some manageable tension to make the good of it feel genuine."

"Huh?"

Jessica laughed. "Trust me. You'll see."

Allen moved out of the house a week later. He seemed to do it in a dutiful way, without resistance and any show of annoyance or guilt.

Jessica didn't want to remain in the marriage bedroom and moved into one of the larger guest bedrooms, which was situated closer to Macy's room.

Late that fall it came as no surprise when her daughter was accepted with full scholarship at Wellesley in Massachusetts. She was accepted not only for her brains but her physical abilities as a baseball and lacrosse player. Her father found out and called to congratulate her. He also asked to speak with Jessica to see if she was doing okay. The brief conversation was congenial.

There was no discussion of separation or final divorce. He spoke as if nothing had happened between them, as if he were on a long sabbatical and would eventually return. When he told her he still loved her, Jessica thanked him and said goodbye.

Macy breezed through her senior year of private high school. She enrolled in several college-level courses, one on advanced writing where she had to write short stories and poems and then critique those of others in the class. Although she loved to write, she had been reluctant to enroll in the course because she didn't think she was good enough. It was her English teacher who had convinced her to enroll.

That decision would eventually change the course of her life.

Macy and her mother visited the elite college that following spring. She had to attend early orientation and then make all the arrangements for housing and such.

The sprawling campus with its private lake, groves of conifers and hardwoods and hills rolling down to vast green meadows was a sight to behold. The architecture of the buildings was spectacular, fusing both Cape Cod arched buildings with elaborate mansion-like structures.

"My God, I'm going to get lost here," Macy said as they toured as much of the campus as time would permit. She visited the massive cluster of resident halls including Pomeroy Hall where she would be living, an elegant edifice near the campus Observatory.

They spent a week in a campus hotel just outside of Boston. While Macy was attending orientation classes, Jessica walked about the extravagant campus, marveling at the buildings and the rustic countryside. She had heard about this highly-credentialed college, seen pictures of it in brochures, but had never imagined a campus of such grandeur.

That August they picked out all the basic necessities for college dorm life and packed the Range Rover with these and sports equipment and two cartons of Macy's favorite books.

Allen would meet them in Boston at a hotel where he would be staying. While he didn't say it, Jessica sensed that he was coming to town not only to see his daughter but for business reasons. When he called upon arrival, she changed plans and asked that he meet them on campus.

Macy had a complicated relationship with her father. He had never been one to coddle her as a child and kept as much emotional distance between them as he did physical distance during constant business trips. She respected him as her father, loved him but had always sensed that he was not fully comfortable around her. Jessica and Macy had talked about this paternal detachment, her mother explaining that it had nothing whatsoever to do with her, that he'd had a problem with his own mother that had probably generalized to all women in his life, including his wife and daughter.

They all met at the admissions headquarters, each embracing each other in perfunctory fashion. Macy held on to him just a little longer than he was accustomed to, causing him to back off slightly and then re-embrace, patting her primly on the back.

After papers had been filled out and signed and Macy had reviewed all the freshmen conditions, they all made their way to Pomeroy Hall and Macy's fourth-floor dorm room. Allen trudged back and forth from the SUV to the room, unloading boxes and three large suitcases full of clothing.

"He loves you and is proud of you," Jessica told her daughter in-between one of his trips.

"Sure," Macy said.

"No, it's true. He's told me that many times. He just doesn't have the ability to show it."

"Mom," Macy began, changing the subject, "I'm so excited about college and studying and all the friends I've yet to meet. I feel so mature."

"I hope not too mature. Independence begins here but it takes time and a lot of good judgment."

"I'm going to miss you, Mom."

"Hey, I'll only be 2,000 miles away. We can meet halfway on Saturdays."

"No, really."

"I love you more than you can imagine, sweetheart," Jessica said, now looking squarely into her daughter's eyes. "You have a brand new iPhone and I expect for you to use it, that is, to call your mother at least once a week. You'll be back for the holidays, and I plan to take you somewhere special on spring break. And I'm always here for you whenever you need to share. Remember that, honey."

When Allen had finished the last of the transfer, he stood in the middle of room, his hands on his hips. "Something's missing," he said.

"Macy's roommate," Jessica said.

"Yes that but something else more essential." He retrieved a silver-plated key fob from his pocket and handed it to Macy. "It's a brand new Mercedes SLS, white with red interior. I figure you'll need it to pick up all your beaus."

"Dad..."

"If your mother agrees to take me to the airport tomorrow, then it's all yours. Let's have a look at it anyway."

"Dad, I don't need a car on campus. I don't think freshmen are allowed to park here anyway. I want to walk and ride around on a bicycle. I'd get lazy relying on a car."

Macy gave her father a long hug and thanked him for being so thoughtful. She rose on her toes and pecked him on the cheek.

Allen looked over at Jessica, shrugging his shoulders. "I guess I won't be needing that ride to the airport."

Jessica accepted a job working for J. Dutton Associates, an advertising firm with corporate offices in San Francisco, New York, London and New Delhi. It was a huge firm that had taken on numerous famous clients around the world. Her position was not in the creative section of the company but rather in the accounting division. Based in California, Jessica soon made division manager and in short time was being called to other offices where she performed the role of executive account reviewer. Highly proficient at what she did, she was not always welcomed with open arms, mostly in foreign divisions whose managers felt she was being sent to spy on them.

She had taken time off at the beginning of Macy's first semester at college. She'd incorrectly anticipated that little problems would require a mother's quick visit or more regular sojourns to keep her daughter's morale up. She was wrong, of course, as Macy seemed neither homesick nor in need of maternal support. She was happy away, enjoying her first real taste of independence and her newly-chosen creative writing classes.

Despite her frequent business trips, Jessica was lonely without daily contact with her daughter. She missed their talks, the baseball and lacrosse games, the complaints and commiserations and all the parenting woes of raising a teenager.

The house in Denver was too big and much too full of memories. It reminded her of Macy, of course, but also of the good days of the marriage.

She soon convinced herself that the house had to go, that she had to sell it and find something smaller and more personal. Macy still had three more years before graduation. The condo or house would have to be large enough to accommodate a college student and visiting roommates and friends. Jessica wanted it relatively close to the airport, so that following long flights she wouldn't have far to drive.

On a partial summer break, having completed an extra course in romantic literature during July, Macy surprised Jessica one rainy Saturday afternoon by calling her from the airport.

"I'm here!" she said brightly.

It took Jessica a few moments to realize that her daughter had taken a secret flight from Boston.

"Oh my God, Macy...you're kidding?"

"You don't want me?"

"Don't move. I'll be there in fifteen minutes," Jessica said, snapping closed her laptop in the office den.

Her daughter looked amazing. She had grown her hair out and lightly feathered it, enhancing her oval face. She wore a pair of white flared slacks and a gorgeous pink lace blouse. Her small bangle earrings reminded Jessica of those she had worn during a comeback of the seventies fashion when she was in college. The mascara drew out her hazel eyes, and the glossy skin-tone lipstick made her lips look inviting. Too inviting.

"I'm writing my first novel," Macy said proudly on the drive to the house. "I think I have some interested editors."

"We'll make sure it gets published," Jessica said, realizing at once that it sounded just like what Allen would say. "On its own merits, of course," she added.

"I just love writing, Mom. It's what I want to do with my life."

"That's wonderful," Jessica said, realizing that Allen would not at all approve of such a whimsical career. Maybe it was just a phase. And if it wasn't, she knew her daughter would become a successful writer if that's where her heart was.

They talked more about the book and the activities Macy had been exposed to at school. She thought her daughter was going to be taking too heavy a load for the coming fall semester. Macy talked about taking a course next summer at the prestigious Iowa Writer's School if she could get in. Her creative writing professor was a successful novelist who'd published several books, heavily influenced by the writings of Joyce Carol Oates.

"Who?"

"She wrote sort of strange novels about strange characters. Noire fiction, so to speak."

"Oh," Jessica said, feeling a little ignorant for not recognizing the author.

Her daughter had almost two weeks before she had to head back to school, and the two of them made the most of it. She told her mother that she wanted to go skiing, and they found a resort in Oregon famous for summertime snowboarding and skiing. Jessica made quick reservations at Timberline lodge on Mount Hood.

"You should bring your bathing suit," Macy said. "That's what they wear up there during the warm months."

"I don't think so."

Jessica and Allen had often taken Macy to the ski slopes in Colorado as she was growing up. She was a natural from the start. Jessica enjoyed the sport but wasn't quite as confident as her daughter. It had been many years since she'd put on a set of skis. She was game now if only to make Macy happy.

They lucked out with the flight to Portland the next day and reserved an SUV at Hertz, from where they would drive the one and a half hour trip to the lodge.

Macy made her mother buy new sunglasses and a light pink ski jacket with removable lining. She also surreptitiously purchased a sexy two-piece bathing suit, hoping her mother might give it a try once she saw others wearing similar beachwear.

Jessica felt a little crazy about it all, the spontaneity, the youthful almost girlish freedom.

On the drive up to the lodge, with the moon roof open and the windows rolled down, her hair tussled by the wind and Macy blaring a song by Maroon 5, Jessica felt, at least for a few moments, like mother and daughter were sisters. By the time they checked in to the lodge, she felt altogether different, snapping back into her role as dutiful mother.

The room in the old hotel was spectacular. Oak timber walls and flooring, a ready-lit fireplace and two king size beds overlooked a line of small chalets and farther down a forest of snow-dappled whitebark and conifer pines.

By 2:30 that afternoon, they'd rented skis and poles. Each had brought their custom-made boots. They moved with the crowd into the main entrance, dragging their equipment and joining the squeak and hobble of others moving outside.

"I want to ride the Magic Mile and come down Coffel's Run," Macy said excitedly as she studied the trail map brochure.

"I'll start on the lower trails until I get my ski feet back. You've skied while at school. It's been years for me."

"If Dad could see us now," Macy laughed.

Jessica watched her daughter as she grabbed her poles and was being scooped up by one of the fast-moving lift chairs. Macy turned and waved.

Jessica took a chairlift to one of the beginner's runs, which from above hardly looked like a novice slope with its moguls and steep descent. At the top she got tangled with her skis, one of them popping off, prompting the young smiling lift operator to stop the lift until she had successfully exited the chair.

"Take care, Ma'am," he said, his bright teeth and copper-tinted sun glasses making him look like quite the perennial the ski bum.

She did fine until she approached the first mogul, which looked huge with its swollen shadow behind it. She probably would have made it just fine had she not given in to the fear and leaned too far forward in her skis. The result was an awkward half-flip, landing her on her rump, causing her to slide helplessly and inelegantly for the next fifty yards to the bottom of the run.

A tall man probably in his seventies reached down to give her a hand when she finally slid to a stop. "First time skier?" he said somewhat pompously. He looked remarkably youthful in his loose alpine sweater, designer jeans and sunglasses. When she stood up, he towered over her by at least a foot. He had a well-trimmed white beard and penetrating blue eyes.

"Thank you. It's been a while," she said and turned away, put off by his condescending remark.

"I'm sorry. I didn't mean to sound that way," he said as if reading her mind. "I'm Harold. Harold Stein." He extended his hand again.

She shook it just to be polite. She gave him her first name. "Thanks again for your help," she added, turning back toward the lift.

"Coffee, perhaps?" he said as she walked away.

Jessica wasn't sure why she'd accepted his offer and as they sat across from each other in a pinewood booth, she wished she hadn't. He went on about his long life, his service in the military, his three grown children and seven grandchildren and how he had mastered most of the challenging runs around the world, including The Streif in Kitzbuehel, Austria. He fancied himself an historian and said he had published several books on the Punic Wars.

Jessica listened politely, thanked him for the coffee and said she had to go look for her daughter. She couldn't believe that in their whole fifteen minutes together he had failed to ask anything about herself except where she came from.

What a conceited jerk she thought, snapping on the skies and then pushing off with her poles towards the area below the lifts where she expected Macy would be waiting.

◆

She'd almost taken the first run to her left and then, realizing it was not the trail she wanted, she'd drifted down to Coffel's Run, stopping short at the crest of the descent. It was an intermediate trail and, despite the warning that snow depth was light in many areas, she decided to make a go of it.

The temperature on the highest slopes was in the forties, ten degrees cooler than down at the lodge. Macy hadn't seen anyone in bathing suits but many of the younger skiers wore shorts and tee shirts. She was glad she'd dressed in her ski suit, not so much because of the cool temperature but to protect her from scrapes and bruises if she fell on patches of bare ground.

At the top before she'd committed to the run, Macy had looked down the trail and the broken copse of pine flanking the woods. In the winter they would have been mantled in heavy snow but now, save for a few spots, they were bare and lush green. The view was spectacular and the cool air held the faraway scent of burning pine.

At the higher level of the run the snow was packed but grainy with numerous icy patches, making for a slower downhill. But soon Macy found her edge and was carving narrow tracks and improving her speed and agility.

A snowboarder had fallen about a hundred yards down where the run elbowed to the left. He was a teenage kid with rusty hair and a spate of freckles on his forehead and cheeks. He had a small gash on the right forearm where he must have scraped a rocky patch.

Macy slid to a stop and peered over her skis. "Hey, you okay?"

"Aw shit!" he said without looking up. He got on his board again and, looking back to thank her, he twisted to a halt, gawking at Macy as if he'd suddenly seen his soul-mate. A skier zipped past and yelled at him to move.

Obviously irritated but still gawking at Macy, he turned and sped down the trail as if trying to outrace her.

Midway down, the trail steepened and Macy found herself having to really concentrate, employing every skill and instinct she had. Patches of exposed rock whizzed past, a slight mogul here and there and coming up a bottleneck of skiers at the every edge of the run, where a fully exposed ledge of rock glistened in the early afternoon sun. The gridlock caused several approaching skiers to fall and one brave one to actually leap into the air, successfully landing with an expletive just a few feet beyond the rocky shelf.

Macy swung far left of the impasse, now cluttered with fallen bodies and upended skis, and safely maneuvered her way to the deeper but slower snow. As soon as it was safe to do so, she angled back to the edge with the magnificent drop to her right and really got her speed going. There was a closed run used for night skiing just below to her right and then the drop into the pine-strangled forest.

Feeling confident she hit a wide mogul, did a leg-split in the air, landing perfectly with her skis, and then regained speed down a chute separating the two trails.

She wished her father could see her now, his daredevil daughter, and wondered whether he'd really be impressed. She knew her mom would be and was ready to tell her about the pile-up she'd successfully avoided. She planned to make two more runs before the day was over.

Where the two trails merged, Alpine on her left, Macy swung far right, lost her edge, regained it, and then, askew, careened across the night skiing trail below. Her weight was on her left ski when it should have been on the other, and she felt like a cartoon character in slow motion about to fall on her face.

But she didn't. Instead, still in suspended motion, she helplessly slid over the flag markers and found herself ducking thick branches on a downward slope that was not part of the trail. Pine needles whizzed by, one branch slapping her cheek.

Soon the off-trail became a leaf-laden pathway with broken branches and only intermittent patches of snow and ice. She was slowing down rapidly, her torso twisting as she did, trying desperately to regain her balance, embarrassed and furious at herself for screwing up what should have been an easy run back to the lodge.

Her skis stopped at the edge of a ravine, ramming into a log hard enough to snap off one ski. Her body sailed over the edge and into a long granite shelf.

A flash of white. And then all went black.

◆

A light fog enveloped the lodge with enough moisture to cause windows to dribble and walkways to become slippery. A soft haze caressed each lamplight.

It was almost seven o'clock, and Jessica stood inside the ski patrol chalet, shivering, her hands shaking, her lips and mouth dry from apprehension.

"Ma'am, you said she was alone, is that right?"

"Of course she was alone!" Jessica retorted, frustrated by all the repetition of questions.

"A boy said he saw her midway down Coffel's, so we know she was safe at that point."

The person asking the questions was a tall young man with a light brown beard who squinted at her repeatedly, as if he was having trouble with his contacts. He wore a white headband with the resort's name and logo on it.

"We have a team of six up there now, some hikers in case she went into the forest. We'll find her. Just please be patient. We know what we're doing."

Radios crackled with voices. The place was overly-warm and crowded.

Tears rained down Jessica's right cheek, an eye that always seemed to show emotion before the other. She rubbed at it with the back of her hand and then dropped her head between her knees as she sat in the hard spindle-backed chair.

"My baby," she finally sobbed.

One of the women patrollers rubbed her neck gently and leaned down beside her. "We'll find her, no matter what it takes," she said.

Another hour went by and when the news came, it was not good.

They'd found Macy in a rock-laden ravine well off the main trails. She was unconscious when the medics arrived. They had stabilized her on a backboard, wrapping her tightly for the winch ride into the hovering helicopter.

She was flown directly to the Legacy Emanuel Medical Center in Portland. The preliminary report by the hospital was not good.

Jessica didn't even return to the lodge room to retrieve their clothes. She jumped into the rental and headed west straight for the hospital. At first she was shaking so hard she couldn't catch her breath, her steeled hands gripping the wheel, her eyes in a fixed stare. When the tears came they were accompanied by stabs of sharp pain behind her eyes.

Soon she began talking to Macy in an imploring, whispery tone. "Honey, you've got to be okay. You're going to make it. Mommy loves you. Oh God, Macy, stay with us."

By the time she arrived at the hospital, the nurse who met her told her that her daughter was in critical condition and not stable enough for surgeons to perform the delicate procedure to reattach hemorrhaging vessels in her brain. They'd implanted a shunt to relieve the dangerous pressure inside. All they could do was wait and pray.

Jessica made a scene of it and demanded to see her daughter, threatening one of the surgeons if he got in her way. With nurses at her side, she was finally escorted into the ICU area. Macy's head was bundled in thickly-wrapped gauze, only the lids of her puffy bruised eyes showing. She'd obviously broken her nose. A tracheostomy had been performed. The shunt protruding from the top of her head wound its way to one of the many bags hanging on the stands. Tubes and wires extruded from the girl's body like strange umbilical cords, reminding Jessica of a scene from the movie *Coma*.

She was allowed to hold her daughter's hand and to kiss her on one cheek. Macy's rosy smell, a fragrance she'd held since birth, made her flare her nostrils. She talked softly to her in short bursts of breath, telling her how much she was loved and that she had to be strong and will herself back to health.

The doctors told Jessica that the next twelve hours were the critical period for survival. She should wait in the critical care waiting lounge, where there were recliners and hot coffee. There was a small chapel next door.

Jessica took hold of herself. She washed up in the ladies room, patting her own swollen eyes with a towel, and realized that she had to call Allen to inform him that his daughter was probably dying.

When he finally returned her call, she was in the chapel gazing up over the non-denominational alter at a pair of praying hands. She left the room and in the hallway answered the call.

"She what?" he said in disbelief when Jessica had filled him in what she knew.

There was nothing else to say that silence itself wouldn't convey. She bit her tongue, shaking her head.

"What was she doing on Mount Hood? I thought she was in school."

You stupid asshole. What difference does it make! The words screamed in Jessica's head.

"I suppose I should fly down."

In anger, exasperation and with unrelenting fear about Macy's grave condition, Jessica clicked off the cell and stared at it as if at any moment Allen would dare to call back. He didn't.

Chapter Seven

They could never prove exactly who was behind the assault. Lydia had been hit on the back of her head hard enough for her to lapse into unconsciousness. Pressed by police interviews, it was obvious that she had lost all memory of ever leaving the newspaper office, much less smoking the cigarette they had found outside.

After the police finished interviewing members of the Arrow Point Baptist Church, the local FBI were called in on the investigation. It was clearly a hate crime.

Ethan and Father Danny had nurtured Lydia back to good health, helping out in the office to make sure the paper continued to publish and assisting with financial matters.

It came as glorious news when law enforcement officials finally announced that the Reverend Joshua Gunter and two church officials had been arrested and charged with conspiracy to incite violence through hateful intentions.

Eventually the church was shut down.

Ethan's announcement that he was going to the seminary and then take his vows as a Catholic priest did not come as a shock to Lydia. In fact, she was ecstatic about it.

"He'll make a good one, Lydia," Father Danny said.

"With your guidance, I know he will," Lydia said before reaching over to hug her son.

"I have a calling," Ethan said, adding, "and I want to make you proud."

They never told Lydia the full account of what happened that afternoon in Arrow Point. Ethan, though feeling somewhat vindicated, thought it best to let the experience rest in the past.

He successfully completed his seminar studies and was soon to be ordained. Lydia wanted him to join Father Danny's church and serve the parish in Watertown, but Ethan had a vision of missionary work that seemed stronger than his faith in the Church.

◆

Attractive as she was, Lydia was bound to meet a man. And she did.

William Noyes was ten years her junior. He was a forty year-old professional photographer who worked out of Sioux Falls as a freelance photojournalist. He had worked at National Geographic for five years, traveling to colorful but remote spots around the world. He did his stint covering conflict zones as an independent photographer for five years. He'd been up for a Pulitzer for his work in Sierra Leone and had landed other awards for shots that told not just a story but a book's worth. Once he had been held by rebels in Mogadishu for over a month. It was right after the failed American raid on the city. He had been brutally tortured but survived.

They met accidently when William had entered Lydia's newspaper office asking if it was okay to use their fax machine. He was passing through town following the Iowa caucuses, cameras dangling from his shoulders and a press pass hanging from his neck.

It was not sudden love but rather instantaneous. They couldn't break their stares and were tongue-tied when they tried to speak. Both felt as though they'd met their soul mates. A cup of coffee and donuts, and actually very little words, led to a dinner at Dempsey's Brewery Restaurant & Pub that evening.

After sharing personal stories of their lives and following the long stay at the restaurant with just enough brew to set their hearts aglow, they meandered down North Broadway, holding hands and staring into each other's eyes like two puppy-love teenagers.

William spent the next three nights in a Watertown motel, each morning rushing to the newspaper to help Lydia.

They were married two months later by Father Danny, not inside the church but in front of the peacocks at Bramble Park Zoo. Despite the priest's initial hesitancy to break from Church tradition, he was won over by the couple's enthusiasm and by Lydia's pleading eyes. She had become like a daughter to him ever since Ethan had started his missionary work.

She tried to call Ethan to give him the news but she couldn't get through to the international operator. She sent him a telegram instead, pleading him to make time to come home and meet his new stepfather.

They refurbished Lydia's old house, adding an extension at the rear for Lydia's sunroom and garden patio. William became the newspaper's lead photojournalist, and while there were few events in Watertown requiring a photographer of his status and experience, he did fly out of the state for conventions and to cover the increasing social unrest in many large cities. He was rarely away from Lydia for more than a week and when he was, every night they telephoned each other.

One bright morning in May Lydia awakened early and led William to the just completed sunroom. They sat on a the white rattan couch with yellow water lily prints on the large throw cushions. Lydia snuggled close.

William didn't know exactly what to expect, an admission or announcement, and could feel his heart beginning to beat harder. He had a faint idea, though, of what was to follow.

"William, we're going to have a baby," Lydia said, placing William's hand on her stomach.

"Oh my God! Are you sure?"

"Of course, I'm sure. I went to my doctor. I'm almost twelve weeks now. Can you imagine...at my age?"

That announcement began a period of paternal doting that had William doing everything from cooking to cleaning and back rubs in the tub. They attended both parenting and birthing classes together and when the gender of the fetus was confirmed, the ironing room was transformed into a nursery with pink and white stripes on the walls. A pale white crib and matching dresser took up most of the space of the small room.

William planned to build a girl's bedroom upstairs, taking the old study Lydia had used. Now that their family was growing, they made plans to expand the house farther, adding a whole wing to the side where the old stand-alone garage stood.

Lydia didn't begin to show until her fifth month but she had been wearing maternity clothes since the time she learned that she was going to have a daughter. While she was hardly plump, she had a bona fide bump and loved the sense of carrying a child. Her face took on a radiant look, her cheeks rosy and her skin smooth as an infant's bottom.

People she hardly knew would come up and strike up a conversation about her pregnancy, as though the birth, when it came, would be a community event. Others who were friends or knew her through the newspaper would stop by the house with cakes, pies, roasted chickens and maple sugar hams.

Although she had been pregnant with Ethan twenty-five years earlier, she barely remembered that experience and the clandestine birth under the selfish eyes of her aunt. This time it would be different. She could relish every moment, each kick and tumble of her baby. It was an easy pregnancy, with no complications beyond the occasional episodes of morning sickness.

Despite the circumstances, Ethan's birth had been easy. Lydia, therefore, saw no reason to give birth in a hospital. She and her husband had met a doula during one of the training classes. Diya, an elderly woman from New Delhi, befriended the couple and seemed to take special interest in Lydia's pregnancy. While she hadn't come out and said it, soon it became obvious that Diya was in favor of a home delivery. She had performed hundreds of them back in India, where the practice was all but customary, and when Lydia asked if it were possible she quickly agreed to helping them.

Diya had frizzy gray hair drawn tightly behind her with stick broach pins. Her face was sharply lined, although smoothed at the forehead. Her face spoke of wisdom and long years of experience. When she smiled her lips barely moved, the smile radiating from her eyes and cheeks.

William was not exactly excited by the idea when Diya explained that he would play a major role in the delivery, but with Lydia's beseeching he finally agreed.

Diya offered two positional options for delivery, one involving a warm water bath and the other a squatting birth, which she claimed was the most natural way of passing the fetus.

Under Diya's watchful eye, they rehearsed both forms of delivery and then Lydia decided she would prefer the squatting method. She was actually thinking of William as the latter position required only his physical support from the back. Diya had insisted that the husband's duty during a bath delivery was to sit in the tub along with his wife.

Lydia did have a second examination by her OB/GYN just to make sure mother and fetus were healthy. He tried to talk her out of the home delivery, strongly suggesting that she give birth in the local hospital, but Lydia had already made up her mind.

"Make sure," he had said, "that if there's excessive bleeding or it appears to be a breech birth, you call 911 immediately."

Lydia asked Diya if she was practiced in breech births, for she knew they could be complicated, especially if the umbilical cord became entangled. The doula said she was, that in fact that was the way she herself had been born.

Donations of Pampers, baby formula, jars of food and blankets poured in from well-wishers and friends. These were neatly stored away in drawers and in the small closet of the nursery room.

At thirty-two weeks, Lydia's stomach had swelled to full pregnancy. She had to support herself when she sat down or when taking a bath, even with William's vigilant assistance.

One morning Lydia stood at the doorway to the nursery and just marveled at the scene. Everything was in its proper place: changing table, highchair, infant's car seat, neatly-folded diapers and the crib with its peacock-adorned pink blanket. Everything but the little princess. It was like peaking at all the wrapped presents under a trimmed Christmas tree. The anticipation was enormous.

When the contractions began at the end of her thirty-fifth week, Lydia and Diya calmly went about the planned routine. Lydia had picked the sunroom for the delivery, leaning with her back against sofa's edge with William supporting her from the back. Diya had sheets and towels piled underneath Lydia along with a basin of warm water.

William kept pushing against her back and trying to squeeze his hands underneath her arms and had to be corrected several times.

"Just keep very gentle pressure on her middle back," Diya said as she went between Lydia's legs with a hand mirror. "Good. Good. Five centimeters," she added.

William was sweating now and breathing more rapidly. Soon he began to feel lightheaded.

Lydia turned her head sideways. "Honey, it's okay. I barely feel any pain."

She deeply regretted her comment ten minutes later when Diya announced that she was fully dilated.

"Keep back straight, push, push, push," Diya said as the baby's head began to crown.

It felt like she was passing a watermelon. The head felt so big Lydia was fearing hydrocephalus or some other deformity.

"Push. Relax now. Push. Relax now..."

From behind: "You can do this, honey...push."

At the crest of the next contraction, instead of pushing, Lydia took a deep breath and exhaled. She felt her uterus implode and then, moments later, heard her daughter's first bald cry of life.

◆

Father Danny presided over the christening. The little infant was formally named Emma Anne Andrews-Noyes, quite a mouthful but a name representing William's mother as well as Lydia's favorite forename.

Emma grew into a rambunctious toddler, always in motion, inquisitive and mimicking sounds and words. She was *talking* even before she was walking, and when the two milestones combined, the little girl was everywhere, talking to both animate and inanimate entities around the house.

While Lydia encouraged her daughter to talk to her parents and those friends who came by to visit during those early months, she became increasingly concerned about Emma's invisible *friends* and the long-winded monologues when she was addressing them.

William agreed with the pediatrician that these behaviors were not a sign of mental or emotional dysfunction and that, in many cases, were indicators of high intelligence and awareness.

Lydia and William homeschooled Emma until she was ready for first grade. By then she was reading at an eight year-old level and possessed the vocabulary of a young adult. That their child was precocious, indeed a child of advanced intelligence and capability, continued to concern Lydia, despite William's assuring words.

In the second grade she was tested on the Wechsler Intelligence Scale for Children and scored at a near genius level. The psychologist who performed the test suggested that she be placed in advanced classes. She also tempered Lydia's concerns regarding the child's invisible friends, assuring her that they were just phases she would soon outgrow.

Em, as she liked to addressed by *certain* people including her parents, was sociable among friends and schoolmates but at home indulged in long periods of solitariness, often asking her mother on weekends to serve her meals in her room.

William had finished the upstairs bedroom, designing it to Em's wishes. Bookshelves lined two walls of the room, filled with old classics to young adult favorites by C.S. Lewis, William Golding and Madeleine L'Engle.

Before she completed the second grade she began reading the greats of philosophy and soon indulged herself in spiritual and mystical readings.

One day when William was away on a trip, Emma came into her mother's room very early one morning. Lydia was awake but pretending to be asleep, just a crease of one eye open. Her daughter stood in the doorway for the longest time and then slowly approached the bed. She stared at her mother's face until Lydia couldn't take it anymore and sprung open her eyes.

"Now Em, are you trying to spook me?"

Her daughter went over and sat down on the edge of the bed. She spread open one palm and placed it against her mother's. She whispered something unintelligible and closed her eyes.

Finally she said, "Can you feel it yet, Lydia?"

Sitting straight up in the bed, Lydia chastised her daughter for addressing her by her first name. This had never happened before, although for years she had been calling her *Mother* instead of Mom.

"But your name *is* Lydia," Em argued.

"Children don't call their parents by their first names, honey. I don't mind *mother* but my given name is just not appropriate."

The issue might have been dropped then and there, but Em had a sort of pointed, troubled look on her face. She might have been pouting or just concentrating very hard.

"I love you," Em finally said, "but I don't *feel* like your daughter anymore.

Lydia grabbed her daughter's wrist and sped her into the girl's bedroom. She sat her down on the bed and looked hard into Emma's eyes.

"I don't know what you meant by that rude comment, Em, but it really upset your mother. In fact, I'm terribly hurt by what you said."

Lydia didn't wait for any explanation or further comment. She told her daughter that she was confined to her room until suppertime. She would make her a sandwich for lunch.

Closing the child's door, Lydia went back to her room and cried. Had her husband said to her that he didn't feel she felt like a wife to him anymore, she would have been hurt but able to handle it. For Em to imply that she no longer felt like a daughter exacted a deep pain in Lydia's heart. And Em wasn't even eight years old yet.

When William returned later that week he consoled Lydia and tried to convince her that it was just another weird phase of their daughter's maturing process. They finally agreed that their daughter needed some intense counseling and immediately scheduled an appointment with the school psychologist.

Sylvia Lowry, one of two psychologists assigned to the middle school Emma attended, had decades working for the Watertown School District. She was what William referred to as a gifted *active listener* and seemed to understand the therapeutic influence of silence. This was nerve-wracking for Lydia because she wanted direct explanations. And right away. She wanted her daughter to talk, instead of just sitting in the lounge chair looking off into the distance.

"Go on and tell Dr. Lowry why you don't *feel* like my daughter anymore," she finally blurted out.

William reached over and held her hand.

"Am I not a good mother to you?"

Sylvia Lowry didn't intervene, but when enough silence had passed, she said, "Em, would it be okay if just the two of us talked?"

Almost two hours passed before the psychologist came out to the corridor where Emma's parents had been waiting. She smiled warmly at them and then led them back into her office.

"Where's Emma?" Lydia asked, concerned that something had happened.

"Oh, she's with Rick, a very good social worker who wants to do some more testing. She'll be just fine, Mrs. Noyes.

"Lydia...please."

Sylvia Lowry pulled a third chair right in front of the two parents and reached over and held out each hand to them. She took a deep breath and nodded.

"I guess I don't have to tell you that you have a very gifted daughter. Not only is she intelligent well beyond her years but she has developed...let's say *spiritually* in ways that not even I can explain. I am not referring to religiosity, although she has her strong views on that, but rather in a supernatural way."

"Oh my God," Lydia said and looked over at William.

"I'm not talking about ghosts and spirits per say," Lowry continued. "Supernatural thinking goes beyond the limits of possibility and into a realm of quite profound ideas and conceptual reasoning. One of those concepts involves miracles, not necessarily divine ones but spiritual ones perceived by very intelligent minds.

"There have been many books written on the subject and there are countless experts in the field. I don't profess to understand it all but I guess it could be referred to as a form of heightened transcendentalism. I really don't think there is anything wrong with Em emotionally or psychologically. When you look at your daughter she looks like any eight year-old child. Inside, though, at least intellectually, she is conceptualizing on a level neither one of us can truly understand."

"Will she grow up normally?" William asked.

"Ah," Sylvia said. "There's that impossible word again. What is *normal*, Mr. Noyes?"

"I mean, will our daughter develop socially? Will she enjoy birthdays and going on vacations?"

"If you are asking whether Em will enjoy family life, I would say yes, but she will need intellectual stimulation, in this case academic challenges."

Lydia sat forward in her seat. "Should I allow her to call me by first name?"

"Of course not. Regardless of her intellectual advancement, that is not socially acceptable at her age. If she makes further reference to not feeling that you are her mother, I wouldn't suggest that you not punish her in any way. Show your disapproval and later on, as you feel comfortable, ask her why she feels that way. While Em may show signs of being intellectually advanced, emotionally she is still a child. This causes conflict and may possibly explain why she tests you in this manner."

"You mean she wants Lydia to react?" William asked.

"Probably. She may even test you."

"Well, she will not be allowed to call me by my first name. It just isn't appropriate. I will accept *Dad* instead of *Daddy*, but that's as far as I'll go."

Sylvia Lowry, a gentle and sensitive professional in her field, grabbed both of their hands again. "Be patient with Em," she said, but also be patient with yourselves."

Ethan had yet to meet his little sister in person but he had been sending her regular postcards and letters. He had called Lydia several times on those occasions when he could get through and even spoken briefly with William. Little Emma, though, was shy, even reticent to speak with her stepbrother.

Lydia made her son promise to come home next year, even if it was only for a few days. She had not seen him since he'd graduated from the seminary, which was almost a decade ago. She had nurtured a gathering sense that his dedication to his missionary and church work had caused their estrangement.

They would finally come together as a family during the Christmas holiday next year.

Emma had not shown any curiosity about her brother. She seemed not impressed that he was a priest and serving others. Lydia couldn't blame her, though, because Em had never been able to put a face to his name. He was just a big brother living his own life somewhere else in the world.

In all fairness to Emma, she *had* attempted to prepare her parents for the departure. She had told her mother about what was soon to happen, that she was going to be gone for maybe a week, that she would be safe and that they shouldn't worry about her.

She knew they had called the psychologist and even met with the social worker while she was in school. They were preparing for a physical departure, that she was planning to run away, but of course they were wrong.

The important journey was going to be a spiritual one, a *passing through* that only Em could fully understand at a level that was far beyond what parents and teachers could comprehend.

It was essential that she go. It was her mission in life. She didn't want to upset her parents, to make them suffer and worry, but they better get used to these spiritual departures. She had been chosen.

Her mother had begun sleeping with Em in her room, sitting in a lounge chair by the door, covered with one of her childhood blankets. She would hear her mother finally doze off to sleep and that's when she would practice her departures. Sometimes she would only be gone for a few minutes; other times the departures took longer. Much longer.

One night Emma found herself traveling at supersonic speed, lights and colors enveloping her as she whizzed through a nothingness devoid of meaning and reference. She opened her eyes to the terrified look on her mother's face and the sight of her father rushing into the room.

She had obviously stopped breathing, which she knew was not uncommon during deep departures.

Her mother began sobbing and then she cradled her in her arms so tightly, Emma could hardly breathe.

Her father rushed to the door to let the paramedics in. She could hear them trudging up the stairs, radios crackling, asking questions as they made their way into Em's room.

"I'm fine!" she finally blurted out after being prodded and attached to various medical instruments, including a heart monitor. She pushed the paramedics away. "See, my blood pressure is fine, my heart is fine, my eyes are fine and I haven't lost any of my faculties!"

"Honey, you're not fine. You were blue in the face, taking no breaths and for nearly a minute you weren't responsive. I think you need to be examined in a hospital."

Emma turned to one of the paramedics, a stout woman with curly blonde hair. "It's up to me. I do not want to go to the hospital!"

The woman smiled and patted her hand as if she were a young child. "I'm afraid it's not your decision, honey."

Her mother insisted with the paramedics that she be taken to the hospital for evaluation. She sensed that her father might have been on her side, but he seemed reticent to go against her mother's decision.

Realizing that she really couldn't prevent them for taking her away, Emma understood that she would have to change her plans. She had wanted more time to practice, to accustom herself to the nothingness, the other side. She had wanted more experience returning, which was the more difficult and dangerous part of the undertaking. Having familiar surroundings...her bed, her room and *Locum*, her best invisible friend, made it all easier to phase back into this realm.

Her mother wanted to ride in the ambulance but the paramedics said they should follow in their car.

Strapped onto the ambulance gurney, Emma asked who the paramedic with the curly blonde hair was.

"Honey, my name's Freda, and you're going to be just fine. I promise you that. Now, I need to start an IV line. Do you know what that is?"

"Yes, I'm used to it. It doesn't hurt anymore."

"So you've been in an ambulance before?"

Emma nodded, waited for the needle to be inserted, and then leaned back against the flat pillow.

There wasn't much time.

"Freda?"

"Yes, honey."

"I don't want you to be scared. I'll be just fine."

Freda leaned over and smoothed her palm over Em's forehead. "Of course you're going to be fine. If you promise not to be scared then I won't."

Summoning all of the psychic energy she could, eight year-old Emma closed her eyes and imagined the far light on the other side, and then prepared for her eviction.

Chapter Eight

E than became a priest following study and graduation from the Cardinal Muench Seminary in North Dakota. His first parish was in a small town just outside Fargo, pleasant during summer months but brutal in the fall and winter. He remained there almost two years and then, unable to bear another harsh winter, he moved south, first to Oklahoma and then New Mexico, just south of Truth or Consequences. Here he found a more hospitable climate and his first encounter with desert living.

Saint Catherine of the Sea was a small parish. The church was old and had been abandoned when a new one had been built in neighboring Williamsburg. Father Ethan asked for and received multiple donations from a group of businessmen in Albuquerque and had been able to rebuild the church from the ground up. His parishioners were limited at first but soon swelled when he began advertising and offering free breakfasts following weekend masses. He stopped short of BBQ cookouts on Sundays.

As the only priest at the church, Ethan lived in a backroom bedroom and made himself available for daily masses, confessions and occasional weddings. Every few months or so visiting novitiates and priests would come and assist with mass and church duties. Several women parishioners took it upon themselves to perform housekeeping chores, for which Ethan was more than grateful.

Father Ethan became popular for his down-to-earth sermons, which were largely based on what Father Danny had taught him about speaking directly to the people and not from behind the alter. Varying from Vatican doctrine, he often approached those sitting in the front pews and shook hands as he went on with his sermon.

He performed the Sacrament of Penance in a similar manner, not with a wall and screen separating him from the confessor but with a head blind if the individual requested it. Most found it helpful to see and feel the presence of the priest. Often times when emotions interfered with the person's confession, Father Ethan would hold their hands and feel the turmoil in their hearts. Sometimes he would embrace them and pat their backs in commiseration.

This humbled interaction shifted the focus of sinner and forgiver, lessening the Vatican's view that priests and lay people served the God on sharply different levels.

Father Ethan became a priest of the people, a collaborator in the faith and love of God. News of his divergent church manners reached the local archdiocese and soon he began receiving requests for an explanation.

Undaunted, he continued with his liberal views, feeling increasingly distant from Vatican dogma and the formality of priesthood.

His church thrived, though, and soon the congregation swelled to over 600. Visiting priests increased threefold and Ethan had to set up a formal schedule, shortening visits to just three months.

A young priest named Timothy Segal arrived one cool winter day in January. His application revealed that he was only three years out of the seminary and shared a church in Las Vegas with two other senior priests.

Tim was a natural with the congregation and began helping Ethan out at the confessionals. He was a little more intellectual than the kind of church leaders Ethan was accustomed to. If Ethan had not known better he would have guessed that Father Tim was of the Jesuit order.

They had long theological discussions on subjects varying from Vatican II and how the Pope was trying to modernize church views and practices, to how to reconcile what both believed was the reality of evolution with New Testament teachings. They thought alike and were soon getting the church involved in missionary work in Appalachia and, eventually, in refugee camps in north Africa.

"Here the Methodists have it right," Ethan said to the priest as they were organizing a missionary trip to a refugee camp in Sudan. "The church needs to go where the fundamental needs exist in the world."

Only one of them could go with this group. Before Ethan could say anything, Tim announced that he would stay back and run the church until Ethan returned.

Five church members would be accompanying Father Ethan. As none of them had ever ventured out of the state, passport applications were necessary. He was able to secure funding for the trip outside of church coffers thanks to the business group in Albuquerque.

Two days before the group was scheduled to depart, Tim approached Ethan and asked him if he would hear his own confession. Save for the introduction, they departed from the customary process and Tim came straight to the point when he said that he thought he was in love with a woman with whom he'd had a carnal relationship.

"Ethan," he said. "I'll surely be excommunicated and have to leave the church."

Ethan gave it some thought. "I guess that depends on what you plan to do."

"I think God has told me what I have to do. We've been talking for many weeks now, not in formal prayer but in silent conversations when I go on long walks. My relationship with God feels totally out of the church, if that makes sense."

"No, I fully understand, Tim." He took the priest's hand in his. "This is wonderful to hear."

Expecting to be asked to leave the church immediately, Father Tim was stunned by Ethan's remarks.

"Did you think I was going to have you excommunicated right here and now?" Ethan laughed. "Or that I would have the conviction to report this to the archdiocese?" He turned and, lifting the priest's chin, looked directly into Tim's downcast eyes. "How much do you love her?"

"What?"

"How deeply in love are you with this woman? May I know her name?"

"Mary. And I am deeply in love with her."

"Then you should marry."

"Mary's Catholic and has always wanted a church wedding. No priest would marry us now...and if they did it wouldn't be valid in the eyes of the Church."

"I'll marry the both of you right here in our church. The sacrament is waiting for you whenever you wish."

Tim squeezed Ethan's hand. They embraced. "There's something else," the young priest said.

"You wish to marry two women?" Ethan said sarcastically.

"Mary is pregnant."

◆

Ethan remained another month after the other church members returned to New Mexico. There was so much to do. He worked with other charity organizations helping on the front lines where refugees were amassed, many in conflict regions of the northern continent.

When the Red Cross, the Salvation Army and other notable organizations were forced by policy to pull out of a dangerous region, Father Ethan remained there at his own peril. Often he lived among the camps, distributing water and food sent in by Unicef, Catholic Relief Services and other aid organizations. He survived the first wave of the Ebola virus, administering an unending number of last rites. He learned to provide advanced medical aid and to assist in makeshift hospital tents.

The work took its toll on Ethan. He wasn't eating well, sleep was a rare thing and soon he succumbed to infections and a nagging respiratory disease. He hadn't taken a break in over a year and was at last sent to the southern region of Africa to rest and recuperate.

He stayed in a clinic in Johannesburg for two weeks, garnering his strength and stamina, and then intrigued by visiting some coastal areas, he departed for the eastern coast. He found Coffee Bay at the confluence of the shimmering waters of the Indian Ocean and lush verdant hillsides. It was the most beautiful place he had ever visited in his life. He had never before seen such vibrant greenery, vast undulating hills and such azure skies. It was such a contrast to the squalor and chaos of the northern conflict regions.

Feeling guilty for neglecting both his missionary work and his beloved church in New Mexico, Ethan soon caught a flight back to Johannesburg on a bush plane owned by a member of a nearby nature reserve who was heading there for supplies. The plane was an old refurbished Piper J-3 Cub, basically a two-seater with little space for supplies.

The pilot was an animated transplant from Australia with long gray hair wound tightly into a short ponytail. His name was Alfred and he talked endlessly about the reserve and his love of South Africa. Seated in the front, Ethan could hardly make out a word for the clatter and roar of the engine. Not wanting to be rude, he smiled and nodded occasionally when the pilot tapped him on the shoulder.

They hit a rainstorm just east of the Drakensberg Mountains. Rain pelted the small plane like bullets, hammering the fuselage in such a loud raucous, Ethan thought he would surely lose his hearing.

Alfred laughed and then leaned forward, handing Ethan a small headset. Suddenly, the pilot's voice boomed in his ears.

"Ain't noise-cancelling, mate," he said of the headset, "but far better'n losing your 'earing."

They dropped precipitously in a sudden downdraft, the engine screaming and Ethan's breakfast at the back of his throat, until the pilot pulled out of the fall.

"Fuckin' shit!" Alfred said, as he finally leveled off again, followed by, "Sorry, Father."

In those 20 seconds of free-fall, Ethan had managed an *Our Father* and two *Hail Marys*. "You are a damn good pilot," he said hopefully.

The plane obviously had no inboard radar, its pilot relying on radio reports from nearby towers. This storm hadn't been announced and had taken the pilot by surprise.

Their second encounter with a stall occurred following a sudden updraft about ten minutes later. Some of the small crates in the rear of the plane broke loose from their restraints and were soon tumbling forward towards the rear seat.

Ethan turned around in time to see one hit the pilot's head.

"Shit!" Alfred said, adding, "She'll be right, though."

The engine was sputtering and bucking as the rain-blast intensified, the blur of its propeller winding backward, appearing as if it was reversing its direction.

They were loosing altitude, this clearly evident by the sober look on Alfred's face when Ethan turned around again.

The priest made a sign of the cross, blessing the pilot and the suffering plane. And himself.

"Don't give up on me yet," Alfred said, adding seriously, "but we got Buckley's chance up here. Find me a highway or even a dirt road, Father."

Ethan recognized Verkykerskop on the left, a mesa-type hill overlooking green land and the same-named town. He saw a roadway passing west of the town and rapped on the side window to alert the pilot.

Alfred dropped the port wing to get a view and then leveled out. The stick was shaking ominously.

"We got a fair go if I get over that shack," he said as the starboard wing rose precipitously.

"God forbid, it's a church!" Ethan cried out, suddenly overwhelmed by the irony.

They must of clipped something on their right, a pole or part of a tree, and the fuselage shuddered with a screech.

What happened next was nothing short of miraculous, but very soon terrifying. Alfred had managed to land the Piper on the straightaway of a dirt road, hopping a few times, careening off the shoulder and then spinning around so that Ethan's windshield was facing the muddy road in the opposite direction.

It looked like one of those Indian caravans or a painted hippy van, with swirling purple and yellow and red designs on its sides and roof, along with a white peace sign on the front.

Ethan was horrified to see that the driver hadn't noticed the plane blocking the road. His head was turned and he was speaking to the passengers on the loudspeaker. The vehicle's windshield wipers, Ethan noticed, were eerily out of sync, one flopping helplessly one way, the other jerking to the left. No doubt even if the driver had his eyes on the road he probably wouldn't have been able to spot the oncoming disaster.

But he did. The bus swerved hard to its left, raising on two wheels, and then skidded past the tail of the plane, only kissing the skin of the rudder.

"Crikey!" Alfred exclaimed, patting Ethan on his shoulder and then exiting the plane to speak with the bus driver.

Ethan watched them standing in the now drizzling rainfall, the driver appearing ecstatic by the way he was jumping up and down and then mimicking the wings of the plane with wide swings of his arms. There was no animosity between them as there might have been in a near mishap in a car. In fact, they embraced each other. Two young boys hopped out of the bus and came over to the plane, one of them peering into the window.

When Alfred returned after seeing the bus continue on its journey south he was very apologetic to Ethan. "It's one thing killing myself, but a holy man like yourself.."

"It wasn't your fault, Alfred."

"That doesn't matter."

"You are a miraculous pilot," Ethan said, shaking the pilot's hands fervently.

Alfred said he would get a tow truck to pull him back into town. He said that the bus driver would be completing its round trip and would pick Ethan up on his way back to Johannesburg.

From Ethan's point, it all seemed so casual, as if planes landing on highways were a common and mundane daily event, as were near-collisions with buses. It all had been unnerving, if not downright terrifying. Maybe part of his life had flashed before his eyes, not so much his past but what lay ahead, the little church in New Mexico, Father Tim and Mary and those feelings of purpose that compelled people forward in their lives. Some called it destiny.

◆

Father Tim had failed to tell Ethan just how pregnant Mary was. When the priest picked him up at the airport in Albuquerque, they were all there: man and wife and a lively one month-old boy.

Mary, was an attractive young woman with curly strawberry hair, freckles and blue eyes. She was breast-feeding the baby in the passenger seat.

"Tim has told me so much about you, Father," she said.

"I bet he did. But how did you guys get married? Certainly not in the church?"

Tim leaned back slightly. "Father Michael, another visiting priest, from Sierra Vista. I hope you don't mind. We had to get married before..."

"Of course," Ethan said, happy for Tim and Mary, but disconcerted that the news would travel that his church was condoning, and even advertising, the marriage of priests. "I suppose little Tim was baptized by Father Michael?"

Both priest and wife glanced back at Ethan. "No," Tim said. "We were waiting for you to return to perform the Sacrament."

"And we didn't name him Tim," Mary said. "Meet Ethan Avery Eagan."

The infant was fast asleep, making little bubbling noises as he breathed, his chubby cheeks occasionally twitching.

Handed the baby, Ethan cradled the boy in one arm and blessed him with his free hand. "With a name like that," he said, "he's bound to have a unique and adventurous life."

Once he was back to his sermons and organizing the work of the church, Ethan knew that his personal missionary work was over. There was so much to do with the church and its growing congregation. Perhaps that decision was made on a muddy roadway in South Africa.

The word did get around and soon Ethan was having to explain to eager priests that his marriage service could not be accepted as real in the eyes of the archbishop, much less the Pope himself. While he said that in God's eyes it probably didn't matter, he made it clear that he would no longer be permitting visiting priests to marry in his church. He was saddened by his decision and while he had no qualms standing up to the Vatican, he was concerned that the local archbishop would start nullifying the marriages he had performed or overseen.

When Tim and Mary questioned him on the validity of their marriage, he could only say, "You are married and blessed in the eyes of God."

The word did get around but not in the way Ethan feared. A group of priests who called themselves Catholic Priests Against Celibacy took a more formal and sensible approach to changing cannon law.

Ethan allowed them to meet in his church on Wednesday afternoons before scheduled confessions. They were a practical group of young clergy who seemed determined to have the Vatican reconvene on the matter of celibacy. It had been discussed for years, but now was the time, the group said, to have the Pope and Vatican leaders formalize a change in the Church's long-held practice of priest celibacy.

Father Ethan soon took on the issue of women serving as priests. Here the Church was entrenched, basing the prohibition not on any canon law but rather on divine law dating thousands of years past.

"This one is going to be easy," he told Father Tim and Mary during supper. "We can bypass the Church altogether and deal directly with God, a more sensible divinity."

He received his approval during evening prayers.

Within six months he had added extra space to the church and officially (without the Archbishop's knowledge) opened Saint Catherine of the Sea Seminary.

Three women applied to the school, which was taught by Father Ethan, and within a year the first of the novitiates was ordained. Her name was Mother Sue Yazzie, a Navaho descendant who was married and had three young children.

Mother Sue added ancient tribal hymns to the mass, along with folk and pop music. A piano replaced the small organ in the church, and church members were encouraged to sing along or, if they had the talent, play one of several guitars next to the piano. An old CD player was wired into the sound system, and it was not unusual to hear songs by popular performers like Maroon Five, Taylor Swift, Eminem and Nicki Minaj in the background during sermons. Mary became the sound mixer and deejay.

Rockin' Masses, as Mother Sue referred to them, were held on weekends at noon. More conservative versions of mass were said by Father Tim during the early morning hours, giving churchgoers, mostly older formal Catholics, an option for the more traditional service.

Despite his own endearing memories of serving mass with Father Danny, Ethan did away with the practice. Again, it reinforced the concept that deity and lay were somehow divided in the eyes of the Church. In Father Ethan's church everyone served mass, church members, visitors, children and most especially those down-trodden souls who appeared, perhaps with only a few hours of sobriety, at the church door.

The word must have gotten around, for soon the small church couldn't contain all of the Sunday's churchgoers. Buses from around the state arrived, emptying their disappointed passengers in the front grounds of the church. Ethan did his best to accommodate all who had made the effort to travel to his church by extending masses and even holding special services in the parking lot.

One day he told Father Tim, "Why do we need the confinement of walls? Jesus preached from a mountainside, didn't he?"

Again with financial assistance from the Albuquerque group, Ethan was able to purchase two acres of desert land to the west of town that included a rather large butte. It was only half a mile from the church itself and well within walking distance for churchgoers.

Except during the brief monsoon season, Father Ethan, Father Tim and Mother Sue led the congregation from the church grounds to the sacred grounds of the butte.

On one Sunday in September almost 800 people convened for mass on the mount. They walked four abreast from the church, winding their way through part of the town and then up the dusty red slope of the butte. It took the better part of an hour to complete the trip and caused such a traffic congestion, mainly from the line of incoming buses, that the local police had to designate one-way only streets through the town.

A newspaper in Albuquerque got hold of the event and published an article about the rather unusual practices of Father Ethan and the Saint Catherine of the Sea church.

The reporter had come down along with a video crew from the local television station. While the article was well-written and focused more on the human interest angle, the television reporter targeted Mother Sue, exposing her as the only female Catholic priest in the world. The interview was intrusive and reported as if a politician had fallen from grace, with little jabs of humor and vindictiveness mean to arouse the court of public opinion.

Within a week an archbishop from Albuquerque visited with Ethan, officially condemning his outlandish church practices and saying he would be petitioning the Vatican to have him excommunicated.

With Father Tim and Mother Sue at his side, Ethan almost lost his temper and had to walk out of the meeting, leaving only the enraged archbishop standing in the church's office with his aides.

Ethan had felt it for weeks and now knew that he was at a turning point in his life. He was forty, defrocked in the eyes of at least one bishop and sharply doubting the version of faith in God that his own upbringing had taught him.

In a last sad meeting with the other priests, he turned over the church to Father Tim, advising him to change its name and return to a more traditional format of service.

"Never!" Father Tim said, shaking his head.

Mother Sue took Ethan's hands into her own and held them. "Perhaps the name change is wise," she said. "But Rockin' Masses are here to stay."

"Are you leaving us?" Mary said.

"It really has little to do with all this," Ethan said. "God has called me in a different direction and I must follow."

"Where?" Tim asked.

"Well, I don't know for sure. It's more of a direction than a destination, so I must trust my faith."

Mother Sue smiled. "You surely mean God's will?"

Ethan exhaled a deep breath. "No, it's never been God's will. It is based on my will and faith in myself."

They had a last supper together the following evening, Mother Sue concocting a hot vegetarian meal of red peppers, tofu, squash and edamame over whole-grain pasta. Father Tim and Mary brought the red wine and bread.

"There'll be no Judas here," Father Tim said, sounding a bit ominous until he broke into cheery laughter and draped his arm over Ethan's shoulders.

"If you only know a direction," Mother Sue said, "will you share it with us?"

Ethan sighed. "West," he finally said.

The next morning, after the long drive to Albuquerque, he boarded a plane for California.

He would never again return to his beloved church in Truth or Consequences. Or to any other church.

Chapter Nine

Pilot Scott Anderson, in a calm professional voice, informed the passengers that they were passing through the western edge of the unsettled weather mass causing the turbulence.

He looked over at his co-pilot. "I guess you know what that feels like back there?"

"Like riding the ass of a big horn," Ted Granger said in a thick, drawn-out Texan accent.

A few minutes later there was a rap at the cockpit door. Scott looked up to see a familiar face on the LCD screen and then unlocked the door.

Stacy walked in balancing two cups of steaming coffee in her hands. Once the pilots grabbed the coffees she took a seat on one of the small jump seats behind the co-pilot.

"How's the girl?" Scott asked.

"Her temperature dropped to 100 and it looks like she's coming out of the post-seizure sleep."

"As soon as we get in range I'll advise the airport to have an ambulance waiting."

"Are we going to have turbulence all the way there?" Stacy asked, adding, "Even the priest looked a little green."

Scott advised her that there might be some more rough weather ahead, just west of the mountains.

"Can't we climb over them?"

"METAR shows them topping at 45K, not exactly a feasible altitude. Even if we could, we'd miss the normal ILS signal and would have to go around from the east. Golden would probably charge us for the extra fuel."

"So what's the plan, Captain?" Ted asked as if he didn't already know the answer.

"It thins out a bit to the south," Scott explained to Stacy. "So we'll make an 85 heading about fifty miles ahead and try to sneak in south of the storm. We'll be dropping some altitude, so be prepared to advise the passengers."

As she'd expressed in the past during rough weather landings, Stacy said, "We all have faith in you, Captain."

"What about me?" Granger said.

"I don't know you," Stacy said, meaning it.

She'd had a strange feeling about the young co-pilot from the moment he'd stepped aboard. Mostly she'd been offended by his cool come-on when Scott had taken a bathroom break and she'd brought him the Coke he ordered. He'd gone on in his Texas drawl about how he preferred California women compared to all others. He'd asked her where she would be staying in Denver before her flight back. Ted Granger was the kind of crude womanizer, a egocentric extravert who saw women as convenient prey. She had met her fair share over the years, most of them drunk passengers whose inhibitions had deflated along with their commonsense.

She left the cockpit and smiled warmly at the passengers, some of whom were asleep on their pillows.

One elderly couple asked if they would arrive on time. She reminded them about the stormy weather and said she knew the captain would try his best.

"Bless us all," the white-haired woman said, a comment that had been said in a way as to infer that the flight might be in peril.

"We're going to be just fine," Stacy said with smile.

She passed the priest and the attractive woman at his side. The nuns smiled up at her as she looked for the little girl in the back drawdown seats. Stacy was relieved to see her trying to sit up, a white blanket draped over her shoulders. She sat down beside her for a few minutes, explaining to the girl that her fever had broken and that she was going to be fine.

Stacy let Nancy, the only other veteran flight attendant aboard, know that she was taking a bathroom break. Inside, she sat up straight and rolled her head around her shoulders, feeling the knotted tension relieve. She and Scott were due for a twenty-four layover in Denver, per FAA rules. She planned to sleep for twelve of those hours.

She opened the door and was suddenly blinded by a jarring flash coming through the windows on the starboard side of the plane. The cabin lights flickered.

"Jesus! We've just been hit by lightning," Nancy whispered.

Passengers were understandably startled and asking questions as Stacy made her way forward to the cockpit door. When it opened she went inside and asked Scott if they had really been hit by lightning.

He didn't have to answer.

It was like a horror show. Through the front and side windows jagged shards of lightning were spider-webbing across the now darkening metal sky. The heads of the pilots lit up against the stuttering flashes. The hairs on the back of Stacy's neck felt alive.

"We took a hit," Granger said calmly. "Nothing to worry about."

Stacy knew that it wasn't unusual for planes to be hit by lightning. In all but a few cases, struck planes suffered no damage. "How long is this going to go on?" she asked.

"Not long," Scott said, turning sideways with a smile.

As she was leaving she heard Scott making an announcement to the passengers, assuring them that the plane hadn't been damaged and that things were proceeding normally. He reminded them to close their shades if they wanted to avoid the bright flashes.

The second hit, probably near the tail, caused the lights to blink again and then go out. Small LED battery lights lit up the aisle and the ceiling. Several passengers screamed.

Ten seconds later the light came back on. And stayed on.

Back in the galley Nancy said, "And they say lightning never hits twice."

They both hurried forward into the cabin to help frightened passengers, a majority of whom were obviously alarmed by the second strike. They repeated what the captain had originally said about lightning having no effect on the structure of the plane, that it happened all the time.

It started with just a pungent whiff, registering instantly in Stacy's mind. She'd smelled it before only once in her flying career. It was the kind of caustic odor they trained you to detect, identify and react to immediately.

She went to check on the microwave ovens, her mind trying to convince her that something had burned in one of the them.

Nancy was already on the phone with the cockpit crew.

"Fire smell, possibly electrical," she heard Nancy say, turning toward Stacy with a statuesque face.

Ted Granger appeared within a minute and made his way back toward the electrical panel.

"Shit!" he said as he crouched down by the opened panel.

Stacy peered over his head and saw the small fireworks of sparks to the left of some fuse switches.

"Oh no," she said involuntarily, the words just escaping with her breath.

"Shut up!" Granger said. "Give me a thick towel."

She let Nancy accommodate the rude man and made her way into the main aisle. The odor was barely detectable, but obviously passengers' concerns had been heightened by the co-pilot's harried presence. As trained, she checked overhead cabinets and then the rest of the bathrooms before entering the cockpit.

"How bad is it?" Scott asked.

"It's in the electrical panel next to the switches. You need to teach that co-pilot some manners."

"Nothing shows upfront here, so it's not in the main circuit. No alarms that I can see."

He asked Stacy to sit in the other seat and check the fire warning signals. No signal lights were on.

Scott told her to get back with the passengers and make some sort of announcement to calm them. "Tell them it's all under control...and that's coming from the captain."

A warning light must have turned on, and she heard Scott curse as she passed through the cockpit doorway.

Although barely detectable toward the front of the plane, the mid-section and aft areas were now rife with the penetrating odor of burning wires. Several passengers were coughing, many holding folded handkerchief to their mouths.

As she passed, the priest asked her if there was anything he could do to assist. The woman to his right said the same thing. Stacy thanked them and then headed back to check on the girl.

Using a high-frequency channel Scott called in to the nearest ATCT, after identifying the plane and it's altitude.

"Go ahead GA, " the Salt Lake tower responded.

"Lightning strike. Dealing with possible inboard fire. Aft, behind the galley," Scott reported in a casual but no nonsense voice.

"Descend to 21 thousand and then I'll give you approach vectors to SLC on runway 16 Left."

"Roger that, sir," Scott said.

"Are you going to need equipment?"

"Yes sir."

As if taking command Granger reminded Scott what he already knew. Despite the fire, they would have to descend gradually to avoid pressure sensors going off and causing the oxygen bags to drop, not exactly what you wanted when there was a fire aboard.

But they had to get down fast. Rules changed when there was a fire event.

Granger dialed in the altitude numbers, a slow drop of one thousand feet to begin with. Scott changed the heading.

They were still at 37,000 feet and decided on a moderate descent by deploying the spoilers. At that rate, it would take approximately five minutes to level off at 21,000 feet.

If the smoke intensified they would have to take the risk of a very steep descent and the possibility of the fire spreading into the cabin.

Scott was going to do everything he could to avoid that scenario. He telephoned back to Stacy what was going to happen and that they should prepare passengers by telling them that they were making an emergency landing in Salt Lake City. He advised Stacy to hand out moistened towels to help filter the air should more smoke flood the cabin.

"Scott, we're going to be okay?"

"Of course. We'll toast with a beer on the salt flats."

Moments later, she felt the plane begin its steep descent.

Both had been unnerved by the lightning strikes. Jessica had grabbed and was still hanging onto Ethan's arm.

The pilot's words while initially assuring fell mostly on deaf ears after the second lightning strike.

She noticed the odor before Ethan did. She looked back towards the rear of the plane.

"What's wrong, Jessica?"

"They must have burned the coffee. Can't you smell it?"

Just then the co-pilot hurried past and disappeared behind the galley curtains.

"Now I do," Ethan said.

Within minutes the odor intensified and began to burn his nasal passages. He gave Jessica his handkerchief, found another stuffed in his pocket and held it to his mouth.

As he had hoped, his presence had a calming effect on others. The two nuns were crossing themselves and then they looked back at Ethan with trusting faces.

A flight attendant moved hurriedly down the aisle towards the cockpit, and after several minutes returned.

Ethan asked the woman if there anything he could do to help out, Jessica echoing his offer. The flight attendant thanked them, assured them that it was under control and then moved towards the little girl.

Jessica sat down in her seat stiffly, the handkerchief still pressed to her mouth. One hand reached the empty seat for Ethan's.

Ethan leaned over and said, "Did you know that once in a bush plane over South Africa I watched the pilot land the plane on a dirt road in front of an oncoming bus?"

It too fell on deaf ears.

As if possessed by a need to witness what was going on outside, Jessica raised the window shade, her face suddenly illuminating with coruscating flashes of light.

"Aren't you interested in what happened?" Ethan said.

She had barely followed the story, her jumbled thoughts darting from Allen to her will and how she wished she had amended it to include him as a beneficiary. As it stood, all of her money and investments were to be left in a trust for Macy and the rest divided between Wellesley College and several charities.

"Well, we landed successfully with not even a scratch. You see, I knew we would. Just as I know everything's going to be fine now."

The flight attendant reappeared and began walking slowly down the aisle from aft forward, explaining in a calm voice that the pilot was going to land the plane in Salt Lake City and that they should soon expect to feel the plane descending. She repeated several times that everything was under control. Her voice trailed off as she moved towards the front of the plane.

Ethan thought something had caught in his eyes, for they felt grainy and soon burned as if teargas had hit them. He wiped them with his handkerchief, blew his nose, and then began to cough.

The smoke was thickening and spreading.

Jessica asked Ethan to move next to her. She was leaning over the armrest and was now snuggled tightly against him.

◆

Scott looked at the panel where the red warning light had lit up.

Granger had just returned and slipped into the co-pilot's seat. "Damn, it's not in the fuse panels," he said as if Scott wasn't already aware of it."

"Aft cargo," Scott said calmly. "The panel must have caught fire because of the heat buildup. "What's back there?"

Granger grabbed for the cargo manifest and began reading a list of items. "No O2 canisters," he joked, referring to the Florida jet decades past that had crashed in the Everglades with no survivors.

"Nothing flammable?"

"Some hospital supplies, mainly hydrogen peroxide and chlorine bleach containers."

"I'd guess something got loose back there during the turbulence," Scott said.

He radioed Salt Lake. "Golden 100. We're at twenty-nine thousand, continuing descent."

"Cleared to twenty one, Golden 100," the controller said.

All of a sudden gusts of heavy rain pummeled the windshield, intensifying until it became obvious that they were descending into a hailstorm. As if assaulted by a barrage of machineguns, the fuselage shook and a cacophony of clattering and tremors rose to a deafening roar.

"That's all we need now," Scott heard Granger say in his headset.

It got worse. Hail the size of hardened marbles battered the windshield. Like spray paint, the windshield turned into a spattering of small white craters as the outer layers of the heavily-forged glass shattered against the impacts.

Warning indicators were lighting up everywhere, indicating combustion even in the midsection and forward belly of the plane. He hoped that they were false alarms probably due to lightning interference.

"This is fucking crazy," Granger said and began tapping on the indicator lights.

"Retract the spoilers," the pilot said.

◆

It felt like they were falling out of the sky. Oxygen masks dropped and dangled like torn umbilical cords from the overhead panels. The plane started shaking violently.

Ethan helped Jessica with her mask and then looked around to see if other passengers needed help. He managed to break free from Jessica's grip, climbing against the descent, and helped a man behind them and then the two nuns.

He was startled to see that the little girl was not in her seat.

Back in his own, Ethan buckled in and held the mask over his nose.

Jessica had her hand cupped over her mouth underneath the mask, doing her best to keep her breakfast down. The terrified look in her eyes was obvious.

"We're going to be okay," he said, repeating it much more loudly when Jessica shook her head as if she didn't want to hear it. He knew, though, that he was equally trying to convince himself. Soon bags in the overhead containers were tumbling onto passengers and shooting down the aisle towards the back of the plane.

A flight attendant was careening down the aisle almost in mid-air. She was on her side sliding, desperately attempting to grab at something to slow her propulsion. Ethan leaned into the aisle and briefly held onto her arm, but she slipped through his fingers, moments later disappearing under the wildly-twirling galley curtain.

There were things on the ceiling, some items still in mid-air. Loose passengers masks were floating eerily above their heads, along with necklaces and strands of long hair. A gray toupee hovered like a saucer over one gentleman's head.

The sound was ear-splitting.

For a second Ethan imagined that the plane would be torn apart by the g-force of the wild descent. He imagined them pulverizing even before impact, a word that had now cleared his thoughts of any possible hope for survival.

He shut his eyes and held Jessica's hand firmly, knowing at any instant that she would be torn from his grip and that they would, together at least, meet with the instant absorption of death.

Again, no vision of his own life passed before his eyes, this time not even the future. But a countenance from his past, calm and compassionate, rose like an angel into his mind's eye.

It was his mother's young but determined face.

The pilot pulled back on his yolk. Scott's hand was shaking as he felt the cumbersome 737 pull out of the dive, slowly leveling off at 15,000 feet.

Granger looked like he'd seen a ghost up close. He'd been holding his breath and now, as Scott looked over, he exhaled in a high-pitched wheeze. He was sweating heavily.

The odor of smoke was faint but clearly detectable. Both pilots had their masks on.

"Salt Lake. Golden one hundred here..." Scott called out.

Silence, a long hushed pause, interrupted only by the sound of both pilots' breathing.

Granger repeated the call. "Salt Lake, can you read us? Golden one hundred. Fifteen hundred and holding. Possible fire aboard."

There was a faint crackle of static, perhaps a voice intermixed, and then silence.

Scott looked at the navigational panel. In a controlled but solemn voice, he said, "We're way southeast of the vectors, well out of range.

Their heading was 95. To avoid the hailstorm, they'd traveled 200 miles southeast of their previous position and were heading into the first ridge of the mountain range.

"The ground will be coming up at us," Granger said. "We gotta climb to twenty four thousand."

Scott had already pulled back on the yolk and increased engine speed.

A voice broke through the radio static: *Montrose center....*

"Where the hell are we?" Scott said as he tried to reach the responding tower.

"Easy."

The plane engine's screamed at a deafening pitch. There was a sudden jolt and a drop to the right.

"Number 2 flamed out."

Granger fumbled with the auto-feather switch. He looked like he'd just seen a ghost. His eyes were wide open, a blank look on his face.

"Ted! For chrissakes, give me a hand."

"Shit."

The black box voice recorder was recording the sounds in the cockpit from various microphone positions. Only Granger was vaguely aware of it at the moment.

"Hold it. Hold it."

"Level out now."

"Yeah, there..."

"Fuel shutdown number two."

"Crazy shit..."

"Mayday...mayday! Golden one hundred."

Silence except for the scream of the left engine.

"That's it, easy."

"That's not right."

Almost thirty seconds of silence.

"I've got it."

"You're going to fuckin' stall us."

"God almighty...we're going down!"

The sound of the stick shaking.

Pull-up! Pull-up!

PART TWO

"To the well-organized mind, death is but the next great adventure."
— J.K. Rowling, Harry Potter and the Sorcerer's Stone

Chapter Ten

She was rising from a depth at an implausible rate, shooting up from a vast and bleak darkness that at first held her ascent and then suddenly let go. It was as if a pocket of air at some great depth in the ocean had been released, soaring up wildly and desperately up to the surface.

Macy opened her eyes to a gossamer bright light and blend of sour scents and faint voices. She suddenly felt like gagging. It felt like someone had a hand down her throat. She tried to cough but no air escaped her lips, just a gurgling sound where something was taped to her throat.

The first nurse who approached leaned over her face. There were tears in her eyes and a wide, astonished smile. "Macy, it's okay," she said in a voice that sounded somewhere between startled and exultant.

Other nurses rushed over. One of them was on the phone. A large man in a white coat took her hand and then dropped it. He peered into each of her eyes with a small flashlight.

She couldn't stand the thing in her throat and tried to reach her hand to tear it out.

A hand restrained her effort.

Time began to slow down.

Soon a familiar fragrance, a hand on her forehead and then a face nuzzling against hers.

"Baby, it's me. Thank God! Honey, can you hear me?"

Macy recognized her mother's voice and attempted to respond but her thick, swollen tongue got in the way. She squeezed the fingers inside her right hand. Tears were now flooding her eyes.

More doctors entered the room and took their turns examining the patient. One asked who she was, a witless question considering the fact that she knew that her name was on her chart.

Soon she felt the cool air passing through her tracheostomy incision, which burned from the dryness. She knew what it meant and tried to answer her mother. The words sputtered through the tube.

A feeding tube ran into her nose. She gagged and signaled for it to be removed.

"She wants it out!" Jessica said.

One of the physicians nodded and then a nurse began the slow process of removing the tube, stopping at several points when Macy's eyes squinted with pain. When it was finally out the nurse lifted her head and had her sip from a cupful of ice cubes.

She showed Macy how to make sounds by pressing on the inflatable tracheostomy cuff.

"Where am I?" The voice came out in a raspy falsetto tone as if she were exhaling a lungful of helium.

She felt her left wrist being untied. A burning sensation in her groin made her cry out. She reached down there but a hand stopped her.

"One thing at a time, Macy," the nurse said.

She felt weak yet itching with energy, her skin tingling as it was slowly awakening to old but familiar sensations.

◆

During the next week Macy fought to remain awake but her weakened body needed slumber to heal itself. She drifted through strange sensations and levels of gauzy awareness.

The tracheostomy tube was removed in stages, shorter tubes replacing the larger ones to acclimate her trachea and allow her lungs to handle more air.

The day the wound was closed and she was finally able to speak Macy cried and held her mother's hand.

"How old are you, Macy?" someone asked.

She blinked her eyes rapidly. "Seventeen, I guess." Her voice still didn't sound like her own.

They asked her other stupid questions, like her father's name, who the president was, the month and date and if she remembered what had happened to her.

"I was skiing and hit my head, I guess." She coughed.

Macy heard her mother talking to others in the room. She asked several to leave, that she needed to spend time with her daughter.

"Oh baby, it's a miracle!" She raised the hospital bed, repositioned Macy's head on the pillow.

"How long have I been here?"

Her mother started crying again. "A long time," she finally said.

"How long, Mom?"

"Almost a year. Ten and a half months."

"Shit. Are you kidding?"

"You were in a medically-induced coma for six weeks. The rest of the time you were in your own world. Macy, it's a true miracle that you made it back to us."

"Where's Dad?"

"I'd tell you if I knew. Baby, maybe that's not a topic to get into right now."

"Am I still in school?" Macy asked.

"Of course. Anytime you feel well enough to return."

Macy leaned forward and placed her head in her hands. "I got pretty banged up, didn't I?"

"You fractured your pelvis, right leg and wrist. The surgeons had to place a small metal disc at the top of your skull after they operated. You had brain swelling."

Macy felt the top of her head, assuming there would still be missing hair there, but felt no hair loss, only tenderness when she touched it.

Her mom tried to laugh but it spilled out as a quavering yawn. She inhaled and wiped at her tears with the back of her wrists. "You've had multiple surgeries but now everything's healed completely. I arranged for you to have physical therapy every day so that you wouldn't lose muscle tone. You see, in my heart I always knew you'd come back."

They hugged again, both of their eyes closed, pressing small smiles against each other's cheeks.

"Mom," Macy said, pulling away, "Get them to take this thing out of me, shoving her hand down to where the catheter tube was taped to her thigh.

The procedure was done by a rather large nurse with round thick glasses. "Breathe out slowly, honey," she said.

Macy was finally unattached. No more tubes and confinement to the bed. When she had to pee she showed off in front of her mother, pretending a ballerina's *échappé saut* and almost falling to the floor.

Soon she was walking down the hospital corridors, peaking through open doors and waving at patients. She spent more time in the small courtyard, regaling in the sunlight and the fresh spring air.

She was released a week later, following innumerable scans from her head to her legs, blood tests, brain tests and interrogations by neurologists, pediatricians, surgeons, a psychologist and social worker.

Jessica had gathered a bagful of cards sent to her by her friends and family. She had to deflate all the *get well* balloons and stuff them inside the large bag.

A nurse named Alma with a round Scandinavian face stayed by her side and eventually wheeled her out to the exit. She told Macy that she had cared for her when she was in ICU and during many of the early surgeries. She loved books and had given her mother some of the great classics, including works by Ibsen, Joyce, Faulkner and Steinbeck.

"I always knew a miracle would come," she said, her hand on Macy's shoulder.

Macy thanked her but said she couldn't remember any of it but that maybe some of it would come back to her later.

Other nurses and physicians lined the path towards the main entrance, waving and smiling and clapping, making Macy feel as if she'd just finished first place in a marathon.

Waving back through the car's window, she became emotional, overwhelmed by the attention and love showered upon her at the hospital.

She was surprised to see that her mother had sold the old house. The new one was not quite as large but was in another exclusive section of Denver. It was a three-floor red brick condo with an arched entryway and French windows, a manicured lawn with hedges and gray-stone walkways, all well maintained by the condo association.

A woman was waiting for them at the entranceway. Macy was still a little weak and the woman had to help her from the car and up the walkway.

"This is Hattie," her mother said. "She's been with us ever since I moved."

"Miss," Hattie said after she had been introduced.

"Call me Macy."

Inside they had Macy ride the stair lift to the top floor, her mother holding her daughter's hand, Hattie bustling up the steps with the suitcase and filled paper bags.

"It's not quite the Magic Mile," Macy said and then, with her mother's help, stood up from the chair and was lead to her room. It was quite large with two windows and harlequin walls, mainly coral in tone. There was a hospital bed in one corner, on the other side a French white poster bed with canopy.

"I was planning to have you transferred when they'd weaned you off those tubes, with your own nurse and visiting therapists," her mother said. "I wasn't going to leave you in the hospital forever."

Macy looked at the hospital bed with an expression that left no question as to what she thought about its placement in her room.

Her mother said, "Honey, it'll be out of here tomorrow."

With fresh new towels, loungewear and a gold-plated hair brush and comb, Macy was left to take her own bath in the adjacent bathroom.

She was swallowed-up by the lathery pink bubbles, only her head and the tops of her knees poking up through surface. She washed, first her hair and then the rest of her body, and then leaned way back in the tub, her face almost submerged, her hair fanned out on the surface like a large spreading stain.

She must have remained in that position for quite a long time, for Hattie and her mother knocked on the door several times to make sure she was okay.

"Fine," she sputtered several times.

When she stood out of the tub and started patting herself dry with the thick towel, she noticed obvious signs of the aftermath: bedsores on her elbows, backside and on the heels of her feet. There were surgical scars on one ankle and at the sides of her upper thigh and one at the joint of her arm. When the mist had cleared from the mirror, she noticed little scars near her eyes and a slight concavity at the crest of her brow. It caused her left eye to appear slightly occluded. When she smiled she noticed a chipped front tooth. The tracheostomy scar didn't look as bad as she feared it would.

To her amazement, her breasts looked fuller than she had remembered them, her nipples extruding and pink.

It was obvious that she had lost weight for, despite the enlargement of her breasts, her chest had a slight caved-in appearance, one shoulder carrying a little higher than the other.

"I guess I should be grateful," she whispered at her reflection in the mirror.

They ate an early dinner that day, Hattie serving Swedish meatballs over whole-grain fettuccini and soft sourdough bread.

They talked mainly when Macy had questions, about school and when she could go back, about some of her friends and finally about her father.

"Macy, you know your dad. He's off living his own life somewhere. We hardly keep in touch."

"Did he call when I was in he hospital?"

"Sure he did," Jessica lied. "He visited several times. He was very concerned."

"Does he know I'm out of the coma?"

"He was informed by several people, Macy."

"I don't guess I'll be seeing him anytime soon?"

"If you really want it," her mother said, "I'll somehow make it happen. Before the accident, I guess...well, you weren't so interested in spending time with your father."

"I don't know...things have changed. In a way, I'm a different person. He's my father and I feel an obligation to at least attempt to warm up to him."

Obviously startled by what Macy had just said, her mother held a blank look for a few seconds and then said, "Honey, somehow I'll get you two together. In fact we'll call him tonight."

Later, after calling her father and leaving several messages on his phone, Macy was suddenly overwhelmed with the day and felt totally exhausted.

Hattie had brought her some herbal tea and sugar cookies on a small china plate. She left daughter and mother in the bedroom and slipped inconspicuously into the hallway.

"I'm too tired to talk any more," Macy said, reaching to give her mother a hug.

"I love you, sweetheart...my miracle girl," her mother said and then tucked her in. She put a small wireless button on the round glass bedside table. "In case you have a bad dream or want me to come in and give you a backrub. Just buzz me. Okay?"

Too tired to read, Macy watched her mother exit and then lay in the darkened room. She yawned several times and then waited for sleep to overcome her.

But it didn't, at least not for another hour.

She thought about coming out of her coma, the weird sensations, the orderly business around her suddenly becoming frenzied, faces approaching with incredulous expressions, her mother's first words. It was like being born again.

The portal through which she'd escaped the coma felt dark and now impenetrable to thoughts. It was there like a walled-in cave, behind it some miraculously-suspended life, or was it death from which she'd been evicted?

Life and death, separated by the nebulous partition of coma. Perhaps not a partition at all, but an incomprehensible overlap, a transition like birth, a wormhole in time, an elected continuance.

Under the weight of such wild imaginings, she finally drifted off to sleep.

◆

Jessica hadn't had the heart to tell her daughter the truth. After last night, she didn't think she ever would.

Sure, Allen had been involved and had made periodic visits to the hospital to speak with the cadre of medical professionals who seemed to be on his side.

After three months he had insisted, along with the group of doctors, that Macy was simply in a vegetative state. Brain death had occurred. She would never emerge from that terminal state, would never be aware of her surroundings, would never recognize people, never breathe on her own. The ventilator *had* to be removed, Allen had argued.

It was costing him a fortune to keep his vegetable daughter alive only for the purpose of appeasing Jessica. They had fights, irascible bouts that had resulted in their being asked to leave the hospital. Soon lawyers got involved. A judge granted Jessica an injunction, but Allen's attorneys were vicious right-to-die advocates. She lost eventually. The presiding judge sided with medical advice and evidence and scheduled a date for the ventilator to be pulled.

Another brief injunction. And then the day came.

Two lawyers were present, along with a priest, hospital officials and a deputy sheriff, who was there, Jessica guessed, to restrain her were she to interfere with the procedure.

There was no motion following the shutting down of the ventilator. Quickly, Macy's face turned slight blue, her skin paled. A physician was monitoring the large overhead panel, slowly nodding his head.

They had been right. She had been only a vegetable, a non human kept alive with oxygen, nutrients and the maze of tubes that provided life-sustaining services.

Suddenly, Macy gasped, her eyes wide open and then started shaking as if in a seizure.

A doctor said he detected faint brain activity but that it could be some renegade cluster of neurons firing off their last electrical activity.

But then her eyes suddenly closed, a possible sign of voluntary movement. She started breathing at a rhythmic pace, color flushing her cheeks.

"That's it!" Jessica had screamed at all of them. "She's alive. What other evidence do you need?"

By the time Allen had scheduled a visit to the hospital, Macy had slipped back into a light coma. They had increased the oxygen flow. A majority of her doctors now felt she was not in a vegetative state, that some brain activity remained. It was enough evidence for Jessica's lawyers to get a six-month injunction. The judge wanted a new panel of doctors to begin their evaluations. He even suggested that Macy be moved to another hospital. After an emotional plea from Jessica, he withdrew his decision.

Allen was furious. He looked down at his daughter and saw only her lifeless body. He continued with his insistence that she be taken off all life support.

Jessica made it a point to always be in the room when Allen was visiting. She'd made arrangements with several of the nurses to warn her immediately if they heard news of his impending visit. In her mind it was outlandish and morbid to think he would be capable of harming his daughter, but the instinctive feeling was there.

Jessica wanted a divorce but her lawyers advised that they might have to compromise on a medical settlement for their daughter. As long as she was married, Allen was legally obligated to pay for most of his daughter's medical expenses not covered by his company's medical plan.

She had planned to move Macy into her new home well before the end of the injunction. If her daughter were meant to die, it would be in a bed in her own home, not in a sterile environment being treated by, what Jessica knew to be, skeptical and perhaps overly-ethical physicians.

But now a miracle, and here she was, with all of her brain function and physical capabilities. Macy had survived despite all of the medical predictions that she wouldn't.

Jessica had taken paid leave from her job and when that leave ran out, she had asked for and been granted a leave of absence. She was told that her position would be held for her for as long as she needed.

◆

Two weeks after her return from the hospital, Macy became somewhat of a celebrity in the neighborhood. After the story was posted online, cards and emails were soon pouring in from across the country. Soon a local television station called, asking if Macy would agree to an in-home interview.

In a strange way Macy wanted to share her story. She first wrote about it in her journal and then attempted to shape it into a short story. She eventually agreed to the television interview. When the interviewer arrived with her crew and had set up all the lighting and fitted Macy and Jessica with microphones, the reporter rehearsed with some practice questions.

"Are you sure you're okay with this?" the young Asian woman asked.

"Yeah," Macy said. "But it would be better if you don't ask any questions about my father."

The first question was so idiotic Macy just starred back at the interviewer. Finally she said, "How would anyone know what it feels like to be in a coma? Coma means no feeling, no awareness, no nothing...."

"I'm sorry. That was an insensitive question," the interviewer said, indicating to the cameraman that they would start over.

The question was rephrased. *How did it feel coming out of the coma?*

Macy tried to be honest, highlighting the sensations, the sounds, the smells and the eventual feeling of the presence of her mother.

She explained that there was no connection at all for the first minute or so, simply as if she accidentally entered a scene that had nothing to do with her. She said that she knew she was alive the first time she took her first breath when the tracheostomy tubes were finally removed. She said she wasn't really frightened by the experience, only that she had felt intruded upon.

"Ah, maybe like a birth?"

"I never thought of it that way, but maybe so."

"But you would never go back," the interviewer said.

Where did they find these kind of dimwits? Macy thought, holding back her immediate reaction to the question.

"No Ma'am," Macy finally answered, looking directly into the camera lens in hopes that somewhere out there in TV land someone would connect and feel her frustration with the lamebrain interviewer.

She was asked a few more questions about her physical and mental abilities and whether she wanted to share more personal details of her experience.

Macy feigned memory loss and said she couldn't remember anything more.

The remainder of the questions were for her mother, who was sitting beside her at a predetermined distance so as not to interfere with head shots. The queries were aimed at the maternal heart, the agony of not knowing if her child would survive, the legal controversy and the injunctions and, finally, what it felt like the moment her daughter came out of the coma.

Eventually national media picked up on the interview and requests came in to appear on several morning shows and an appearance on CNN.

Macy decided to forego the interview invitations, and the notoriety. She didn't want to dwell any longer on what had happened to her during the past year and was ready to move on with her life. She wanted most to get back in college and then on to the Iowa writers' program. She wanted to finish her novel and begin another. She missed her friends still at Wellesley, those who had not graduated since her coma and convalescence. Mostly she wanted to be independent again.

She returned again for the fall semester. It was to be her senior year. She settled in as if there had been no intermission. She became co-editor of the *Wellesley Magazine* in which she published several of her own stories.

Macy's body healed. She put on a little weight and had her hair cut, and could be recognized by her white jeans and flirty sweatshirts and her charming good looks as she scurried about the campus.

And soon she had a boyfriend.

Jessica was elated by Macy's romantic affair. She was amazed that she even had time for herself and the relationship.

Macy had been calling her mother weekly, usually on Sundays, and when she casually mentioned Greg, a fellow senior at Boston University she'd met at a party, Jessica had squealed with delight.

"He's a journalism major and a really neat guy," Macy said.

"I'm so happy for you, sweetheart."

"I really love him. It's a serious relationship."

"I'd love to meet him."

"Well, that's actually why I called," Macy said. "Would you mind if Greg stayed with us over the Christmas break. He will pay for his flight, of course."

"Absolutely. We'll start making plans."

Jessica returned to work at the advertising agency but had requested that her business trips be limited just in case something unforeseen were to occur with her daughter.

She never realized how much of a toll the vigil at the hospital had taken on her. Even though Macy was now safe at college, the palpable absence at the house left her on edge, sleepless and mostly worrying that her daughter might relapse. It was a foolish thing to worry about, she knew, but idle time made for rambling imagination and mindless thought.

After her first day back at the firm, her temperament and worries changed for the better. Better sleep, more rational thoughts and less time for listless contemplation.

A good friend from work who had supported her throughout Macy's ordeal began asking her out for lunches and soon dinners at romantic restaurants. She was taking it slow for emotional reasons and because legally she was still married to Allen. If he found out that she was dating, she could well imagine the malicious reprisal from his cast of attorneys. Macy was still a minor, and she had no doubt that he would interfere with the custody of their daughter.

Michael was a good-looking man with a kind heart and solid character. She had known him for a long time and trusted his intentions, which seemed to match her own. He too wanted to take it slowly.

It was not unusual for them to be seen together at local restaurants, along with some of Jessica's other coworkers. The real first date occurred at her home, where Michael insisted on preparing her a surprise meal.

She gave Hattie the evening off and cleaned up the kitchen before Michael arrived, grocery bags in hand. He kissed her on the cheek and demanded that she stay out of the kitchen until had had finished his work.

"Are you ordering me out of my own kitchen?"

"Yes Ma'am, I am."

"Can I take a peek?"

"No Ma'am, you can't. But you can handle the wine and the settings."

In less than thirty minutes, Michael appeared with two steaming plates of sauté bourbon chicken with chives on a beds of white rice, with hollandaise asparagus as a side vegetable and sourdough bread, Jessica's favorite.

It was the first time Jessica had been alone with Michael. She felt captivated by his southern ways and good looks and by what she felt was a trusting relationship.

"So Macy's bringing her beau for the holidays?"

"I'm so excited and so thrilled that she has a boyfriend. It's been a long time. She so deserves it."

Jessica filled him in on how they met and what Greg planned to do with his life.

"A journalist? You know, that was my initial major in college."

"So what happened? How did you end up in a stuffy ad office?"

"Life happens, you know," Michael said in a slow exhalation. "I joined the Air Force after college...and it took me places I'd rather not talk about. Let's say that a turn of good fortune landed me here."

"It's strange how we meander through life, having no idea what doors may open, or pathways diverge...and suddenly we're here, at the present moment. It goes so quickly." She stopped and looked down at her plate. "Michael, this is delicious."

"I'd like to say it's an old family recipe, but the truth is I found it in a recent edition of *Good Housekeeping*."

"Bachelors are always great chefs," Jessica said, realizing that it was sort of a lame comment. She dipped her fork into the soft asparagus and then took a sip of the robust red wine.

Michael let Jessica talk, about her daughter, the holiday visit and how great it was going to be to have a young man in the house.

Then he said, "Having the family together at Christmas is wonderful."

"And you?" Jessica said.

"No immediate family, I'm afraid."

There was a long pause and then Jessica's eyes lit up. "Please plan to spend Christmas day with us. It would be so good to share the holiday with you."

"I'll have to rearrange my schedule...and I'll be flying out to Iowa the week before. Honestly, Jes, I don't want to interfere."

"Rearrange but please be here. Macy would want it too. In fact, I think you should stay over Christmas Eve and be there when we open up gifts."

"But it would be an intrusion..."

"Michael, please promise me." She got up and went over and draped her arms around him, snuggling against his broad chest. She wanted to kiss him, *really* kiss him, but it didn't feel appropriate given that they were really just friends. *What was she thinking?*

Michael had no problems showing his feelings for her. Just at the moment when she was about to pull away, he leaned up and kissed her on the lips, not a passionate intrusive kiss but warm enough to set a beat to his heart.

"My heart says I have no choice," he whispered. "I'll be here."

Chapter Eleven

The tower at the Montrose Regional Airport in Colorado had picked up the plane's primary and secondary transponders, a faint blip on the screen reading out altitude and speed of a commercial jet identified as GA 100.

Although a small regional airport, they had been updated a couple of years ago with new high-tech radar equipment and served as the only station in that area to be able to track planes in that mountainous region.

Dana Sanders spoke through his headphones to the ATC manager. "We've got a secondary that appears way off course," he said in the trained, flat voice of a controller.

He tried to make contact, looking hard at the west sector of the radar screen. He magnified the blip and noticed that the altitude reading had changed. With every two sweeps of the radar, the reading fell again. It was now showing an elevation of 17,000 feet.

Five minutes later when the transponder reported another 2,000 foot drop in altitude, Dana called his manager again.

Jack Hollander, a heavyset man in his sixties with a fringe of white hair on his otherwise shiny bald head, approached and leaned over the console. He had been in the business for over forty years, and looked it.

"I think it's the plane that called in a mayday south of Salt Lake. They reported that it fell from their screen thirty minutes ago. Jesus! It's way off its flight plan, if it's the one out of SFO."

Dana nodded his head. Two fellow controllers had approached, their eyes glued to the screen.

"Golden 100, Montrose Center here. Squawk seven seven zero. Repeat squawk seven seven zero," Dana called out, instructing them to change to the emergency responder frequency.

He listened for a reply, and then made the call again.

"Heading seventy-five," one of the other controllers said, tapping at the screen.

"It shouldn't be down there," Dana said.

Hollander loomed like a shadow over this shoulder. "They're not going to make it at that altitude," he said solemnly.

"There's a gorge just north...here," one of the other controllers said, sliding his finger tip up the screen.

"Golden 100, Montrose Center, change heading to zero six eight. Repeat. Change heading to zero six eight degrees."

Hollander knew that no other ATC centers in the area would be able to detect the plane's transponders. The plane was too far south of Denver and separated by high mountains. They were the only ones able to make radio contact.

"If they hold that altitude, they might make it through," Dana said. "But they gotta move up to zero six eight."

In his ten years as a controller, Dana Sanders had witnessed a fair share of emergency landings at the airport when he worked at Denver International and, unfortunately, three fatal crashes involving private planes. He had seen green laser incidents involving sadistic citizens whose intent was to blind pilots with laser beams. One of those pilots landing at Denver had sustained permanent damage to his retina, which ended his flying career. During his training years he had heard black box voice recordings of doomed flights. He could well imagine what it was like inside a cockpit during emergency conditions.

Although his senses were trained to focus on the radar screen and on the many positions of planes he was assigned to follow, his ears alert for breaks in the rush of static in his headphones that signified impending calls from pilots, Dana could never shake the human element of his role.

According to information just in, Golden 100 out of San Francisco had 115 souls aboard including the pilots and crew. They had run into trouble with lightning, as reported by the Salt Lake tower, and had lost power in the number two engine, apparently put out an electrical fire and miraculously pulled out of a death dive.

Now they were about to slam into the side of a mountain.

As much as Dana attempted to remain detached and professional, he couldn't help but wonder how much the crew and passengers of that plane had been through. And what was surely to happen if they didn't change course.

Almost robotically he repeated his calls, watching the screen for any indication that the course had been corrected. He had to urinate badly but wasn't about to hand over to another controller now. It was his plane, he felt, his primary responsibility with so many lives hanging in the balance.

He sensed Hollander over his right shoulder again, the heavy cigar scent on his breath, the concern and concentration in his silence. He continued trying to make contact, his voice slightly more raised, more eager to break through. He wanted to hear that pilot's voice. He wanted to let him know that they had been following him, that someone else knew about their harrowing experience. He wanted to be able to congratulate him, to promise him a beer.

"Nothing," Hollander said, shaking his head.

Denver called to see if they'd made contact.

"Primary and secondary transponders, but no voice," Hollander said.

"Any other aircraft in the area?"

"I'm afraid not."

"Please advise..."

"Roger. Good day," Hollander said, trying not to let his gut reaction show in his voice.

Dana was staring, anticipating the next blip on the screen, and when it didn't happen he just froze.

He tried to make contact again, and then when Hollander put a hand on his shoulder, Dana said flatly, "I think they went down."

They waited for the next several sweeps of the radar.

Hollander called back Denver to report what had happened.

He was holding one end of the headsets to one ear, still stooped over Dana's shoulder.

"Sonofabitch. I can't believe they went down." he said, sweat beading on his forehead.

Dana made one last frantic call to the jetliner and then dropped his head.

"Son, it's bad shit but there's nothing we can do about it. It's over."

Hollander told him him to take a break.

Dana didn't make it to the toilet. He was leaning over the drinking fountain, coughing out the last of his vomit.

Chapter Twelve

Jessica had everything prepared. A nine foot spruce pine stood in the living room set against the main window. She draped it with old-fashioned bulbs, the large multicolored ones whose weight splayed each limb, making it perfect for decorating. It had been a custom in her own family to wait until Christmas Eve to trim the tree with tinsel, so she was going to have Macy, her boyfriend Greg, and Michael have a go at it.

She spent a solid week buying presents for everyone, items she knew Macy wanted, others suggested by her daughter for Greg and then special ones she hoped Michael would enjoy. They were wrapped in expensive foil paper with imprints of traditional Christmas figures: snow sleds, snowmen, trees, Santa's various reindeer, angels, Father Christmas and bucolic scenes of snowy cottage landscapes. Hattie handmade the silken bows, wrapping each present with fine ribbon.

Macy and her boyfriend were to arrive in less than three weeks on December 22nd. Michael had assured her that he would be there on the 24th.

Jessica had been called to a convention in San Francisco, only a five-day affair from which she would return in plenty of time for the Christmas season.

She had called both Macy and Michael on the morning of the flight but had been forced to leave each a message on their phones when the calls went to the recordings. She knew she would make contact with both once she arrived in San Francisco.

Golden flight 70 was packed and overbooked. She'd arrived late at the airport due to yet another overnight snowstorm, but had just barely received her confirmation when the airport agent announced that the flight was full. It was coming up on the holidays and people were getting an early jump on travels.

She watched an angry couple with a child confront the agent, threatening to sue the airlines if they weren't let aboard the flight. Others in the gate lounge were getting riled up, shoving their boarding passes in the woman's face.

When she found her seat in the forward business section of the plane, Jessica noticed that three seats had not been filled. She shook her head, irritated that the airline hadn't allowed the plane to be filled to capacity. She imagined the couple with their young child sitting in those empty seats, getting the chance to arrive at their destination on time.

It aggravated her so much that in mid-flight she asked one of the first class flight attendants why those seats were left empty.

"I guess they were no shows, fellows up late last night and with not enough coffee to get over their hangovers in time. Happens all the time."

It was an insensitive comment with rude implications about business class travelers.

"Do you care at all, Miss, that there were quite a few ticket-holders not allowed to board the flight?

The young woman with slightly bloodshot eyes nodded slowly in a way that suggested she knew she would have to deal with at least one problem passenger on the flight.

"I'm afraid that's not something I can do anything about," she said, flexing a big smile and moving on down the aisle.

I bet you were partying with at least one of those men, Jessica thought meanly, instantly recognizing that that response was out of character for her. She had been up late the night before, awakening too many times during the night, and wasn't in the best of humor.

The rest of the flight was uneventful, although they arrived fifteen minutes late at San Francisco International Airport. The convention driver was in a glum mood, probably because of the longer wait, but answered Jessica's questions about the forecast and at what time tomorrow the conference would start.

It was a bright, crisp early afternoon in the *City by the Bay*, with temperatures in the high fifties, with a cerulean sky broken by lazy flotillas of clouds. There was a faint scent of fresh fish in the air, the kind that teased the palate for oyster, crab, calamari and a variety of whitefish served on the Waterfront.

Jessica's room was on the top floor at the West San Francisco hotel, her window overlooking the cityscape and in the distance the Oakland Bay Bridge.

The conference was being held at the Moscone Center, just a two-minute walk from the hotel. That meant that Jessica could sleep until eight and still make it to the conference tomorrow morning at nine. A chilly night was predicted but, thankfully no rainstorms. She was looking forward to a respite from the bad weather back in Denver.

Her call to Macy that afternoon went through. She had just gotten back from a literature class and was looking forward to a night out with Greg.

"What's the weather like there?"

"Scrumptious," Jessica said, remarking that she was going for a walk after dinner. "I've got to get you here one day, Macy. San Francisco is such a romantic town, always bustling but not like New York or Chicago. I guess I'd call it an adventurous city."

"Greg and I have talked about visiting there one day."

"One day? Now, there's a definite sound of planning in that statement. Your relationship is serious?"

"Yes, Mom."

"Do you mind if I ask *how* serious?"

"We'll talk about it when we get home. Don't get too worried. I'm not pregnant."

"Thank God for that."

There was a pause in the conversation and then Macy said, "Guess what, Mom? I was accepted at Iowa."

"The writing program?"

"Yes, yes, yes!" Macy said. "I just can't wait."

Jessica told her daughter how proud she was and that it was cause for an extra celebration over the holidays. She had tears in her eyes when Macy said that there was an incoming call from Greg beeping on her cellphone.

"Do you mind, Mom? I can let it go to voicemail..."

"Honey, go ahead. We'll talk later."

Jessica went to the window and watched the snake of taillights wending its way over the crowded Bay Bridge. A faint mist rose off the water. The temperature would rise into the mid-sixties that day.

Everything seemed absolutely perfect in her life. Her daughter was about to become a famous novelist, and Jessica had a new man in her life. It was almost Christmas and, although she had told no one yet, she had just received a sizeable bonus in her paycheck.

The one-week conference purporting to host some international advertising consortiums as well as some of the most creative organizations from across the United States, was poorly planned, with several individuals failing to attend. Each day didn't go quite as scheduled, with some speakers extending their time at the dais and causing late lunches and failed appearances.

Jessica was disappointed but not enough so to let it impinge upon her excitement about Macy's impending arrival in Denver. Conventions were conventions. Some were well organized and others were just a flop.

The only good thing about this one was that it was going to let out two days early. Jessica decided to try to change her flight, though she knew that possibility was next to nil considering the holiday reservations. She was eventually told that she would be placed on a waiting list for flight 100, which was scheduled to depart early tomorrow morning.

She decided to take the chance and called the reservation desk in the hotel, explaining that she would be checking out in the morning, one day early.

Jessica got to bed early after a seafood platter dinner had been delivered to her room. She'd ordered a dry white wine and a side dish of asparagus. The dinner was light as was the wine, which relaxed her and made her look forward to slipping under the sheets.

She checked her iPhone and saw that it was still snowing in Denver and that more was on its way. She called Hattie to check on things in the house but mainly because she needed to hear a friendly voice.

"Hattie, it's Jessica.

"Yes, Ma'am."

"Just because I'm away from the house doesn't mean you can't address me as *Jessica*. My goodness, how long have we known each other?"

"Sorry...Jessica," Hattie said. "It's an old habit. I've been in this business for a long time."

"All okay there?" Jessica asked.

"There was a caller late last night, close to midnight."

For a split second she thought that it was Macy and that something was wrong. She immediately asked Hattie if it was her daughter. She was told that it was not.

"I don't mean a telephone caller," Hattie explained. "Someone at the front door, in from the storm. She wouldn't come inside and wasn't dressed for the weather. I pleaded for her to come in to warm up but she just stood there."

"What did she want?"

"She never spoke. She just starred at me."

"A woman?"

"No, she was a little girl, maybe nine or ten. She was wearing nothing but a flimsy nightgown, and the strange thing, Jessica, was that she wasn't shivering or even wet from the snow."

"Oh my God. What did you do?"

"I told her that I would get her some hot chocolate and cookies, hoping that would entice her inside. When I returned the door was wide open and the girl had vanished. I hope you don't mind but I had to call the police to see if they would help find her before she froze. They came right away and called for a search..."

"You did the right thing, Hattie," Jessica interrupted.

"Well, the search went on all night, and then they came back in the morning and insisted that I give them your cell number. I don't think they believed me, Jessica."

"Well, I do, Hattie. But you should have called me."

"I'm sorry. I knew you had important meetings and I didn't want to inconvenience you and I..." The sudden pause elongated into silence.

"Go on, Hattie," Jessica said.

"Well, the next morning when the police came back I...well, how can I say this, Jessica...?

"What?"

I wasn't so sure that it had really happened."

Hattie was sobbing now.

"Do you believe it happened?" Jessica said.

"Maybe it was all a nightmare or a figment of my imagination. I just don't know anymore."

Jessica told her that she probably would be coming home a day early if she was lucky and got a seat on the flight. They would talk about it tomorrow and then Jessica would contact the police herself. She reassured Hattie that she had done nothing wrong by calling the police, even if she wasn't sure the incident had happened. Her reaction to what she believed had occurred was very appropriate. She left her housekeeper feeling better and eager to sort things out the next day.

Jessica took an extra glass of wine to bed but not before unwinding in a hot bathtub. It was the kind of tub that had nozzle jets around the sides and on the bottom which would have easily lulled her to sleep if she hadn't kept her eyes open.

The king-size bed had extra pillows with lavender-scented sheets and one of those massive arching headboards, expensively tufted and almost as soft as the matching bedspread pillows.

◆

The next morning Jessica awoke late and had to scramble to dress, collect her bags and call a cab. She must have had a bad dream because she was feeling an odd anxiety about flying. She'd flown for decades and never had any qualms about flying. She wanted to make it on the flight but yet wouldn't be disappointed if she didn't. In fact, by the time she arrived at the airport she was hoping they would tell her that the flight was already filled.

And she wasn't disappointed. Inside the gate she was told that flight 100 was overbooked. The next flight to Denver was early that afternoon. Relieved in an strange sort of way, Jessica sat in the gate lounge planning out what she would do for the next five hours.

She heard the last boarding call for Golden 100 and then collected her carry-on bag, reminding herself that she would have to pick up her suitcase at the baggage claim in Denver as it had already been taken aboard the departing flight.

As she was leaving the gate, a flight agent rushed up to her and said there been had last-minute no-shows and that a seat was available on flight 100.

"They're not in first class, Mrs. Gibson, but if you don't mind the rear section you can board the plane."

Jessica froze with indecision, feeling at once panicky and irritated at such an irrational reaction. She took a deep breath and said that she would take the seat.

She walked hurriedly into the gate and down the jet bridge to the waiting stewardesses at the boarding door. Passing down the aisle of packed seats on both sides, she saw the Catholic priest on the left near the rear of the plane and the two nuns behind him on the right.

Whatever trepidations she had felt before boarding, upon seeing the priest Jessica felt almost overcome with relief. Surely, a plane couldn't be safer when a priest was onboard.

Approaching and realizing that her seat was next to his, Jessica smiled at the man, trying her hardest not to show her relief.

The priest moved over, insisting that she take the window seat.

Remembering the sight of the nuns in the rear, Jessica's reassurance soared.

She felt silly for having succumbed to such childish apprehension.

All these years of safe flying and never a problem she thought.

As she sat back, Jessica's cell rang. It was from Macy.

Chapter Thirteen

A week before they were scheduled to leave for Denver, Greg convinced Macy to cancel the flights and to prepare for a road trip instead. He said it would be romantic and give them both a chance to drive through so many states.

"How long would it take us?" Macy said.

"Well, it's a twenty-nine hour drive straight through. I figure with both of us driving we could make it in under three days. Even if we decide to become adventurous and stop over a few nights here and there, we'd arrive in plenty of time to celebrate the holiday weekend at your Mom's.

Checking the route online, Macy said, "If we take the toll roads it would be faster and I could stop by Iowa City for a few hours."

"Iowa City?"

"The workshop, dummy. I guess you haven't heard that I've been accepted there?"

"Yeah, I'm sorry. I wasn't thinking. Sure, Honey. That would be okay."

Macy called her mother just as she had boarded the plane. She said she couldn't talk, that the plane was about to take off but that she would call Macy at the airport in Denver as soon as she disembarked.

"Great," Macy said. "It's just more good news to tell you. I love you, Mom."

Their classes were over and they had little left to do but plan the trip and pack.

"Just pack your things and we'll leave by noon," Greg said.

"You mean now?"

"Sure. I've already packed all my stuff in the car."

Macy had a cross look on her face. "How the hell did you know that I would agree to this crazy idea of yours?"

"I know you."

"The hell you do. I have writing to finish up."

"I'll drive the whole way, Macy, and you can sit in the back with your laptop and write to your heart's content. There's even a USB plug back there."

"I love you, you bastard!"

"Iowa City, here we come," Greg said and immediately began helping Macy pack.

◆

They got to Buffalo in just over six hours. Greg's arrangement had been perfect. Macy had been able to write stretched out in the back seat while Greg was plugged in to his favorite station on iHeartRadio.

They'd stopped once before for a bathroom break but now they needed to fill up with gas and buy some munchies.

The sides of the streets were piled high with plowed snow. At the Shell station where they refilled so much snow had accumulated on the roof, two attendants were attempting to clear it with large snow shovels. Melting stalactites fringed the roof gutters in front and on the sides, dripping under a nearly-warm, mid-afternoon sun.

While Macy went inside to purchase the food, Greg clicked the filler nozzle on automatic and then checked his smartphone for weather updates for the next leg of the trip well to the south of Chicago. No big storms were predicted.

Greg made a run for the restroom when Macy returned, and then they both sat in the car drinking their sodas and eating an assortment of candy bars. She had brought Greg a tall cup of black coffee for the road, thinking he might need it, but he told her that *Hit Nation* on iHeartRadio was all the caffeine he needed.

"In some states it's illegal to drive wearing headphones," she said.

"These aren't exactly headphones. They're pods. I can hear what I need to hear around me."

"I rather doubt that."

Greg turned with a grin, his mouth almost full. "Back there you were reading out loud something you wrote. I just remember the words *exsanguination* and *Cassie*. Is she one of your characters?"

"You were eavesdropping, Greg!"

Greg laughed. "I was listening to ambient noise."

"Touché!"

They got back on Interstate 90 heading for Cleveland, both full of sugar and reignited energy. They made pit stops in Cleveland and South Bend. At the latter stop Macy noticed that Greg was a bit wobbly when he got out of the car and yawning heavily. He had already finished the coffee. She suggested then that they pull over at the next rest stop and sleep for a few hours, but Greg was adamant about continuing on.

"Do you want me to drive?"

"No. That wasn't part of the deal, remember? I'll be fine," Greg said.

They continued, driving through sudden snow squalls spawned by brisk winds from the lakes. They were hit broadside several times, the car jerking out of its lane and then Greg overcorrecting and causing it to lurch back.

Macy climbed into the front. She grabbed for her smartphone and began searching for motels. Greg looked relieved.

"Damn!" she said after completing several calls. "All the major chains are filled up for the night. If we can make it to Elkhart, there is a Holiday Inn Express with two queens and a kitchenette. That's about another three hours. Can you make it, honey?

"I'll make myself make it," Greg said bravely.

Macy quickly made the reservation using her debit card. She told the staff member that they probably wouldn't arrive before 1:30 am. She asked if there were any chicken places near the motel and was told that Popeyes wasn't too far but that they closed at one in the morning.

After the reservation was confirmed she called Popeyes and ordered a bucket of assorted fried chicken, drinks and apple tarts, requesting that the food be delivered to room 140 at the motel at the latest possible hour before the restaurant closed. She added to the total a handsome tip.

Macy looked over at Greg and began to massage his neck. "Honey, warm beds and Popeyes await us."

◆

They checked into the motel at just past one thirty. The temperature was 19 degrees, and Greg was shivering as he loaded the last of the bags onto the baggage trolley. Since it was after-hours Macy had to use the code the reservationist had given her to get into the lobby.

The night shift receptionist was a petite young black woman, perhaps around Macy's age. She wore short bangs and thick reading glasses and had an accent from the deep south. Macy couldn't help but notice that she was reading a copy of *Love and Lies in the River City* by D. Elaine Fields. Macy had purchased the e-book on Amazon but hadn't read it yet.

Yawning, she asked what the book was about.

"My hometown. Richmond. Well, it's not really about the city but the drama takes place there, romance and tragedy, you know."

Macy told the young woman that she was about to read the novel herself.

The receptionist's eyes raised as Greg pushed the cart toward the elevators. "Sir, we can have someone do that for you."

"Thanks," he said. "I think we'll manage. By the way, what time is checkout?"

"Eleven a.m., but don't worry if you're late. By the way, the order from Popeyes is already in your room."

They took separate showers and then sat down on one of the beds and, famished, opened the still-warm bucket of delivered chicken. For the next five minutes they said nothing, almost devouring the entire container, licking fingers, occasionally going for the Cokes.

Macy turned on the local TV station, looked at the weather and a recap of the day's news. It was almost all political stuff, more people already talking about jumping onto the Republican wagon, some candidates already preparing their spring appearances in Iowa, where Macy hoped to be by tomorrow afternoon.

Both wearing only tee shirts, Macy's with a Wellesley logo reaching down to her knees and Greg's a sleeveless football jersey, they collapsed into one of the queen beds, their backs to each other, yawning out loud as a respectful message that there would be no fooling around tonight.

◆

Jolie, the night clerk, had paused her reading and was eagerly imagining the love-couple upstairs. She had been smitten by the handsome young man, and with too much time on her hands, she was imagining her own novel, embellishing it with her own passionate chapters.

"Now Jolie...," she said out loud, cautioning herself against such compelling notions. She didn't have a steady boyfriend but had enough experience in near-carnal pleasures to let her imagination to take colorful flight.

Before soon, with heavily lidded eyes and abbreviated drops of her head, she lay her head down across her arms on the desk and was soon fast asleep.

◆

Macy awakened suddenly as if someone had poked her in the stomach.

Greg was cuddled up against the other side of the bed. He was snoring deeply, but that's not what had awakened her.

It was unusually cold in the room, as if the air conditioner had accidently turned on. She got out of bed and went to pee. Coming back from the bathroom, she checked the thermostat and saw that it was set at 72 degrees.

Macy peered out of the curtained window and blinked at the haloed street lights in the parking lot. There was frost at the corners of the window. In the distance she could hear the rhythmic clinking of a loose flag post halyard. An empty soda can rolled swiftly across the tarmac and hit the curb.

An eerie feeling of loneliness made Macy's face go blank. Maybe it was the wind and the cold outside or the sudden awakening. She rubbed at her arms and tried to shake the feeling. It was as if something was out of place, not there anymore, a vague sense of loss and sadness, the kind of feeling when you wake up from a sad dream without knowing where the sadness came from.

She lay back down on the bed and observed Greg's back expanding as he took a deep breath and then settled back into shallow, effortless breathing. She wiggled over and cupped herself against his back, her knees drawn slightly and pressing on the back of his thighs. She wanted to put her arms around him.

The closeness, the feeling of his dormant warmth, made her eyes heavy. Soon she fell back asleep.

Greg's alarm went off at eight, a low buzz, but neither were awakened by it.

When he finally opened his eyes and stared at the nightstand clock, he couldn't believe it was eleven thirty.

He'd had to snake his body away from Macy's, so close was she to his. She was now in a fetal position, her arms crossed over her chest, her legs drawn up, just revealing a strip of her panties.

He got out of bed without waking her and turned on the coffeemaker.

He finally had to wake her. "Hey, sleeping beauty..."

Macy licked her lips and slowly raised her head from the pillow. "Oh God, I feel like I've been run over by a truck."

"You sorta look like it. Here, take some coffee. It's after eleven."

"I had a horrible night," Macy said, sitting up and drawing the covers over her shoulders.

"Do you want to talk about it?"

"No."

"Cheer up...we might have to fly but I think we'll make Iowa City by this evening."

Greg heated up the raspberry sweet rolls in the microwave. Dressed and already packed, they sat on the Rayon sofa, mounds of sticky cellophane and paper napkins piled on the coffee table.

They checked out of motel, apologizing for leaving so late.

Inside the car, Macy said, "I can't believe we overslept. Your phone alarm must not be working."

Grey shrugged his shoulders. He got onto the expressway and accelerated to the posted speed limit. Macy remained in the front seat.

Four and a half hours later, as the first exit signs for Iowa City showed up on sign posts, Macy's phone rang.

Greg was sure it was a call from her mom. Noticing the curious look on her face, he guessed it was not a familiar number. She clicked it on after the third ring.

"Who?"

Macy's expression suddenly dropped from her face.

Greg glanced over, instinctively slowing the car.

"Dad? What do you want?"

Macy listened silently for nearly fifteen seconds, her face turning pasty-white, her mouth contorting into a silent *no!*, followed by a gleaming flood of tears.

Greg quickly pulled the car over onto the shoulder.

"How do you know for sure?"

"How long have you known?"

"Have they found the wreckage? She may be alive..."

In the ten seconds of painful silence that followed, Greg saw his girlfriend's face age by years, her dripping mascara painting the edges of her face like an eerie clown, her eyes bulging with tears, her hand cupped around the phone, shaking convulsively.

The sudden *no!* exploded from her lips in an octave that didn't sound human.

Greg wrapped his arms around her.

She screamed into his chest, a long muffled cry.

And then she fell limp in her seat as if deflated by some enormous exhalation of energy.

Chapter Fourteen

She was barely breathing. Her O2 sat was hovering around 65, and she'd gone into a seizure for about a minute. Her pulse was steady but registering around 45 bpm.

Freda had made the ambulance driver pull over once because she thought they were losing her. She was sure that they would have to intubate the young girl.

During the emergency Freda had let her training take over. After relaying her patient's data to the emergency room doctor, she placed her hand over the girl's chest to monitor her breathing. She now had the time to recall exactly what little Emma had told her about not worrying. It was as if she knew what was about to happen.

But Freda had witnessed this before in her career as an EMT. There was once a man being transported for heart pain who showed no abnormal cardiac rhythms. He smiled up at Freda and said that he was about to die, thirty seconds later succumbing to a fatal myocardial infarction.

She wasn't going to lose this young patient. She updated her condition to critical, and the driver turned up the steady wail of the siren, red and white lights thrashing through the darkness around.

"Emma, don't you go anywhere!" she called out, suddenly unable to feel the young girl's chest movement and seeing that her breathing had stopped.

"Pull it over!" Freda shouted. "We have to intubate her!"

Hardly able to keep up with the speeding ambulance, William slammed on his brakes as he saw the flashing lights ahead on the side of the road.

"They've stopped again!" Lydia cried out, opening the car door before William had fully stopped, almost losing her footing as she raced ahead to the back door of the ambulance.

"Em...Em! Oh God, what's going on?" She banged at the rear door with all the energy she could muster.

William came running up behind her and put his arms around her.

Through the frosted windows Lydia could see murky figures moving urgently about under the fluorescent lighting. Muffled voices were interrupted by sharper radio vocalizations. "Code 25. Repeat Code 25," were the only words she could make out.

Recognizing the code, William said, "She's stopped breathing." Trying to console his wife over his own anguish, he held her in a bear hug. He knew she would attempt to break the door down.

"Nooo!" she cried out in a voice of such torment William buried his face against hers.

"I know Em will be fine!" William said, sounding more like he was demanding the outcome. "Let's pray for her."

"Fuck the prayer!" Lydia wailed. "Ethan, Ethan...where are you now that we need you?!"

Less than five minutes later the ambulance sped off. Lydia and William scrambled back to their car.

Once at the hospital, they caught a glimpse of their daughter as she was whisked down the corridor to the trauma room. She was naked from the waist up, one EMT leaning over her head manipulating an Ambu bag, the other, a woman, straddling her upper legs ready for a sign that compressions had to be initiated. The look of frozen panic on the woman's face was enough to prompt Lydia to scream out again, "Nooo..."

They were led to a small waiting lounge, where one nurse sat down next to them and explained what she knew about what was happening to their daughter.

Possibly a seizure. Respiratory arrest. Possible cardiac arrest. Your daughter is in the best trauma center in the area.

The nurse grabbed for Lydia's hand and said she would remain with them until the doctor came.

The comment was meant to comfort them but in Lydia's mind it was a sober hint that her daughter was losing her battle for life.

◆

They sat in the hospital chapel until a priest arrived. Lydia was cradled up against her husband in the pew, no longer screaming, no longer sobbing, no longer beating her fists against the doctor's chest. All hope and energy had been extinguished.

A tall man wearing a white collar sidled in beside William. "I'm so sorry for your loss, Mr. and Mrs. Noyes." He reached over to put a hand on Lydia's shoulder. She didn't move.

The priest said a short prayer and made a sign of the cross over the grieving parents.

The doctors allowed Lydia and William to view their daughter in a corner of the trauma bay. They had dressed her in a blouse that was much too large and removed all tubes, including the intubating instrument. Her hair was matted and she had small bruises on her arms from the needles. Her skin had a horrible chalky color to it. The profound stillness of her daughter had finally convinced Lydia that it was over, that Emma was dead.

Lydia sat up and told William that she was ready to go home. It had been four hours since Emma had passed, four hours for her to accept the truth and garner the courage to leave her little body at the hospital.

When they returned, the house had a chill void to it, as if many people had died in it overnight, their souls already departed.

Lydia couldn't bring herself to view Emma's room, but William did, standing inside, looking at the books on the shelves, the unmade sheets on the bed, stunned by the silence and Emma's absence. He let himself cry, heaving with inconsolable sobs, tears flooding his face. He began to shake as if some gelid blanket had been thrown over his shoulders.

He found Lydia at the desk in her office.

Sensing his presence, Lydia said almost matter-of-factly that she was making a list. "I'll make the arrangements at the funeral home and later on go by and pick out a coffin. I'll buy a plot at the cemetery. I need to buy our baby a funeral gown, something attractive but not too frilly. I'll have her hair done the way she always liked it and bring her favorite necklace."

She turned around to face William. "And I want to write her obituary."

◆

Later that morning before leaving for the funeral home, she called Father Danny. He wept on the phone in a coarse ragged voice that showed his advanced age. He would meet them at the funeral chapel and prepare a special mass.

Lydia thought about calling Ethan but found herself feeling suddenly bitter toward her son. He had never made the effort to meet his sister, was always too busy helping others, hadn't even called in months. Later she would write him a letter.

That evening, after picking out a white coffin and meeting up with Father Danny, Lydia managed the courage to finally enter her daughter's bedroom.

At first she just stood there as if nothing had happened. It wasn't real. There had been some terrible mistake.

And then the truth settled upon her, a cold weighty mesh, an inescapable loss.

Then suddenly she felt Emma's presence in the room, a warmth, a familiar fragrance, an image of her face.

She went through some clothing drawers, running her hand over each garment, rubbing it slowly, occasionally lifting items to smell them. She found a box in one drawer that contained Em's jewelry, her favorite anklets, charm bracelets and a shark's tooth leather necklace.

She found the diary tucked under her daughter's undergarments. It was white and had a gold clasp on it. She took it over to the bed and sat down. She thumbed through the pages. They were mostly filled with entries. Between the cover and the first page there was a note. It was dated yesterday. One sentence, with her signature below.

When *I die I wish to be cremated and my ashes spread over Pelican Lake.*

Chapter Fifteen

Macy and Greg had driven straight through to Denver, switching the driving every four hours. They made it in less than ten hours.

Her father's words were still in her mind.

Driving had enabled Macy to begin the numbing process of accepting at least her father's version of the accident. There had been matter-of-fact certainty in his voice, as if reporting a news story, and only hints of compassion for his daughter. She was angry at him for not finding out where she was and coming to tell her face-to-face. He shouldn't have told her, not all of it. He could have said, simply, that her mother had been in an accident and was in the hospital.

How could he know even now? He'd said they hadn't found the plane, that it was just missing. His stupid presumption was that her mother was dead.

Macy remembered her mother's last words just before the plane had taken off. She didn't have time to talk, that she had to turn off her cell. And those last three words: *I love you, honey.*

Her mother was alive, and Macy knew it, even more certain now after evaluating her father's message. He wouldn't make it up but with misinformation he was bound to have drawn the wrong conclusion.

Greg said little during the rest of the trip, only agreeing with Macy when she told him that it was impossible for her mother to be dead. When they'd stopped once for gas on I-76, he'd held her and rubbed her back, traffic whizzing by behind them on the cold interstate.

They'd hit moderate snow in Nebraska but it was largely a dry snow, collecting on distant farmlands and side roads but swirling like dancing serpents across the pavement ahead. The closer they got to Colorado, the heavier and thicker the icy crystals became, soon covering the roadways and blanketing all that was visible beyond.

Even at four o'clock in the morning, the outskirts of Denver were a mess. It was like a pre-rush hour gridlock, the snow piling so heavily on vehicles and streets that it almost caused a whiteout in the haze of the street lights. Windshields of oncoming cars were reduced to twin trapezoidal carve-outs beneath jittering wipers, totally obscuring occupants inside.

As Macy saw signs for the airport, she abruptly directed Greg to drive there. She yelled at him a couple of times when he missed a turn. When they finally arrived she told him to drop her off in front of Golden Airways.

She burst through the entrance and proceeded straight to the counter under the brightly-lit logo, where a just-arrived agent was yawning.

"My mother was on a flight out of San Francisco and was supposed to arrive here yesterday morning...don't know the flight number, only that it left California early in the morning...her name is Gibson, Jessica Gibson..."

The young woman behind the counter, well dressed with a white blouse with the Golden logo on it, looked at the screen in front of her and then back at Macy. She said that flight 100 from San Francisco was still listed as delayed, but then a man approached Macy from the side and asked her to follow him.

"I'm not going anywhere!" she said in a loud enough voice to draw the attention of some gathering passengers.

"Miss, please," the man said. "We have some information but you'll have to come where the other relatives are gathered in a special lounge.

"I demand to know where my mother is!"

"Miss, you'll have to calm down."

"Don't tell me to calm down!"

Another airline official arrived and put her arm around Macy's shoulders. The touch felt cold and intrusive, but Macy knew she would have to comply in order to get the information that she needed.

The tall slender woman with gray hair escorted Macy to a door well behind the Golden Airways counter. She turned as they walked down the narrow corridor, saying, "Officials will share with you everything they know at this point."

She was led into a large room filled with people, some walking nervously about, others sitting in rows of chairs, heads bent over, sobbing softly to themselves. She took a seat next to an elderly Indian woman with a parched face and hard, penetrating eyes.

They sat there for a minute and then Macy asked the woman what they had told her about the missing plane. She turned and gave Macy a stubborn, anchored stare, then shook her head.

"Are they sure it crashed?" Macy asked nervously.

"Missing," the woman said. "That's all they've told us."

"How long have you been here?"

"Don't know...since yesterday."

"How often do they brief us?"

The woman turned squarely at Macy and seemed to be gazing into her eyes. There was a glint of softness in the stare. She reached over for Macy's hand.

"Your name?" she asked.

"Macy. My mother is aboard the flight."

The woman squeezed her grip. "My stepdaughter Krishna," she said.

Shouting began in the front of the room near the podium. Out of nowhere a woman began wailing, followed by another person and then someone began banging against the podium. It went on for several minutes until finally an airline representative appeared through a side door.

"We want answers!" a small group said in unison. "We want the truth!"

The man who appeared had his jacket off, his pale blue dress shirt rolled at the sleeves, dark patches of sweat staining his armpits and the collar of his shirt. His face was puffy and red, and the veins in his neck bulged prominently.

He tapped his fingers on the stick microphone and waited until there was a lull in the din. "Ladies and gentlemen," he said. "All I can tell you is what I announced half an hour ago."

Macy squeezed back as the Asian woman held onto her hand.

"Flight Golden 100 is still missing. It dropped from our radar center at eleven hundred hours yesterday morning. We don't know for certain but they might have attempted a landing at Salt Lake and then changed their mind. They disappeared somewhere over the mountains southwest of Denver. That's all we know. I'm sorry, I wish I could tell you more."

"Do you have proof?" a man yelled.

"Have they discovered the wreckage?" another demanded.

The sound of the word *wreckage* made Macy's stomach turn. It conjured up something her mind was unwilling to accept. She stood up suddenly. "If there's no wreckage found then you don't know for certain the plane crashed!"

"Yes! That's right," a woman several chairs away rebounded.

Someone started chanting, "No wreckage, no crash!" Others followed suit.

No wreckage, no crash.

The whole scene became rowdy, the official at the podium trying the quell the uproar by repeatedly tapping his fingers on the microphone.

The chanting and sobbing went on until their energy was spent, and the voices slowly faded, one by one, extinguished by sheer exhaustion. The silence that followed smelled of weariness and sweat and a wrenching stench of hopelessness.

Grief counselors suddenly appeared and began making their way down the aisles. Two priests and several non-denominational clerics filtered through the crowded hallway door.

Macy couldn't take it. She ran down the aisle toward the exit, burst out of it as though propelled by a blast.

In the corridor, running toward her, was Greg.

At Denver International later that morning they were interviewing via satellite conference the two Montrose air traffic controllers who had followed the last radar blips from the transponders of Golden 100 flight.

Present were two FAA officials, an airline representative and the head controller on the monitor.

"No possibility of error, a UFO?" one of the FAA men asked.

"The plane was clearly identified," Hollander said. "Transponders don't lie."

"Recon?"

The airport official said, "One plane and three rescue choppers from Crested Butte. Snow's pretty bad up there and visibility almost nil. They're waiting for the next break."

The FAA man asked what they had told the next of kin.

"The truth. That we haven't spotted any wreckage yet."

"I don't think we should tell them if and when we do. You have to be careful how it gets out to the media. Anyway, we can't confirm until we have boots on the ground."

"Any VIPs aboard?" the other FAA man asked.

"Doesn't appear to be."

The FAA men continued to confer with the airport manager, reviewing the passenger roster and then downloading the map of the flight plan of the doomed plane, quickly determining approximately where the trouble began for flight 100.

"Was there an onboard fire reported?"

"That's on the Salt Lake tape. After a lightning hit. Then they dropped to nineteen thousand."

"A flameout?"

"Probably. A Mayday call came in."

"Where?"

"Salt Lake." The FAA official shook his head.

"Last word from rescue?"

"About an hour ago. They've triangulated a probable area but the weather is thick, almost impossible for the choppers."

"They've got to get down there before the whole damn thing is covered up with snow."

"National Park Service has SAR ground teams ready as soon as we give them coordinates."

◆

They ate an early lunch at CRÚ, a small tavern-like pub at the airport. Greg ordered chili and sauerkraut hotdogs and mugs of chilled ale. Macy had said nothing since being served and only dipped her spoon into the chili bowl a few times before putting it down.

Greg watched her from across the booth table. She'd told him all that officials had shared about the missing flight. He felt helpless and wished there was something he could say or do to make her feel better. The news, although not yet conclusive, felt cold and real to him, a devastating event that would change both of their lives. He was more of a realist than Macy was and wanted to begin to process the healing that was the urgent next step. But if Macy held out hope then he would support her in any way he could. For Greg, the important person to save now was not her mother but Macy herself.

Greg caught a glimpse of a news crew rushing past the tavern, equipment handlers and a well-dressed woman in a green suit, a makeup artist dabbing her face as they walked.

He told Macy that they were probably about to have a news conference.

"What?"

"A conference for the media."

"I don't want to go back there."

There was a recorded football game on the overhead TV. Greg got up and went over to the bartender and handed him a twenty, which he refused. The station was switched to CNN to a few boos from the customers.

The veteran anchorman was talking about the missing flight, behind him a smaller screen showing an empty podium. The picture switched to a tracking map showing a red arc from San Francisco to a black star near the base of the Rockies southeast of Denver. The anchor with a gray beard and black-rimmed glasses was talking with his guest, an aviation specialist who sat across the news table. Occasionally, smaller windows appeared on the screen showing the somber faces of other expert guests.

Greg knew that Macy wanted to hear any new information about the flight, but only if it was good news. She didn't want to hear about sightings of a charred wreckage, of pillars of smoke and flames licking up from the blackened surface of a mountainside.

Fifteen minutes later, Golden Airways had assembled a team at the podium. The camera drew back to show the chairs with the news reporters sitting in them. As one member of the team drew forward and tapped on the microphone, the image zoomed in to reveal a man in a black suit with gray hair and moustache.

"Ladies and gentlemen, my name is Gars Strohm and I am president of Golden Airways."

Greg watched as Macy sat up straight in her seat. Her expression was grim, her stare accusatory.

"This is our second news conference," Strohm went on. "I am afraid that we have no new information about Golden flight 100. The crash site has not been identified, though our team has narrowed the search area to about a hundred square miles. Projected coordinates suggest that the plane went down somewhere between Portland and Ironton. We don't believe the flight passed beyond the western ridge of the Rockies. Currently the weather does not permit helicopter searches or ground rescue and search teams. The snowfall is heavy and the area just too large for ground teams."

A reporter stood up. "Is terrorism being considered."

"Not at this point. All evidence suggests an onboard situation."

Another reporter, still seated, asked, "I've heard there was a fire onboard. Was White Sands conducting any missile tests that morning?"

"No. That has already been confirmed."

The reporter persisted. "There's a confidential report indicating that a missile was launched at eight hundred hours and that it had to be destroyed."

"We've heard no such report," Strohm said dismissively.

"If it *is* true, then the plane could have been shot down."

"I strongly doubt that. Listen, we all are looking for answers, especially for loved ones, and stirring up that kind of speculation is only going to make things worse for everybody. All we know for certain at this point is that Salt Lake Control lost contact at about 10:00 a.m. Mountain Time. There was a brief radar contact at Montrose Regional Airport at 11:45 a.m. Central Time.

A woman stood up. "Would a crash like that be survivable?"

Greg swung out of the booth as Macy pushed her way past him and made a run for the door. He threw the twenty dollar bill on the table and ran after her.

She seemed to be heading for the survivors' room but passed it and began throwing open doors along the corridor. Greg could hardly keep up. He saw two airport guards at the very end and then Macy disappearing between them following a brief scuffle.

The security men were already inside the news conference room when he got there. Macy was shouting at the startled speaker.

"My mother is on that plane! You're not telling us the truth! You don't know what it feels like..." And then she fell through the arms of the guards and landed on the floor.

The room was silent, although most eyes were turned towards the back. They tried to drag Macy back to the door like some crazy protestor. Her anguished sobbing filled the room. A camera swung around.

Greg launched himself at one of the guards, breaking the man's handgrip on Macy. He helped her to her feet, his arm protecting her face.

One of the guards was pointing a Taser device at them.

"Go ahead. In front of national television!" Greg touted the man.

Macy stopped at the door and then turned around. Most in the room were standing up looking back at her, empathy etched on their faces.

"I'm sorry," she said and then let Greg take her outside.

◆

The snow had let up some as Greg drove Macy home. The traffic was terrible but felt strangely comforting to Macy. Time was no longer of the essence. She wanted to think without distraction.

She watched the unplowed roadway ahead, white on white for as far as she could see, red brake-lights pulsing in the white blur, and heard the crunching squeak of the tires and felt the insular contraction of pain in her heart.

Her world had been turned upside-down. Nothing mattered anymore, not school, not writing or the workshop, not the once-exciting feeling of returning home and, maybe, not even Greg.

Hattie must have seen them drive up for she greeted them at the entrance, her eyes red and full of tears, her arms hanging at her sides.

Macy went to hug her and held on as the woman began to shake in her embrace.

"Macy, baby...I'm sorry," she managed, looking up into her eyes. "I didn't know. She changed her flight. I Didn't have your cell number."

"Hattie, I need for you to be strong because I'm losing it fast. Please be strong for me."

They held each other again. "Macy, girl, I will...I will," Hattie said.

Greg introduced himself, and Hattie wrapped her arms around his broad chest and held him as one of her own.

"Was my father here?"

"Your mother gave me the day off yesterday. I think he was here when I was gone but I'm not sure."

"Bastard. He should have left you a message," Macy said and then asked about her mother's boyfriend.

"Michael?"

"We need to notify him."

"I'll find his number, Macy. Don't worry. Let me handle things."

Macy suddenly felt exhausted. She told Hattie and Greg that she was going to catch a nap in her room. Greg said he would get all the current contact numbers from the airlines and keep his eyes glued to the news.

"Honey, you need to rest too."

"Don't worry about me."

Even before Macy made it to the stairways, Greg and Hattie began looking up phone numbers and arranged scratchpads on the kitchen table.

Macy heard the television go on downstairs as she took off her coat and then cuddled under it, soon, mercifully, drifting into a cocooned slumber.

◆

Gars Strohm, President of Golden Airways for the past fifteen years, had always prided his company for not having a single fatality during their operational years.

Strohm had been a commercial airline pilot for Swiss Airways for ten years before raising the substantial capital he needed to fulfill his dream of owning his own airlines. He had a couple of friends in Congress and, as a result, found financial backers for establishing his company, originally called Golden Express, a solid competition for UPS. It failed within two years, its planes about to be swallowed up by competitors, but with Strohm's determination and willingness to offer better service at cheaper rates soon recouped his losses when it converted to passenger service. He had kept his pilots and crews by making every employee a shareholder in the new company.

In truth Strohm was not ready to accept that one of his planes had gone down with all its passengers and crew aboard. He had never prepared himself for such a tragic situation and felt it incomprehensible that he would soon be confirming what could only be the instant deaths of so many people. As a former pilot he was a realist. There was no hope whatsoever when planes ran into mountains. Flat areas with no trees, rivers and even oceans...perhaps there were fluke miracles in those cases.

His PR people had vetted every word of his announcement and had advised him how he should respond to questions from the press. Though he was uncomfortable with their advice, he understood protocol and making sure that no unconfirmed information be shared with the public. No doubt the company's attorneys and accountants were scrambling about, worrying about individual and class action suits and the possibility that the company might fold because of financial losses. In truth Strohm couldn't care about the prospect of another financial collapse. His focus was on the passengers' deaths and family members who were suffering unimaginable grief. Nothing could make him feel worse. He thought he could face anything at this point.

But not a young woman whose mother had perished on one of his planes. He understood her anger and frustration, as well as all the other suffering souls in the survivors' lounge. But he could not console them. The PR people used *hope* as a method for buying time, for delaying the law suits. But to Gars Strohm it was an unconscionable way to prolong the agony of survivors.

Upon completing the news conference, Strohm broke away from his team and demanded to be left alone in his temporary office suite. The afternoon was waning, as was the light for the waiting search teams, and he knew there wouldn't be any news until tomorrow at the earliest.

He called his wife and told her that he would again be spending the night at the Denver airport.

Later, he watched the rerun of the news conference and was disappointed by how he had handled some of the reporters' questions. The answers sounded laconic and perhaps a little dismissive. He watched the young woman bursting in at the back and the despicable way authorities had handled her. The woman's voice made his stomach wrench. He turned off the news channel and covered his face with his hands.

He thought of his own daughter, grown up with children now, living in Melbourne. She was a commercial pilot working for Qantas, and undoubtedly was abreast of the news. She had been on a flight back to Australia with a two-day layover. He thought about calling her but soon realized it was still very early in the morning in Sidney.

He had close friends he could call but he didn't want to burden them; it wouldn't be professional. His wife was a comfort and he loved her dearly, but she was too emotional when it came to company problems. He wondered if she understood the grave magnitude of having one of his planes go down and the deaths of so many, many people.

His head now pounding, Strohm took two Advil capsules and drank a glassful of water. He lay his head down on the desk, over his thick arms.

A devout Catholic, he said a prayer and then recited the 23rd Psalm.

◆

The phone rang, the red one. Gars Strohm looked up at the clock suddenly, realizing that he had fallen asleep. It was a little past five. The phone rang again.

"Gars?"

"Ya..."

It was Monique, his personal secretary and friend. "I'm holding a call from the Coast Guard..."

"Coast Guard?"

"They've already notified search and rescue. They think they know where the crash site is, Gars."

Wild imaginings raced through Strohm's mind. The plane must have crashed into waters, maybe a lake or river. Perhaps there were survivors...

Monique went on. "They got a call from someone named Billy who lives on one of the Ute Reservations in the mountains. He claims that his son witnessed the crash."

"Oh my God! Where?"

"Just east of Uncompahgre Peak"

"Jesus! Where's that?"

"About 176 miles southwest of here."

Strohm closed his eyes. His heart was pounding, hot tears welling in his eyes. He took a deep breath. "Okay, Monique, put me through."

Chapter Sixteen

lthough it wasn't exactly within their purview, the Coast Guard chopper was the first to arrive on the scene. There was deep snow and no discernible pathways or trails leading up to Uncompahgre Peak. You couldn't even see the branches of trees, only what looked like dark ghostly skeletons where the wind had stripped the upper branches.

It was only an hour before dawn. There was just enough light to make out the snowy terrain below them. Both pilots of the MH-65 sensed that the crash site was not far away. If they didn't find anything in the next hour they would probably have to return to base and try again in the morning.

In addition to the poor visibility, the chopper was causing a blizzard of its own. The updraft generated by the rotors was making the hovering unstable and nerve-racking for the pilots.

Lieutenant Dusty Wellborn, a veteran of the Guard, had experience with mountain rescues off the coast of Oregon, but few had involved heavy snow.

"There. That's the national park," Dusty said to his co-pilot, pointing down at a vague snow-smothered structure south of the peak.

The woman was using infrared binoculars. "Okay. I think I've got something," she said. "Half a klick at one thirty, past the peak."

"Yeah."

"There's definitely something down there."

Hovering over the spot, Dusty took the binoculars. The pale green image showed massive dark forms on the snow-blanketed mountain. Slightly to the northeast shone a faint cluster of white and possibly the impact zone.

They went lower, a spume of snow catching the tail rotor and causing the fuselage to sway to one side.

"Easy... What kind of thermal reading you got?" Dusty asked his co-pilot as she pointed the thermal radar gun just to their right.

"It's hot. Definitely. Right there. Coordinates?"

"Yeah, got it," Dusty said and radioed the position to search and rescue.

There were two other choppers not far south of their position and they were coming in with their rescue teams, although it seemed hardly likely that anyone down there could be rescued.

A ground team would be making its way from the southeast and would probably be there within the hour.

Dusty called Buckley Air Force Base in Aurora and confirmed their position. He told them they were looking for ground space to attempt a landing. They were told not to touch anything until the team of investigators arrived.

"Until the wreckage is examined, it's a crime scene and not the Armed Forces jurisdiction."

"All we want to do is determine if there are survivors," Dusty said, realizing at once that the possibility was a foregone conclusion.

As the sun rose and illuminated more of the area, they came around and approached the point of impact from the west. A small but fairly level plateau could be detected just at the top of the ridge, just enough area for three wheels. The windblown surface showed packed snow.

Dusty made a decision to go down and hover over the location just to make sure all wheels when lowered would hold them at an acceptable vertical position. One slip and they would flip and careen into the next ridge.

"Gear down," Dusty said.

"Down. Fifteen feet," his co-pilot instructed.

"Blowback is manageable."

The chopper landed almost perfectly, its tail pointed away from the wind, all three wheels on hard surface, just a slight tilt to starboard.

"That ridge is pretty vertical," Dusty's co-pilot said as she took over controls and watched the pilot slip out of the sliding door.

It was about a 70 meter walk to up to the crest. His communication lanyard dangling from his helmet, Dusty eased himself up the slope and crouched at the precipice.

A gust of wind caused his communication line to slap against his closed faceplate. It whistled eerily in his ears as it slipped through the opening at the base of his helmet, assaulting him with the frigid air. He pulled the visor off. His eyes immediately glossed with tears.

Peering over the edge, Dusty saw the outline of the wreckage about forty meters down, a long smudge of blackened snow in a patchwork pattern, probably a hundred meters long. Ghostly snow-covered shapes protruded from the mountainside. One was a small section of the tail. The snow had appeared fairly deep from the air but Dusty could see that the wind had sculptured shallows along the steep mountainside.

The stillness assaulted him. He could smell the acrid odor of engine fuel and burned material. A spire of smoke rose and flickered in the wind, probably from one of the engines.

The scene was static and incomprehensibly serene, as if something sacred had occurred there.

He walked farther along the ridge and was struck by another odor, malevolent and sickening, which Dusty remembered from one tour in Afghanistan before he joined the Coast Guard. It struck a memory of the aftermath of a car bomb.

Then the deathly odor wasn't there. He'd only imagined it.

Futile and almost ludicrous as it felt, he called out for survivors. "Anybody there? Can somebody hear me?!"

He repeated his calls several times and at one point thought he heard a voice, a singular anguished cry that drifted up the mountainside and faded into the soft whine of the wind.

His heart pounded as he leaned over the ridge, his shoulders and arms dangling over the edge. He spent the next ten minutes calling out.

"Is there anyone down there? This is Lieutenant Wellborn from the Coast Guard."

Silence.

"For God's sake, can anyone hear me?"

He suddenly imagined people huddled together under a piece of the wreckage, a snow cave, an intact piece of the fuselage, survivors waiting to be rescued and returned to their families, their homes and loved ones.

He heard nothing more and was now fully able to grasp in his head that a plane and all its passengers had disintegrated upon impact. This was no longer a search and recovery mission.

◆

A twenty-member SAR team from the Rocky Mountain center in Boulder had been brought in to prepare for recovery. They had landed their chopper in what turned out to be the only stable surface at the top of the mountain ridge near to where the Coast Guard had landed.

A NTSB team was on its way.

They had begun their rappel to the north side of the wreckage, where the snowpack was more dense and offered better stability for rappelling equipment. They operated in teams of two, one anchoring the rope, the other making the descent.

At the base where Billy and his son stood, they looked like snakes unraveling down the mountainside.

The boy was mesmerized and fearful. He knew more than the climbers that the mountain was not to be trusted. Even *Senawahv* had abandoned it.

The big man with white hair had stopped taking pictures and now was holding a notepad.

"Son," he said. "Now, you actually saw the plane crash into the mountain?"

The boy nodded.

Billy said, "He traveled to the peak of Uncompahgre and climbed to the crest...and that's when he saw it."

The boy nodded again and opened up a palm to simulate the belly of the plane sweeping over.

Billy explained to the FAA individual that his son could not talk, that he'd been traumatized by what he had seen.

"When you saw the plane go over before it crashed was there any fire?"

The boy thought for a few moments and then nodded his head. Using one palm as the side of the mountain and the other hand as the plane, he slammed them together and then used his flared fingers to indicate an explosion and fire.

"How far above was it?"

The boy turned to his father and used Ute sign language to explain.

"Maybe ten horses high, he said. Not more than fifty feet," Billy explained.

"I rather doubt that," the man said. "He would have been swept off his feet if it was that low."

"My son does not lie," Billy said.

"Does he remember anything else?"

The boy used one quick motion of his hand to his brow for the succinct answer.

"He can't tell you," Billy said.

"What do you mean that he can't tell me! This is an official investigation."

Billy stiffened, his jaw squared. Finally he repeated, "He can't tell you."

There were now around thirty people at the staging area between Uncompahgre Peak and the crash site. Ground teams were assembled here, along with snowmobiles and other small vehicles. The rescuers were dressed in either bright orange or yellow outfits, some with vests. The body baggers had on white uniforms. They would be the last to be called to the crash site if any remains were to be found.

By nine o'clock the search area had been gridded. Red flags would be used to signify dangerous areas like crevasses, yellow ones aircraft wreckage, and green ones human remains.

The rappellers were using their hands and picks to dislodge dark stains in the snow where evidence might lay.

Billy and his son had been allowed to remain where they were, about two hundred yards from the wreckage. The man saw plenty of yellow flags, a few red ones, but no green markers.

He explained to his son about the flags then shook his head slowly. "That is not right," he said, referring to the lack of body markers. He could only deduce that everything had burned or been obliterated by the impact.

The boy explained to his father in sign language.

"The mountain took them?" Billy repeated.

The boy used one hand to sweep over the other.

"Yes," Billy said. "They are on the other side."

◆

The active search was called off later that night. Six Colorado State troopers remained to guard the site. A generator powered the tall LED light stands on either side of the wreckage, lighting up the side of the mountain, giving it a strange Hollywood movie scene effect.

Rodney Blake, one of the patrol members, had a flare gun with a box of plastic shells, as well as several rounds of stun gun ammunition. He knew from past experience that hawks and other predators were known to feed on remains. He was ready to use his cache of ammunition in that event, but seriously doubted whether it would be necessary.

There were no green flags, and the word had gone around that all of the passengers and crew had simply vaporized upon impact. It reminded him of the Flight 93 in Pennsylvania on 911. The crater the plane made when it hit the ground at 500 miles an hour had consumed all but miniscule fragments of fuselage and human remains.

The lack of green flags indicated nothing of human origin was in the wreckage. Not a finger or a fingernail, a strand of hair, a bone fragment...nothing. Just thinking about it raised goose bumps on the back of his neck.

Blake lit a cigarette in the artic night air, the flickering of his lighter yellowing his cupped hand. He began walking to the outside heater blower that had been set up for the troopers and run by a separate generator. It was going to be a long night.

Feeling the powerful radiant heat, he took off his gloves and began rubbing his hands briskly. His face and clothing soon warmed. For a moment all seemed as it should be, eerily normal.

He thought of his wife and three children back in Boulder, the decorated Christmas tree and the kids' presents and how much he missed being there with all of them. Christmas was just two weeks away. Headquarters had already approved his three-week vacation when he had to return to duty and serve on this mission. That his family was together and safe brought almost as much warmth as the roaring heater.

Blake's speaker-mic crackled beneath his jacket and a voice called his name.

"Blake here."

"It's Jeff. I think you'd better come over here. Something's moving up there."

The Lieutenant scrambled over the shallow ridge and hurried up to where the Sargent stood. "You're kidding, aren't you?"

The Sargent was using a green laser light, the end of its narrow beam bouncing nervously at the top of the wreckage.

"Right there," he said.

"I don't see anything," Blake said, using his night binoculars to focus on the area.

"I swear I saw something move up there."

"Probably a bird or coyote."

"No, Lieutenant. It was a figure of some sort, moving north to south."

Blake rubbed at his shoulders and smiled. "Maybe you should plant a white flag up there."

"White flag?"

"They're used for sightings of ghosts."

Chapter Seventeen

Lisa Morales was enjoying the last day of her vacation in Acapulco when she got the call on her cell. Against the brilliant sunlight on the beach, she rolled over and sat up dizzily, cupping a palm over her smartphone to see who was calling. She answered on the third ring.

Monique looked at her from the adjacent blanket, her heart-shaped sunglasses slipping down her nose, exposing pale semicircles above her eyes. She watched the austere expression on her friend's face. The silence gave her a good indication of who might be calling.

"Yes. Yes," Lisa said in almost a military cadence. Her eyes were focused as if she were memorizing every word of the caller.

When she hung up the phone, she bent down and grabbed her towel and bag. "Gotta go," she said to her friend.

Monique gathered up the rest of their beach stuff and hurried behind Lisa as she half-jogged to the beachfront hotel.

"Ah shit!" Monique groaned, referring to the hangover from last night's escapade, now made worse by soaking in the sun for half the day.

In her room Lisa called the Acapulco International Airport and got a priority ticket on the next flight to Denver. It would be departing in less than two hours. Had she been at home in Tampa she would have been placed on an immediate military flight from MacDill Air Force Base.

As a junior member of the Go Team for the NTSB, Lisa would be part of the investigating team looking into the crash of a passenger jet. This was her third assignment involving a plane crash in so many years. While many of her friends thought this a gruesome job, Lisa saw it quite differently. Her job as part of the NTSB investigation was to assemble a puzzle from thousands of pieces of physical evidence located at a crash scene and then, after all data and material had been analyzed, to provide an accurate explanation as to what may have caused the crash. In Lisa's mind it was to help prevent future disasters and, more importantly, to give survivors the facts they needed to accept and then grieve for their loved ones who had perished in the crash. Accurate and detailed information of this kind wouldn't make the pain and anguish go away, but it would provide a logical rationale for what had occurred and why it had occurred.

On the plane Lisa reviewed the NTSB investigative manual and then reread the email she'd received at the airport. She would be the fourth member of the team investigating the downing of a Boeing 737-300 that had apparently slammed into the side of a mountain near Uncompahgre Peak in the San Juan Mountains of Colorado.

The only other information provided in the email was that the impact area had been located and that there were only fragments of the plane left.

No human remains found at the crash site.

This last part of the message said it all to Lisa. The jet had been traveling at maximum speed and probably in a near-vertical descent.

She located two members of the team at Denver International and then they took a priority flight to Grand Junction just northeast of Uncompahgre Peak.

Their main base of operation was at Grand Junction. Here they met up with the other two members of the Go Team. After surveying aerial photos of the crash site, the investigator-in-charge Chad Erlick provided each their assignment.

Lisa's preliminary duty was as structural investigator, which meant that she would be looking for mechanical remnants of the destroyed plane. This would include locating the *black boxes* if they had survived the impact. Located in the tail section of the plane, both the data and voice recorders customarily had good records of survivability in air crashes, assuming at least that the tail assembly remained mostly intact. As of yet, no pings had been detected from either recorder.

Based on an aerial view of the limited size of the debris field, only Lisa was assigned to this task. On-site officials reported seeing a small section of the tail and just tiny fragments of the fuselage. High velocity impacts with granite usually pulverized the structure and contents of a plane. Even the ground produced the same effects in vertical impacts, one of which Lisa had investigated two years ago.

With their investigative equipment on board, all four members of the team flew to Montrose, the closest staging area to Uncompahgre Peak. They were flown there in a large twin-rotor Chinook helicopter.

Lisa sat in front nearest the cockpit and was able to get a good view of the harsh, craggy mountain-scape ahead. Darkness came hard and fast in the mountains. She asked the pilot how far Montrose was from the crash site and was told that it would take less than 20 minutes by helicopter.

As she was the only female member of the team, she was given a room to herself at the motel in Montrose, a small sprawling town in the Uncompahgre Valley with an incredible view of the San Juan Mountains. Sixteen inches of snow remained on unplowed areas and the main road in town still bore evidence of the heavy snowfall, with crusted ice and banks of hardened snow flanking the road.

They remained there long enough to change clothes and grab a bite of food before heading for the crash site.

Onboard the Chinook Chad turned to Lisa with a devilish smile. "Just think. This morning you were languishing on a beach under an Acapulco sun..."

And a hammering hangover, she wanted to say but thought wiser for it.

By the time they arrived at the site the eastern face of the mountains was draped in evening shadows. Some areas sank into complete darkness.

They circled over the area and saw that some of the recovery teams were already searching the mountain face.

Chad made a decision not to land the team that evening and, instead, start as early as possible the next morning.

"We break at 0600 hours and arrive at the crash site at 0630. Any questions?"

Ordinarily an instant sleeper, Lisa was still tossing in her bed at midnight. She had been reading a summary of the type of material Uncompahgre Peak was composed of. It was a hard igneous granite, a volcanic type originating from ancient volcanic activity. That seemed very relevant in Lisa's mind. Volcanic rock like Mount St. Helen was much more porous and would tend to absorb impacting material.

How could a 100,000-pound aircraft almost vanish into a hard-granite mountainside? Sudden and violent compression should have resulted in massive dispersion of material. It was an irritating enigma that caused Lisa to toss and turn for almost an hour.

◆

The sun was breaking, bathing the eastern slopes of the San Juan Mountains in aurora-like streaks of gold, red, pink and yellow against a fading navy-blue sky.

The NTSB team was flown on a twin-engine Sikorsky provided by the Coast Guard. It was large enough to fly the team and much of the equipment. A second drop would be needed for some FAA officials and the rest of the supplies.

Lisa sat at the door window trying to make out the crash site. Since the impact had occurred in a deep crevasse on the western side of mountain ridge, deeply-carved shadows obliterated the view.

The pilots flew around in a tight circle and then one of them pointed at the ground, indicating the small flat ridge where they were going to land.

As they descended Chad reminded them that they might have to rappel down into the crevasse. He said a rope system had already been rigged which would make the descent easier for the inexperienced. Lisa wondered whether one of the older Go Team members, a man in his sixties and somewhat overweight, would be able to safely navigate the descent.

Each wore a gray and neon vest with NTSB insignias and white hardhats. They had been given the choice of wearing the customary tan pants or jeans. Lisa chose the latter.

She was surprised to see that a rope ladder had been constructed for the members of the team. The first to go down was Sam, the eldest investigator. Leaning over the side, she saw him jump from the last rung of the ladder and land on his feet with a slight bounce.

So much for overweight seniors, she thought. She learned later that Sam was a decorated Vietnam war hero who, in the early years of the war, had made nearly a thousand parachute jumps over enemy territory.

Down on the small ledge between Uncompahgre Peak and the impact wall of the mountain, Lisa took off her goggles and looked up at what should have been broken wreckage and bodies and was astounded by what she saw: almost nothing. She had prepared herself for this, but the scene was just plain creepy.

A small chunk of the tail of the 737 lay at the bottom on the ledge. As the sunlight caved in on this side of the mountain, only tiny objects reflected back, miniscule remnants of the fuselage.

Nothing. There should have been larger pieces of wings and certainly engines. Fragmented remains should have been there, too. It hardly looked like a crash scene.

A shiver slithered down Lisa's back. This wasn't right. The magnitude of the impact had been all-consuming, an instant vaporizing event the likes of which she had never witnessed before.

The charred remnant of the jet's tail section, about the size of a refrigerator, sat firmly on the ledge. Lisa first took a dozen pictures of the object from different angles and then marked it with an identification number which would later be marked on the crash site map. The object was so disfigured that only the trained eye of an investigator could verify what it was...or what it had been.

The tail remnant would be hoisted by helicopter and transferred to a hanger in Montrose in an old warehouse on the edge of town. There Lisa would embark on the hopeless mission of finding the black boxes...or what was left of them.

The largest pieces of the wreckage besides the tail object were no bigger than marbles. The rest was just a fine dust of charred aluminum. By late afternoon all of it had been bagged and ready for transport to the assembly hanger.

Although it wasn't part of her responsibilities, Lisa used the rappelling equipment to begin a zigzag inspection of the charred wall of the mountainside. It blew her mind that no one had found even a sliver of human remains. There had to be something there: a fingernail, a piece of hair or skin, a smudge of residual life.

It became an obsession by the time she finished the last unsuccessful sweep of the mountain face. She thought about her parents and how they would feel if she perished in a crash and no one was able to offer them evidence of her remains. It would be unbearable for survivors to hear this.

As hard as she searched, Lisa Morales could find no evidence whatsoever that human beings were aboard Golden flight 100.

Chapter Eighteen

When Lydia received news of the plane crash and the death of her son, she collapsed dead-weight in her husband's arms. It had only been a month since Emma's sudden death in the hospital. They had cremated her remains at her daughter's request and were waiting for the ice to melt on Pelican Lake to spread her ashes.

"I've lost them both," Lydia sobbed in William's arms. "God has forsaken me. He is cruel and I hate Him!"

William was in survival mode. He hadn't even begun to process the death of his daughter. And now this. He had steeled himself since Emma's death, suppressing his own emotions in order to be able to help manage Lydia's. His chest hurt from the days-long barrage of his wife's fists.

"Keep to your faith, Lydia," he said now for the umpteen time. And when he did, his wife took her anger out against God.

"Faith in what? A heartless God?"

She had begun pounding again. William took her by the wrists and tried to lower them. "No," he said. "Faith in your children and our own daughter. Faith in their spirits and the meanings of their lives. Don't you see? It's the only way we can survive."

Lydia fell to the floor. She was still a young-looking woman for her age but now, wrenched by grief, her face looked gaunt, her eyes recessed and darkened, her body too small for her clothes.

William sat down beside her and began massaging her neck, feeling the taught tendons beneath the spread of brown and gray hair.

Nobody had called them about the crash. They'd followed the news reports. It was only when the passenger manifest was scrolled across the TV screen that Lydia found the name: *Ethan A. Andrews*. She hadn't even known he was flying to Denver. Or now, so many years later, what he had been doing with his life. She'd read his infrequent letters and knew of his disenchantment with the Church and that he was considering leaving priesthood. But that was all.

And now she would never know all of the truth.

Ethan had never met his sister. They would have gotten along so well, both smart and intellectual and set in their ways.

Within hours of learning of the accident, after William had called the airlines in Denver, they were informed that human remains couldn't be identified, yet they requested hair samples from Lydia just in case.

They followed the news and Lydia revisited the old newspaper office where she had once worked. AP and Reuters were covering the story almost daily as were CNN and other networks.

Only the flight data recorder had been recovered from the crash site. It was badly damaged, and the NTSB reported that it would take some time to recover data if they could retrieve any at all. About one hundred pieces of wreckage were found, none larger than a dime.

No one could explain the absence of human remains, although theories abounded, many religious survivors pointing to God's choice to preserve the passengers in heaven. Spiritual groups had their own beliefs, as well as some reputable but fringe scientists, many of whom pointed to a vaporizing fireball. Or the possibility that no one was on the plane when it hit.

For loved ones like Lydia, the non-existence of remains was a tormenting addition to already agonizing news. She wanted to have something to bury, a part of Ethan to bring home to his family. It become an obsessive notion. Lydia even considered somehow going to the crash scene and witnessing the lack of evidence for herself.

"Maybe we should go," William said. "Not to the crash site but to be among other loved ones. We may be able to find comfort among them."

It was not something Lydia had thought about. Initially, the idea of being surrounded by grieving people felt like the last thing she would want but then, with William's urging, she began to give favor to the notion. Her husband suggested taking along the urn with Emma's ashes.

When the airlines finally called and told her that a private conference had been scheduled in Denver only for the family members of the passengers, Lydia's mind was made up. There might be some updated news.

◆

The meeting had been set up at the Marriot near the airport, in a private conference room that could accommodate four hundred people. There were no news teams and no evidence that this was going to be anything but a very private arena for family members' questions. City police had cordoned off that part of the hotel and stood guard at entrances and exits.

Lydia and William were asked to sign in and were given photo ID tags. They were told that the meeting would last as long as loved ones had questions to ask. There would be a luncheon served by the hotel.

When they entered the large hall, Lydia was staggered by the sheer quantity of people in attendance. The room was filled to capacity. She had expected to see and hear people openly grieving but found instead a sea of stone-sober faces. She thought, like herself, that there were no more tears to cry at this point. Information, any of it, was the priority now.

Chairs were arranged around long conferences tables, maybe thirty or more, with seats to accommodate hundreds of people. Water bottles and soft drinks, along with snacks, were available at each table.

Lydia found two empty seats midway in the room. People at that end of the table turned and smiled respectfully as she and William sat down.

In the front the conference room, on a raised stage, sat a dozen officials. One of them, Lydia was told, was Gars Strohm, the CEO of Golden Airways, two FAA representatives, an NTSB public relations spokeswoman, local police officials and Air National Guard officers. At a table just below the stage sat a group of men and women in casual attire. Lydia wasn't certain, but they looked to be social workers, nurses and clerical members.

The speakers introduced themselves and then Strohm opened the meeting.

"Thank you for coming, ladies and gentlemen. As you may know, we have excluded all members of the media from being in attendance today. We are going to share with you all the information we know up to now in this investigation. This is *your* meeting and I encourage all of you to participate by asking questions and by sharing your views about any information we present to you today.

"Golden Airways flight 100 took off as scheduled from San Francisco International Airport at 8:15 am Pacific Standard Time on Thursday, almost ten days ago. It was bound for Denver and a subsequent return flight to California.

"Somewhere east of the Rockies, well south of Salt Lake City, the pilots made contact with ATC, reporting a fire onboard possibly due to a lightning strike. We can only assume it was an engine fire based on the fact that no fire was reported following their rapid descent to 21,000 feet. The cockpit data recorder indicated that there was substantial turbulence at their originally assigned altitude as well as at the lower altitude. It sounds like they hit a bad storm.

"Last contact with the plane was at 10:40 am Mountain Time by Montrose ATC. There was no voice contact, only transponder data. The plane went down on the eastern edge of the Rockies near Uncompahgre Peak at approximately 11:05 am Mountain Time.

"I am sorry to say that there were no survivors. We have not identified any of the remains."

Someone opposite of Lydia's seat at the table stood up. She was a young woman, looking poised and comfortable, her face an oval of solemnity and conviction.

"There haven't been any remains to identify. Isn't that true, Mr. Strohm?"

The CEO must have recognized her. He dropped his head and then looked up, his hands planted firmly at the lectern. "No, we have not found any remains, although the crash site is still being analyzed."

Someone else stood up. "How do you explain the lack of remains? It doesn't make sense."

"No, it doesn't," Strohm said. "You've probably heard many theories, some of them on the fringe side. Our own forensic experts have no explanation other than...and I wish there was a better word for it...complete *incineration*."

A voice from the rear of the room, amplified by a portable microphone, said, "Then...they didn't suffer? That makes me feel better."

"I am not a medical expert," Strohm said, "but those I have talked with assure me that there was no fading consciousness, just instant death...and no pain."

The young woman across the table stood up again. "My mother was aboard that plane, Mr. Strohm. Don't you think she suffered extremely as the plane was going down? If that's not excruciating pain, I don't know what is."

Strohm nodded and said he was sorry.

Lydia, holding the small urn of her daughter's ashes, stood up and turned about to face the audience. "I lost my son, a man of the cloth, who was the kindest and most selfless person you would want to meet. Four weeks ago I lost my young daughter Emma to a fatal seizure. To say that I am not consumed with grief would be a lie...but over the past several days with my husband's help I have just learned to accept that which I cannot change. That may not be a comfort to all of you now, but the truth is that it is all we can do. I pray that all of us come to our own individual places of peace as time passes."

The young woman had already stood up before Lydia finished her comment. "We can hold people accountable," she said, "and that's what I plan to do."

"You mean sue the plane's manufacturer, the airlines or hold the pilots themselves responsible?" Lydia said. "Some of you may already have attorneys...in fact, one came knocking at my door...who are promising you compensation. I don't blame you for reacting that way. They might promise you final closure. Let's face it: there will be no closure for any of us. There never is."

There were many more questions and discussions among loved ones. Strohm allowed the others on stage to update the audience on any new findings. A clergy member said a prayer just before lunch. Strohm addressed the audience one last time before the break.

"I want each of you to know that Golden Airways is here for you. For those who wish to extend their stay for additional news, we will provide you with accommodations and food at no expense. Representatives will be approaching you this afternoon with substantial compensation offers from our company should you decide not to take legal action. God bless, and I'll see you after the lunch period."

Platters of cold cuts, cheese, bread and an assortment of condiments were placed at each table.

Lydia and William fixed sandwiches for themselves.

The young woman across the table reached over and shook Lydia's hand.

"My name is Macy. I really appreciate what you said, although it's hard for me not to hold someone accountable."

Lydia smiled and said, "You have no idea how hard that was for me. I've had so much anger, mostly at God, for what happened to my son. I made my husband suffer and I think I almost burned a hole in my heart."

"I know where you're coming from," Macy said. "I think each of us in this room has gone through so many stages, you know, denial, grief, anger and hopelessness. Nothing is ever going to bring back your son or my mother. I know that. But the feeling of blame is overwhelming."

Lydia leaned forward. "Please tell me about your mother."

◆

After the meeting adjourned later that afternoon, Lydia and William asked Macy and her boyfriend if they would like to share dinner together.

Snow showers earlier that day had stopped. Under a slate-gray evening, both couples got into Macy's car. The two restaurants they tried were reservation-only and had no openings until much later that evening.

Macy insisted that Lydia and William have dinner with them at her house. She'd called Hattie and asked her if there was time for her to whip something up for a foursome.

Feeling no need to engage in conversation about the crash, at Macy's house they talked about themselves and their interests. William and Greg were both Broncos fans and were entertaining fanciful thoughts about making it to the Super Bowl as a wild card.

Greg was astounded to hear that William had worked as a photojournalist and had been nominated for the Pulitzer while covering conflict areas. He told William that he was mainly interested in communication journalism.

Glad to be off the subject of the air disaster, William was soon sharing riveting stories about his coverage in Iraq.

Lydia had connected with Macy from the onset. They thought alike. Macy, of course, was decades younger than Lydia, but she had poise and a mature way of thinking that was hard not to admire in someone so young.

They talked about Emma and Ethan and then Lydia listened to Macy as she poured her heart out about her mother and the special love they had for one another.

After being served leftover glazed ham and mashed potatoes with chives, Macy insisted that Hattie sit down with them. Her presence was inexplicably comforting for Lydia, almost as if they had known each other before in some other place and time. There was something almost spiritual about the woman.

Following dinner, Macy took Lydia up to her mother's bedroom. They sat on the edge of the bed and talked.

"At least we have something else in common," Lydia said. "We're both writers...that is, I *was* back in the day. But being accepted at Iowa is such an honor. You should be very proud."

Macy's eyes glazed over. "I don't know now if I could attend the workshop. I think I've lost pretty much all of my creative energy. It's actually the last thing on my mind."

Lydia leaned over and hugged Macy. "Your mother would want you to continue your life's dream, Macy. You know that. She's probably yelling at you right now from Heaven."

Macy smiled and hugged Lydia back. "I guess you're right. I'll think about it when I return to college."

Greg had been listening just outside the door. He knocked on it and came in.

"Macy," he said. "You *have* to write about your mother. You know that, don't you?"

"I will...one day. There is so much to share with the world about who my mother was and the love she gave to others."

Downstairs in the living room they all had drinks, Macy insisting this was only the second time in her life that she had drunk alcohol. She sipped on the white wine while the others enjoyed brandy.

Lydia was pleasantly surprised to hear that Macy had already written a novel and was thinking about having it published. "I would love to read it," she said.

"Honestly?"

"Of course," William said. "We'd both be honored to read your work."

"I would too," Greg said. "Macy's always kept a tight lid on her writing."

Eventually the question about Macy's father arose. Without giving it any thought she said, "My father is dead."

"I'm so sorry," Lydia said.

Greg gave Macy a respectful look and said nothing.

The fabrication had slipped out so effortlessly, almost as if it were true or at least wishful thinking. Macy felt bad about it almost right away.

"My father is dead to me," she clarified.

Lydia could feel the hurt and anger from across the sofa. She surmised that Macy's father had done something awful to his daughter to earn that kind of remark.

"My Mom and my father have been separated for many years," Macy explained after an uncomfortable delay. "She had already served him divorce papers before she boarded that flight. He was never good to her and he just wasn't part of my life. That's it, I guess."

"You didn't have to tell us," Lydia said, feeling awful now for having broached the subject.

"Actually, I'm glad you asked. I needed to hear that from myself."

Lydia wanted to hear more about Macy's mother. She was mesmerized by Macy's miraculous recovery from the coma and her mother's vigil by her hospital bed for all those months. She shared the tragedy of her own daughter and how Emma had been such a spiritual child, gifted in ways that few people understood.

She removed the urn from her purse and placed it on her lap, now gently stroking the sides of the vase. "Em was on this earth only for a short time, but I feel she was here for a purpose, a mission and something I still don't understand."

Hattie, who had just entered the room, sat down in a chair. "Your daughter," she said, "is spiritually gifted. I think you know that already, Ma'am."

"Why do you say *is*?" William said. "Our daughter has passed on to Heaven."

"Yes, of course."

Lydia looked at Hattie, abruptly seized by a feeling that the woman knew more than she was telling. "Please go on, Hattie."

"It's really not my place to interfere with religious faith. Belief of that kind is the greatest source of comfort. I guess you could say that I hold a secular notion that we all have living spirits that they are always traveling. Dying is not the end of life.

"Ma'am, when I first saw you sitting at the table I knew that we had something in common. You see, I too lost a child many years ago. She was very much like your daughter. She had spells too."

"Spells?" Lydia said. "I never mentioned anything about Emma's little episodes."

"Seizures," Hattie said. "Didn't you say your daughter died from a seizure?"

"Yes, of course," Lydia said.

"I know your little Emma was very intelligent and highly sensitive. Precocious is the word. She probably had imagined friends and sometimes spoke in strange tongues."

Obviously William was trying to be protective when he stood up and said that it was late and that they should be getting back to the hotel.

Lydia agreed but not before saying, "Hattie, both of our girls were very special, unique in ways that are hard for us to understand. Thank you for sharing that. You know, I feel inside that they would have been best friends had they met."

Hattie nodded and smiled.

At the door, Macy and Lydia hugged again.

"Thanks for coming," Macy said.

"I will be saying prayers for your mother."

"Me too, for Ethan and Emma."

"Would you do us the honor of coming to the service when we spread her ashes on the lake?"

"I'd love to," Macy said and they quickly exchanged cell numbers.

Back inside, Greg and Macy fell back against the sofa, both exhausted from the long day, yet comforted by the visit of their new friends.

Hattie was moving about, clearing the coffee table and sweeping up crumbs.

"In all the years that I have known you, Hattie," Macy said, "you never once mentioned that you had a daughter who died. What was her name?

Hattie nodded slowly, a warm smile on her lips.
"Emma," she said softly.

Chapter Nineteen

Macy opened the door to see Michael standing under the shallow portico, a tall man wearing a flat cap and a thick brown wool jacket.

"Macy?" he said, removing his hat.

They shook hands, an inadequate gesture for both, and quickly embraced each other.

"I'm so sorry, Macy. I should have contacted you earlier. I've been in a daze since I found out."

Macy helped Michael with his coat and asked him to have a seat in the living room. When she returned to join him she just stood there, almost rudely gazing at him.

"You are exactly the kind of man I imagined my mother would be attracted to," she said.

Michael had his large hands planted on his knees. "How are you doing?" he asked.

"Like a rollercoaster. Listen, I'm sorry for you. I know Mom thought of you highly."

"We had a good relationship. We cared for each other. I think every conversation we had included you, Macy. She loved you and was so proud of your accomplishments."

"Do you think you would have married my mother?" The words fell out of her mouth without forethought. She immediately realized that she'd made Michael uncomfortable. "I'm sorry," she quickly added. "That's none of my business."

Michael's eyes were glazed over. "I'm not offended at all. Your mother and I had a very close relationship. I think we both wanted it to develop. There's no doubt in my mind that at some point in the future we, well...would have fallen in love and might very well have married." He smiled at Macy. "At least that was my intention."

"She deserved someone better than my father."

Just then Greg and Hattie bustled through the front door, carrying bagsful of groceries. They went straight to the kitchen to unpack.

My boyfriend and Hattie," Macy explained.

Michael nodded politely. He then asked Macy if she had attended any of the airline's conferences. "All I know," he said, "is what I've read in the papers and seen on the news."

Macy filled him in on the details of the FAA and NTSB findings, adding that the investigation would probably go on for many months. She mentioned the lack of human remains on the mountain. She could see that it seemed to upset Michael. She reached over and placed a hand on his.

"It's both unimaginable and brings me strange comfort," Michael said. "Sometimes I think it never happened, at least not for the passengers, that somehow they went on."

"Me too. My mind tells me that they perished in the crash but my heart doesn't always agree. I've had dreams, strange dreams where I see my mother existing somewhere else, talking in her special voice, almost as if she was striking up a conversation with someone. It's like I am on the outside looking in, if that makes sense."

"We really don't know what happens after death...or if death really ever happens." Michael shifted in his seat.

Macy looked intrigued. "That's a really challenging thought. When I was a young girl I would have strange dreams about death. I'd awaken in that realm and visit dead relatives who were very much alive. It didn't seem a place of suffering, and it wasn't really heaven. It seemed like a place of never-ending awareness."

Michael smiled a thin, knowing smile.

"Macy," he said following a long pause. "I too have had dreams. At first I thought they were supernatural and beyond my understanding. But then I realized they were really scenes of precipices in my life where I've had to make choice."

"Precipices?"

"Points at which I chose to make important choices in an unconscious way. Sometimes they involve accidents where I feel my spirit lifting out of me, or the surgery I once had for a gallbladder removal and found myself observing my body on the operating table. In all those cases I felt that I'd been given an opportunity to actively choose the next scene of my life. I've never felt any fear of death. You know, after decades of having these experiences I have come to believe that there is no death, or at least as we know it, only altered continuances."

"That's fascinating," Macy said. "And I kind of feel that way too when I am deeply immersed in spiritual energy, like when I find myself writing about a character that seems to appear out of nowhere and begins to talk to me and wedges into my narrative or character dialogue. They feel like old souls."

Michael sat back on the sofa. "Where do you think your mother is right now?"

"I think she is waiting to come home. She was so excited about sharing Christmas with all of us. Yes, she is just waiting for the right opportunity. The right moment."

Michael looked at the Christmas tree near a bay window at the other end of the room, brightly-wrapped presents and cards on the silvery apron at the base. It had been almost a month since Christmas. None of the presents had been opened.

Macy explained that they had all decided to put off Christmas. As she said this, her eyes lit up with a thought.

"Why don't we go ahead and hold Christmas tomorrow. We'll pretend it's Christmas Eve tonight."

Relieved, Hattie turned and smiled.

"You'll have to stay with us until tomorrow," Macy said. "I guess you know that you were originally invited."

"Yes. I was honored."

"Then you must. Hattie can cook a turkey."

"Of course," Michael said. "I'd love to."

Macy said, "You never know. Maybe Mom will show up after all."

They had a lite dinner, delicious salads Hattie prepared with lettuce, bell peppers, onions, olives, broccoli tops, artichokes and avocadoes, all topped with a fine vinaigrette mixed with feta cheese.

Greg struck it off well with Michael. He too was fascinated by spiritual experiences and shared with Michael recollections of *flying* dreams when he was growing up.

"How reality changes everything as we grow up," Michael said. "The more we are forced to *think*, that is, to use rationalizing thought, the more our awareness becomes fragmented and restrained by what we think is reality. The realness of life lies in accepting that all is connected."

"Oneness," Greg said.

"Yes, an immeasurable continuance."

"It's fascinating stuff," Macy said. "And it makes me feel better about my mother's death...and all death, for that matter."

She put her fork down, making a clink on the china plate under her salad bowl. "Michael, how do you know so much about this topic? It sounds like you've studied it for a long time."

"While there is a lot out there to read, what I know is intrinsic. It comes from awareness and just being still with yourself. That is, putting yourself in a listening or receiving mode. It's the knowledge we're all plugged into, whether we choose to be aware of it or not. The mystics refer to it as manifest truth."

"We'll it's blowing my mind now," Macy said, feeling the possibilities swirl in her mind. She needed to anchor herself again in something ordinary.

Hattie, who had joined them for dinner, said nothing but Macy could tell that she was not letting one word escape her.

Afterwards, all but Hattie sat around the Christmas tree. Macy's, Greg's and Hattie's gifts were there, along with her mother's. There was also one for Michael.

They played some of Jessica's favorite Christmas songs: *Bing Crosby*, *Nat King Cole* and *The Carpenters*. Macy's eyes glowed with nostalgia as she listened and remembered Christmases past.

Greg suggested that they open one gift, a tradition in his family, but Macy protested.

"Not yet," she said.

Michael looked over at her and smiled. He knew exactly why she had said that.

Chapter Twenty

Since the announcement a weary calmness fell over the passengers sitting in the airport lounge. It had only been a few minutes. Someone was finally going to explain the delay.

Jessica was thinking about Macy and the upcoming holidays. She was contemplating the nature of her daughter's *good news* she had mentioned when Jessica had boarded the plane back in San Francisco.

Everything in Macy's life nowadays seemed to be good news: her pending acceptance at the Iowa Writing Workshop, her new boyfriend, her incredible grades at Wellesley and lastly, most importantly, her burgeoning talents as a writer. She couldn't have made her mother any more proud.

Christmas was two weeks away. A stickler for being prepared in advance, Jessica had already wrapped her gifts and placed them under the tree. She had bought Macy a new Apple MacBook and Greg a tablet, which Macy said he really needed. Hattie was to get a sizeable bonus and a 18-karat gold necklace and locket with matching earrings. She had purchased Michael a good pair of leather gloves and a tartan scarf.

It was going to be a perfect Christmas, more perfect because Allen was finally out of her life.

Not that she cared, but she had heard through a mutual friend that he was engaged to another woman. He was having a house built in Chicago, in a gated community just outside of the city. For Jessica, that wasn't far enough away.

She was frustrated that she couldn't contact Macy now. It seemed ridiculous that cell service wasn't available in this part of the airport.

She noticed that Ethan was staring at her. She turned to the ex-priest and gave him a thin smile and then patted her hand on his.

"Have I grown a beard yet?" he said.

"Just a rough-looking shadow. Nothing to worry about. Yet."

"There's something I didn't share with you about my past," he said.

Jessica laughed. "Oh, no...you were never a priest?"

"I told you that I was going to meet a close friend here in Denver. But that's not the only reason I took the flight."

He looked like he was about to reveal something very personal and probably none of her business. "You really don't have to explain," she said.

"I haven't seen my mother in just over a decade. She lives in South Dakota. A number of years ago she met a wonderful man and they married. They have a child, a little girl named Emma, my sister. I've yet to meet her...and my stepfather."

"Wow!" Jessica said, excited by the revelation.

"After a short stay in Denver, I'm scheduled to take a flight next week to Sioux City. I want to meet my sister and spend time over the holidays."

"That's wonderful, Ethan. You must be excited.

"Terrified, actually. I've been such an inconsiderate son to my mother and have only sent Emma a couple of postcards. There's no justification for it at all. My mother is a wonderful caring person. I won't go into the details, but after a traumatic event in my early childhood she took me home and raised me with love and kindness. She was a perfect mother. She doesn't deserve how I've treated her with my absence."

The distress in Ethan's eyes was evident. Jessica held his hand for a moment and then said, meaning it, "We weren't born to be angels. Of all people you know that, Ethan. You haven't exactly committed a crime..."

"A crime of omission," Ethan said. "But I plan to make it up to them.."

"You're going to be a wonderful brother...I can feel that so strongly. And your mother is going to be so happy to see you. I wish I could be there."

"I wish you could too," Ethan said.

Jessica wondered why Ethan had thought it so important to reveal that personal part of his life. It must have been on his mind for some time and he obviously felt a heavy sense of guilt about avoiding his family. It seemed odd to her that a priest would want to confess something so personal about his life.

She looked over at Ethan, unable to contain the curiosity. "I'm glad you did, but why did you feel you had to share something so personal with me?"

"I've heard too many confessions in my life, Jessica. The Church makes it a one-way process, with the priest giving absolution. You don't know how many times I've been tempted to ask the confessor to hear my own confession."

"You wanted my absolution?"

"The person confessing is the only one who can really forgive. And the process involves sharing."

"You are quite something, Father Ethan Andrews," Jessica said. "I have never met anyone else with such liberating ideas. I'm going to miss our talks."

"And you, Jessica? What are your immediate plans?"

"The honest truth is that I eventually plan to quit my position at the firm. I want to be a fulltime mom and engage in something that is more personally creative, a relationship. I met someone recently who really interests me, a man I think I could easily settle down with if it all works out."

"I'm sure it will," Ethan said.

Macy took out her cellphone to check for service again. She stared at the opening screen on the display and said, "Oh my God!"

Before Ethan could say anything, Jessica dialed Macy's cell and held her own to her ear, almost shaking with excitement. She hoped Macy wasn't in class or in one of her writing sessions.

The cell rang six times and then went to Macy's message center.

Jessica left a message that she was okay, that the plane had landed but that the crew and passengers were being held up for a while. She would probably be home by one o'clock. Then suddenly the phone call clicked off.

Ethan looked over and smiled. "Well, finally," he said.

"I don't know if the message went through..."

Just then the door to the hallway opened.

Chapter Twenty One

Lydia and William were finally heading back to Watertown. It was a clear day, and at 28,000 feet the cloud cover was minimal. As she had been on the flight to Denver, she was not nervous about flying.

She looked out the portside window and, as the plane banked slightly, she could see vast stretches of Nebraska farmland below that appeared like a variegated canvas. Houses were not visible but the larger highways cut through the segments of verdant land like a patchwork of scars.

Their visit with Macy at her home had been comforting and had left Lydia with a hopeful feeling of promise, that there was some meaning to the tragedy. She felt that Ethan and Emma were together. And perhaps Macy's mother too.

Although feeling at peace with her son's death, she couldn't relieve herself of the pain caused by the fact that Ethan had never met his sister. Or was aware of her death.

Ethan, her firstborn so many years ago. The abduction and then their serendipitous encounter on the banks of the river during the circus. While she had once blamed the Church for her son's estrangement, she knew in her heart that Ethan had made his own decision based on his commitment to helping others. How could she have expected him to drop his work and fly home to see his mother and sister?

Why was Ethan going to Denver? And would he have finally contacted her from there? The pain brought on by those thoughts, the blank uncertainty and the reality that she would never find answers, Lydia knew, would follow her to her own death.

She looked over at William, who smiled faintly and reached for her hand. He had an expression of such empathy on his face, Lydia felt he must be reading her thoughts. For someone who had recently lost his daughter, he seemed more concerned about her feelings than his.

Although she had not announced it to William yet, Lydia planned to return to fulltime work at the newspaper. Merely the thought of being confined to the house, weighed-down by memories of her children, brought on an angst and a sense that she would not survive without some form of distraction. Although she had long considered it was time to retire, Lydia felt going back to work was essential, at least in the short term. She was looking forward to routine and being around members of her staff.

Spring would be here before long, and Emma's ashes would be scattered over the lake. It was something to look forward to and to regret, for it would mean finally letting go of Emma's physical remains. Lydia planned it to be a little ceremony for both of her children. She had to say goodbye to Ethan as well.

They arrived back in Watertown by early evening, having driven from the airport in Sioux Falls. They were both exhausted and ready for dinner before getting to bed early.

Lydia passed by Emma's room. The door was ajar, but she couldn't bring herself to walk inside again. She stopped at the entrance and lay her forehead against the doorframe. She could just make out Emma's bed and a pair of pink socks laid across the bedspread.

Lydia knew that one day she would have to clear out her daughter's room and go through things. Clothing would have to be packed along with all of Emma's stuffed animals and notebooks full of sketches. The room would eventually be turned into a guestroom. But not now, not this close to her death. To Lydia Emma's spirit was still alive.

She found it troubling that Ethan *felt* dead, almost as if he had died a long ago time. She knew their estrangement had a lot to do with it, yet she felt guilty and saddened that they hadn't had the time to develop and maintain an adult mother-and-son relationship.

Later that evening after William went to bed, Lydia climbed the stairs to her old office. The redwood office chair seemed to squeak more boldly than ever. The desk was a mess, with reams of papers to one side, books piled on the other, along with stacks of old newspapers.

She knew it was there somewhere. She looked through the side drawers and eventually found the letter stuffed in the back of the center drawer.

The letter had been sent from Sudan five years ago. The handwriting on the envelope was uniquely Ethan's, with bold cursive script so delicately made it could have been created by a professional calligrapher.

Now Lydia only vaguely remembered its contents. She turned on the brass desk lamp and smoothed out the pages. It was dated five years ago.

Dearest Mother,

I am so sorry I haven't written earlier. The work is so hard here I haven't been able to carve out a moment of privacy. I have been helping those who are suffering terribly in this region in the east. They suffer from hunger and malnutrition, as well as those pernicious diseases of malaria, river blindness, sleeping sickness and other visceral conditions. It is a disease-beset country, this otherwise beautiful part of northeast Africa.

That is wonderful news about Emma. She must be quite a darling at this age. I can imagine my sister now as I write. Hopefully, we bear no resemblance (hah!). You must be as beautiful as the last day I saw you. I miss all of you so.

Please say hello to William and to that nutty, wonderful priest, Father Danny, whom I miss dearly.

All my love and affection,

Ethan.

He hadn't even known about Father Danny's death. Lydia had tried to write him but obviously the letter hadn't been received. She wondered selfishly if that news would have prompted him to come home for the funeral.

There were two postcards to Emma, one showing the capital Khartoum and the other a photograph of a huge elephant with looming tusks. They were signed *Love, your brother Ethan.*

A sudden despair came to Lydia and seemed to sit on her shoulders with unbearable weight. She was slowly accepting her children's deaths but the thought that Emma and Ethan would never meet, never develop a relationship was almost incomprehensible to her. The cruelness of that fate pressed against her heart like a branding iron.

Lydia reread the letter and then lay her head down on her arms on the desk. Emotional exhaustion, more than the long day of traveling, made her yawn repeatedly. It was as if that involuntary motion might expel the grief and the worry inside.

Sleep came to her, swallowing her up in its own fathomless yawn.

◆

She opened her eyes to a cold muffled silence. A chill draft in the attic room had raised goose-bumps on her skin. She sat up and rubbed at her shoulders and then heard the familiar moth-like tapping at the window.

She wondered when it had started to snow and how long she had been in her office. It didn't seem that long.

As she prepared to leave, Lydia noticed a soft light pass across the crack at the base of the door. She listened for footsteps but heard none.

Instinct from decades past came to her as she wondered if someone had broken into the house. It couldn't be William for surely his heavy footsteps on the floorboards would have alerted her.

Again the flurry of light rippled across the gap at the bottom of the door.

"Emma?" she said.

Her own words startled her. Here she was addressing her daughter whose very ashes were contained in a vase in her bedroom. Emma was dead.

The light passed again, this time stopping on the far side of the door.

Lydia watched it and realized that it wasn't like any light she had seen before. Not a lamp, not a flashlight or some portable fluorescent device, but the kind of glow she remembered from her childhood emanating from a jar filled with fireflies. There was almost a gentle pulsing to the luster.

She wanted to open the door. She knew who was on the other side. Though compelled to do so, something was stopping her.

"Emma?" she whispered, afraid that her voice might scare away the entity on the other side.

She closed her eyes, a teary tackiness sealing them shut. Doing so made the light disappear. In the crepuscular darkness behind her eyelids she saw Emma's face, not a soft angelic reproduction but instead a living countenance. Her daughter's eyes were open and connected to Lydia's. Her lips were slightly parted, showing a glint from her teeth, and her cheeks were florid, as if she had just come in from the cold.

The child moved her lips but no voice escaped into the airy silence in Lydia's mind. The message resounded in a calming warmth somewhere between her heart and her mind, an affirmation that all was well and she had nothing to fear. An inscrutable message to accept what had happened and for Lydia to go on with her life seemed to translate into a lightness in her heart, almost like a door waiting to be opened to the future beyond.

Meanings then filled her heart, illuminations about life and death and the importance of observance and love. The epiphanies were so powerful, Lydia felt unable to contain them all. The strongest one was about death and the fallacy of human perception. Death was not an end but a wayside point, a resting venue before the journey continued. Living spirits never died. The individual odysseys of life were endless, existing in partitions and alternate worlds and universes, some crisscrossing, others shooting straight to the great common source.

All of these revelations seemed to resound within truths already known. As she became aware of each message, Lydia felt them explode with meaning and relevance, something she had never been open to before.

A love lifted her heart, an emotion unlike any she had experienced before. It was a love of oneness, of common being, yet embroidered with individuality and connection at the same time.

It might have lasted a minute or an hour. Lydia opened her eyes slowly, the light from the desk lamp slowly parting her lids. She blinked.

"Emma, baby?"

The light beneath the door was gone.

"Please come back..."

The cold in the room closed in about her. She blew warmth into her hands and rubbed them together.

As much as Lydia wanted to will her presence back, Emma was gone. That sense didn't alarm her for the acceptance seemed purposeful and practiced. Within seconds it produced an enveloping blanket of solace.

She went to the window and stared out into the blotted darkness. It was still snowing. She felt the cold from the windowpane and then drew down the blind. It felt inordinately cold, and Lydia wondered whether the furnace had malfunctioned. Perhaps a window had been left open during their absence. She turned off the desk lamp and walked into the hallway and then down the stairs to their bedroom.

The thermostat downstairs registered seventy-eight degrees.

William had left the nightstand lamp on. He was turned facing the opposite wall, snoring softly. He hardly moved when Lydia slipped under the covers, just a brief interruption of breath.

Part of her wanted to awaken her husband and tell him what had happened. The greater part seemed to quell that urge, as if what she had experienced was something profoundly secret and personal.

One day, though, it would have to be shared.

Early the next morning Lydia awakened refreshed and in a surprisingly good mood. She had thought the day would have brought continued sadness and mourning. She sat up and saw that William was already up. It was 7:00 am.

Soon the blended aroma of coffee, bacon and blueberry muffins made her feel famished. She put on her robe and slippers and made her way down to the kitchen, where William, standing at the sink, turned, smiled and opened his arms for a hug. He felt warm and strong and curiously youthful for his age. They embraced for an unusually long time, William rocking Lydia in a way that may have suggested that they had been apart for some time.

"I love you so much," he said.

Lydia kissed him on the lips and then snuggled back into his embrace.

"Oh Lydia," he said. "I had the most wonderful dream last night."

Chapter Twenty Two

The girl entered the room, softly closing the door behind her. She walked to the small podium and folded her hands on the top. She looked out upon the waiting passengers as if attempting to make eye contact with everyone in the conference room.

Ethan knew instantly that he was in the presence of someone with vast wisdom and awareness. He felt a calmness settle over the room, almost as if people had been expecting her presence.

She appeared to be the girl on the plane. She was dressed in the same pale blue denims and sweatshirt she had worn on the plane. She seemed to have something important to say but was in no rush to do so. Her presence and the silence seemed to communicate something beyond words.

Ethan felt Jessica reach for his hand. He suddenly felt an overwhelming sense of multiple déjà vu, that this moment had happened before not just once but many, many times. There was a strange feeling of layering, as if each experience was shifting slightly one atop the other, making each familiarity almost vibrate.

He knew now why they were being held in the lounge. It was no longer a mystery or a mundane matter of delay. The message had come to him not as a revelation but a clarity of truth, a truth he had known all along.

He realized that the girl was illuminating that knowledge in every person in the room. Their faces showed it. At times they acknowledged with small astonished sounds, occasionally sharing remarks, sotto voce.

Ethan was enthralled with the knowledge, which seemed to answer every question he'd ever posed about God, heaven, birth and especially death. The puzzle was becoming complete.

The awareness that they'd all perished in the crash was neither a frightening revelation nor a particularly novel one. It was more a reminder. They had known it all along.

No one looked shocked or saddened or in disagreement with the disclosure.

Ethan looked down at his hands and then over at Jessica' face, now flushed with accepted wisdom. It seemed odd at first that they still possessed their bodies. His experience in life had him fixated on ethereal versions of spirit and soul and the notion that corporeal dwelling was temporary. Would they pass into the unknown, the other side, as spirit *and* body?

The answer came to him instantly: *It is a choice.*

As a theologian Ethan wanted to ask her questions. *Who was God, if not a fatherly deity to worship? What was the purpose of death within the experience of life? Why was there so much conflict in the world and why did people have to suffer?*

As if she had been listening intently to his questions, Emma spoke in his consciousness, a voiceless message as clear as if she had articulated it.

It is what you have chosen to believe and experience.

And then began the strangest revelation of all. It must have come as a surprise to Jessica, for she reached for Ethan's hand.

The decision to remain or leave was a voluntary one. Those who left by free will would be able to return to their former reality or other parallel realities. For them the plane crash would never happen. They would be reunited with loved ones and continue on in their separate or altered lives. It was a choice neither correct nor incorrect. No contingencies or consequences. Nothing to expect or not to expect.

There was a long period of silence in Ethan's consciousness. People were obviously challenging the choice with rational thought, while others, he sensed, had already made up their minds.

The young girl continued.

You also have the choice of rejoining other dimensions of your existing lives. You may choose to re-experience a different layer of your existence. If so, you will appear at a different junction in your life, perhaps to change the consequences following a major life event.

Ethan felt Jessica stir beside him.

All death experience involves personal choice. Not only do you choose when it is time for death but you also choose to be born.

The question of God, His existence and relationship to human beings swelled about the room as if the query had risen to a crest and was now washing through the collective awareness in the room.

God is a notion. The faith in that notion is more powerful than the truth that explains it. If you feel God in your consciousness then do not let go of that belief. All of you know the answer as it serves your needs and your chosen reality. When you pass to the other side, the answer will be clearly manifested, but it will not surprise you.

There were more questions by others. Many wanted to know about the existence of Heaven and if there were angels. The nuns were most vocal and seemed to be challenging the girl on this issue. Both had been whispering their rosary prayers, holding the crucifix and beads in a way as if to protect themselves from uncertain influences.

I can only tell you that there is no hell. There is no suffering on the other side. Tribulation and pain are only inventions in our lives. In some cases, they serve important functions in daily experiences. Most of the time suffering is an active choice influenced by early experiences during childhood. Remember that you always have a choice.

A period of time passed without further questions. The girl took a seat, her back against the podium, her legs dangling over the small stage. She looked innocent and childlike, in sharp contrast to her highly-evolved consciousness and wisdom. Finally she continued.

You may feel overburdened now with a feeling that you must now make a choice. That is not the case. All of you here have already made your decisions. You have lived your choice throughout your lives.

This must have been confusing to Jessica. *But you said we still have a choice now. That doesn't make sense.*

Your choice now is simply to be aware of who you are and your original choice. Those of you who have remained true to your choice throughout your lives have no need to correct that choice. For those who have been influenced by the consequences of poor decisions a reawakening to your original choice becomes the choice.

Silence filled the room.

Ethan understood. But he felt a compunction to help others understand what they had just been told.

Instantly, the girl quelled that need.

The two nuns stood up and walked toward the door. The girl got up and escorted them outside.

Four businessmen in the front also went for the door. The co-pilot followed. And then half a dozen more, including an elderly woman who made use of a cane as she shuffled toward the door.

One of the flight attendants rose and followed.

Eventually, Jessica stood up. Ethan looked up at her, feeling neither surprised nor concerned by her action and intention. They stood there for a few moments and then Jessica made him rise. They hugged without tears, without sadness or a feeling that either would be missed.

Before she reached the door, Jessica stopped as if perhaps she had changed her mind.

In Ethan's mind it contradicted what the girl had said about decisions already having been made.

The pause was long enough to suggest she was uncertain and might turn around.

The girl picked up on the indecision. *You can always return, Jessica.*

Ethan's companion and friend walked through the door, the last to leave the room.

The girl turned her attention to those remaining.

Choice is what vibrates the universe. When it becomes unconscious or unaware choice, it becomes truth.

Ethan *knew* this but the truth had never been so well-articulated in his awareness. It now made sense of his own peripatetic life, the many choices, the diversions and the ever-present sense of true direction in his life.

The need to analyze this truth soon faded, and Ethan suddenly felt a magnanimous compassion for himself and for all those he had shared his life with. This quickly expanded to the universe and other universes and beyond.

The next revelation explained that there was no death as humans understood it. People lived and relived many lives. Termination of life did not exist. But there was a further enlightenment for those in the room who felt the need for a sense of total closure of their lives.

Finality and original birth, the girl continued to channel, *is what remains on the other side. For those of you who have made the decision to rest, perhaps because you have lived many, many lives before, there is the comfort of finality. This is an absorption into a vibrant nothingness, a reconnection to the oneness and what you may know as God.*

Ethan sighed beneath an elegant peacefulness for he knew this was his chosen course. It felt like an eternal rest.

Original birth can be likened to a vast, pulsing potential. 'Waiting to be born' is a term many are comfortable using. It can be both instantaneous and eternal, for there is no time on the other side, no beginnings or endings, no measurements whatsoever. It is the miracle least understood at our limited level of consciousness.

Then that miracle is God, Ethan wanted to reply.

The girl must have just become aware of his thought. She looked at him and smiled.

And then a startling truth came to Ethan. The knowledge caused his physical body to tense with such anguish and sadness and love, he trembled. Tears came to his eyes.

The girl seemed to respond as well. She stared at him for the longest time. She nodded her head and smiled again.

Ethan was the last to leave the room, guided by his little sister Emma who, with a cheerful bounce in gait, led him through the doorway.

PART THREE

"You've gotta dance like there's nobody watching,
Love like you'll never be hurt,
Sing like there's nobody listening,
And live like it's heaven on earth."

− William W. Purkey

Chapter Twenty Three

Jessica must have fallen asleep. Her head lay on the priest's shoulder next to her. Embarrassed, she straightened in her seat and then quickly apologized.

The man smiled. "You looked so peaceful I hardly had the courage to wake you," he said.

Dressed in a black suit and clerical collar, the priest held a missal and rosary beads in his lap. He had a kind face and eyes that seemed to draw you into that charitableness.

She heard the captain report that they would be landing at Denver International in twenty minutes.

Jessica couldn't believe she had slept through most of the flight. She remembered having called Macy just before the plane took off. She couldn't wait to get home and call her daughter back. Her husband was finishing his own business trip in Chicago and would be returning home tomorrow. She missed Allen and couldn't wait to share some private time with him. It was going to be a wonderful Christmas, all of them together, including Macy's boyfriend.

Her attention was drawn to the flight attendant guiding a drink cart down the narrow aisle. They were obviously trying to secure everything before the landing.

She looked about the cabin and saw passengers packing away laptops and reading material.

Soon the seatbelt warning light came on. The flight attendant asked them to return their seats to their regular positions. Window shades began to slide open. Jessica opened hers to catch a glimpse of dense swirling clouds.

The plane banked slightly to the right.

A murmuring groan spread among the passengers when the captain announced that it was snowing heavily in Denver. The weather didn't bother Jessica and, in fact, she was looking forward to it and very much hoping for a white Christmas.

The young girl seated several rows behind her cried out, "Yes!" to the captain's weather announcement. When Jessica turned around she saw the girl struggling to get into her pink ski jacket, having a time with it because of her seatbelt. A flight attendant told the girl that she would have plenty of time for that after the plane landed.

It was one of the smoothest airplane rides Jessica could remember. Even the passengers seemed more quiet than usual. No kids screaming, no boisterous behavior by inebriated people, nothing to wake her from her three-hour sleep.

She yawned deeply, heartened by a sense of good fortune in her life. She had a loving husband, a wonderful daughter, a comfortable home and a rewarding career.

She felt she had been especially blessed in her life.

Golden flight 100 landed on time at 10:03 am (MT) at Denver International airport.

As Jessica disembarked the plane she saw the little girl get off the plane in the line before her. She was bouncing about, her small carry-on in hand, seemingly thrilled that she was at last home and would soon be frolicking in the snow.

Jessica's suitcase was one of the first to emerge from the luggage carrousel.

Under a swirling winter sky with snow falling at a rate of two inches per hour, Jessica carefully made her way to the long-term parking area, pulling her suitcase behind her.

She gave one of the young parking attendants twenty dollars to clear off her car, which he did with the alacrity of someone who had performed this service many, many times before.

When he had finished he tapped on her window until she had opened it halfway. He handed back the money, smiling and then tipping his head.

"Just paying it forward, Ma'am," he said and then turned around, looking for the next beneficiary of his service.

"Thank you, and Merry Christmas!" Jessica called out as the snow, soft and lacey and pure, swirled about her like giant white moths having found the eminent light source.

Chapter Twenty Four

She opened the door and stood there for a moment. "Are you okay, Mom?"

Macy came over and lay down on the bed next to her mother. "In my opinion, he was a rotten schmutz."

"Youth over middle age," her mother said with a sigh. "I can't compete with a twenty-eight year-old *girl*."

"He's still a schmutz. He lied to you just like Dad did. It's just not fair. You are entitled to at least one good relationship in your life."

"I read him wrong, honey. I really don't think Michael was ready for a close relationship."

"But he was so genuine-sounding at Christmas and then the two of you going on that skiing trip to Aspen."

"I think that's really when I knew the relationship was going south. Michael was just too distracted by younger women, especially those in tight jeans with bouncy blonde hair."

"He was immature," Macy said. "And very selfish."

"Yes he was, honey. But I'm not a woman with fragile emotions or with contempt in my heart. I survived your father, and I will survive this."

Macy turned and sideways cupped her head in her hand. Wistfully, she said, "I wish you could meet someone like Greg. He's so kind and sensitive and let's me have my space and time. You know, he really likes you, Mom."

"Uh-oh. I don't know exactly how to read that."

"Mom, you know what I mean. Greg has a lot of respect for you. He thinks there is something spiritual about you. You know, he's into all that stuff. He thinks you've lived many lives."

Her mother laughed. "A weary soul, huh?"

"I guess you know that we're pretty serious, Mom."

"It's hard not to come to that conclusion. There's chemistry between you. I sensed that at Christmas."

Her mother swept the hair from Macy's forehead. "You should wear your hair in a broach. You have a beautiful face and you shouldn't be hiding any part of it. You've grown it long enough now."

"Greg likes it this way. I don't know...maybe when I get married and start having kids. After I get my education degree, of course."

"Come closer," her mother said, patting the comforter on the bed. "I want to hug you."

Macy felt her mother's warm and familiar embrace. She nuzzled her face against her neck and breathed in the faint lilac fragrance of the body wash she used. She smelled and felt so familiar, with a sense of sturdy permanence Macy remembered from her childhood days.

"Do you know how much I love you?" her mother said.

Macy could feel the warm exhalations of those words against the back of her neck. She sighed.

"I love you too, Mom."

"I'll always be just a breath away. Always."

Macy gave her a strange look.

Her mother began talking about the divorce hearing coming up in two weeks. Allen's lawyers had finally agreed to the divorce and a sensible settlement between parties. Even her father seemed to welcome the final closure and failed to ignite further conflict in the agreed settlement. He set up a trust for Macy, available to her when she turned twenty-one, and set aside funding for her to finish her studies and continue in graduate school.

Macy felt no more animosity between her parents. They seemed to have shunned their emotional embattlement with one another and were acting as mature adults making sensible decisions for the first time in their lives.

It was as if her father was finally ready to get on with his life.

"I'll always love him," Macy said after listening to her mother. "And in a strange way I'm going to miss him."

"I can understand that," her mother said, squeezing Macy's hand.

"I'm going to make an extra effort to keep in touch with him. At first letters and then hopefully phone calls and visits. Eventually, I want to get to know my father and develop a real relationship."

Months ago, her mother would have made some sarcastic remark or would have derided her father's intentions. But now she only nodded and seemed to be fully supportive of Macy's decision.

She talked about her own newly discovered plans to attend law school at the university, joking that she would probably be the oldest person the world to become an attorney. She wanted to become a defense attorney and hoped to join the Innocence Project to work for the rights of the wrongfully accused.

"It's something I've always wanted to pursue...but never knew it."

"Huh?" Macy said. "That doesn't exactly make sense."

"No, it doesn't," her mother said. "And please don't ask me to explain it."

"Well, it sounds to me like you will be fulfilling your life's dream. I'm so proud of you, Mom."

"But I have to get through law school first," her mother said.

Just then something strange happened. Though they had been sitting beside each other, a few inches or so apart, Macy noticed that she was only faintly aware of her mother's presence. It was as if she had momentarily floated away, leaving behind the vaporous bond of her love for her daughter. Startled by the inexplicable sense, Macy turned toward her mother.

"What's wrong, honey?"

"Oh, nothing," Macy said dismissively.

There was a knock at the door and then Hattie popped her head in.

"Belgian sausage and waffles sound good?" she said in a voice that seemed grounded and curiously validating.

◆

Macy's mother had decided to skip breakfast and have an early brunch later on. She'd said that she had certain things to sort out in her mind and then read some of the pre-law study books she'd ordered online.

Hattie and Macy sat at the breakfast nook, occasionally turning to look outside the narrow bay windows at the kids kicking around soccer balls in the street.

Two weeks ago, some kid had kicked a ball at the living room window, shattering it. Hattie had seen it happen and had run after the scoundrel with a frying pan. She never caught up with him but had returned with a sense that it was her fault. Now she had become more or less a vigilante for the neighborhood, often running to the door and starring down kids whose soccer balls had infringed upon the property.

It was all Macy could do to reassure Hattie that the accident hadn't been her fault and that she shouldn't be so hyped about the kids. They had good property insurance, she had tried to convince the concerned housekeeper.

Hattie then startled Macy with what she had observed during the course of last night. It felt almost as if Hattie had made it up.

"You really scared me," Hattie said. "When I walked by your room late last night, I heard you talking up a storm. I thought you might have been talking with your boyfriend, but then you suddenly emerged from your room and began taking the steps to the first floor, in full conversation with someone."

Baffled because she had no recollection of the experience, Macy leaned back and gave Hattie a doubtful look.

"What was I saying?"

"Oh Lord, all kinds of things. It almost sounded like you were speaking with your mother. You kept saying that you didn't want her to go."

Incredulous, Macy said, "I remember none of it. Why didn't you wake me?"

"In my culture, waking somebody in the middle of sleepwalking is considered dangerous. We believe the soul is trying to make peace with itself, ridding itself of uninvited spirits. The process shouldn't be disrupted."

"Where was I going?"

"Well, you finally shuffled your way to the front door, opened it and seemed to be staring out into the darkness, almost as if you were waiting for someone. Maybe it lasted twenty minutes. Eventually, I followed you as you returned to your room, where I watched you get back into bed. I checked on you several times during the rest of the night. Each time you seemed to be sleeping peacefully and soundly."

"Have you ever seen me to do this before?"

Hattie's face drew into a wistful look of guarded knowledge. "No," she said. "But your mother used to do the same thing when you were in the coma. When I was scheduled to watch you, she would often stand up and walk about the hospital room several times. Sleepwalking too. I never told her about it."

The early morning light spilled into the room through the slatted window, laying a faint striped pattern across the floor. Hattie stood up to adjust the shutters.

"You know, when you were in the hospital for so many months after the accident," she said, "your mother refused to leave your side. A hundred men couldn't have dragged her away."

Macy nodded, wondering why Hattie was digging into a past she didn't really want to recall.

"You were in a deep coma. A lot of medical folk had given up on you. Not your mother, though. During the day she would read to you and engage herself in constant conversation, just as if you were sitting there listening to her. At night sometimes your mother and I would take turns watching you just to make sure you were breathing and to check on all those tubes."

"On some nights," Hattie continued, it was just you and me. The first time it happened I almost rang for the nurse. It's like you were talking, trying desperately to communicate. Your lips were moving as if you were trying to form the words. The doctors explained it as involuntary movement caused by the swelling of the brain. But I knew better. It began to happen more regularly over the course of many weeks."

"What was I saying?"

Hattie shook her head. "I just knew you were preparing to wake up. I would lean over the bed and pinch your arm or a leg. It was to let you know that I was there and could hear you. The nurses who bathed you noticed these little red marks, and I'm sure they thought that we were so desperate we were trying to use pain to get you to wake up. Your mom never asked me. In the weeks leading up to your miracle, I was pinching you almost every night. I knew you had made a decision to wake up, to come back to us."

Macy laughed. "So you abused me?"

"Heavens no, child. I was..."

"Hattie. I'm kidding."

Hattie got up and began to carry the dishes to the kitchen. She stopped abruptly and said, "I think you have a phone call."

Macy listened but couldn't hear anything. "Are you sure?" she said.

Hattie nodded, and then Macy ran up the steps to her bedroom.

It was Greg. "Wake up, sleepy head," he said.

"Good grief. Why so early in the morning?"

"It's 9:30 here. I've been up for hours."

"You've got to respect time zones. So, what are you up to, lover boy?"

"Thinking of you."

"Oh..."

"I had a wonderful dream of us and haven't been able to get you off my mind since then. When are you coming *home*?"

"I emailed you a copy of my itinerary. Do you ever read your mail?"

"Say it again."

"What?"

"*Itinerary*. You sound so sexy when you say it."

"Oh Greg. I'm leaving the day after tomorrow. Eight a.m. on Golden Flight 90. Will you pick me up at the airport?"

"That depends on the compensation, my dear lady."

"I love you, Greg. I'll call you from the Denver airport before I board."

"Love you more, Macy. Much more than you will ever know."

She returned to the kitchen and gave Hattie a long hug. She kissed her on the cheek and then held her hand.

"I'm so glad you brought me back. Don't ever stop pinching me when you think I need it."

Jessica hadn't felt like eating breakfast. She could barely make out her daughter's conversation in the other room. She must have been talking with Greg.

When Macy had mentioned the word *kids* and *education degree* in their conversation earlier, something had ignited in Jessica's mind, a horrible reality.

Kids? What about her writing career?

The knowledge came to her in rippling fragments. When they were pieced together in her mind she realized, as if comparing it to a once-remembered dream, that Macy *hadn't* been accepted into the Iowa workshop. She'd never completed her novel. Her heart wasn't in it anymore. She had switched her major and decided to become an elementary school teacher. She would never become a published author.

There was nothing wrong with aspiring to be an educator. She knew Macy's commitment hadn't been altered. She would make a fine teacher. And Jessica would be proud of her just the same.

But what had transpired to cause such a drastic change?

That knowledge was unavailable to her.

And what about her own decision to study for a law degree? She couldn't remember ever having that desire or even just the inclination.

Something was wrong. Weirdly wrong.

And down deep in her gut, she knew it was *her* fault.

Chapter Twenty Five

Ted Granger grabbed his coat and made for the door. He found his car, a Datsun 240Z, green with tan interior, and jammed the key into the door lock, minutes later weaving in and out of morning traffic as he frantically made his way to the airport.

He had to get there in time.

There were lives to save.

He knew exactly why the plane went down. He remembered now. He had accidentally turned off the auto-feather system right after the flameout on engine number 2. He was certain that it was at least a contributing factor to the stall.

He had to board the plane and keep that knowledge clear in his mind. But he didn't know if it worked that way.

That he was still conscious of what had gone on in the waiting lounge puzzled him. He assumed that a choice to return to his former life would come with total amnesia.

But he knew. At least for now.

He had been late when he'd originally boarded the flight. Maybe not this late. The flight was scheduled to depart shortly after eight a.m.

It was 7:45 and he only had a few miles to go before reaching the airport. He would make it in time just as he had before.

He had been originally late because of his night out on the town. Free margaritas between midnight and three in the morning at the Crazy Horse bar. He had broken FAA regulations and technically was not allowed to fly a commercial plane if less then eight hours had elapsed from his last drink. *Bottle to throttle* they called it. There was still enough margarita juice in his blood to make him fail a sobriety test. As he had before, he was taking a chance.

He knew he had a problem stemming from his days in the Air Force. It didn't seem funny now, but once he flown an F-16 with an open Budweiser between is legs and had thought it hilarious. Some of his buddies did, too.

He still had a slight buzz when they had encountered problems on Golden flight 100. He was convinced that this had caused his confusion when he disarmed the auto-feather feature.

It was different now because he was aware of it.

This time he was clean sober.

He would make up for it now. He would make it a safe flight. The plane would be saved because of what he now knew. None of the passengers would have to die.

As he swung onto North MacDonnell Road leading to the airport, Granger saw the distinct red-and-blue lights of a California Highway Patrol car pulsing in his rearview mirror. He immediately checked his speed. Maybe ten miles over the speed limit.

Shit! Not now.

He slowed down and waited for the patrol car to catch up. He prepared himself for the worst. But the patrol car whizzed by silently and disappeared into the traffic ahead.

Jesus! That was close.

Successfully parked in the long-term parking section, Granger grabbed his bag and ran for the terminal, gate 74. He almost stopped to grab a sandwich at the small tavern.

Not this time.

At the gate he showed his ID and then went through a separate scanner for the flight crew. The TSA officer shook his head.

"When I saw you coming you looked like OJ in the old Hertz ad," he said.

Granger laughed, collected his shoes and items, and made a dash for the pilots' jet bridge.

As he came down the bridge his legs buckled and he fell against the handrail. He felt like he had to vomit.

His hands began to shake. He felt dizzy.

What the hell was wrong?

He took a deep breath and slowly made his way towards the doorway.

Without intending to, he winked at one of the sexy-looking flight attendants as he boarded.

He used his code to gain entry to the cockpit. The pilot and a flight attendant were inside.

"Ted Granger," he said, reaching over to shake Captain Anderson's hand.

Then he grabbed a pen and a small writing pad from his pocket and wrote it down:

DO NOT DISARM AUTO-FEATHER.

He ripped the page from the binder, folding it once and slipping it into his shirt pocket.

As anticipated, the captain made a comment.

As Granger called out the items on the pre-flight checklist, he made mental notes, image associations that would help him remember. In this case he settled for a scene full of feathers, a visual blizzard of feathers. Their flight route was bound to take them through the heavy snow storm over the mountains.

He would make the connection. He would remember exactly what he had to do when engine number two flamed out. He would prevent the stall.

Puzzled by the sudden but ponderous familiarity of his surroundings, he felt a little like an actor who was just asked by the director to repeat a scene. He felt awkward and then apprehensive that he would miss his cue.

The old familiarity broke into a strange layering of scenes.

Fuck! Which one?

He had just exited the restroom and was returning to his seat in the cockpit.

A cold blankness befell him.

It wasn't that he had forgotten something important. He just wasn't aware of it anymore.

Chapter Twenty Six

It was evident now to investigators that Golden Airways Flight 100 had encountered serious turbulence as it came in range well to the south of the Salt Lake City tower.

The data flight recorder, although badly damaged, had revealed no data evidence of a fire aboard the plane but had confirmed a flameout on engine number two. It also detected a pulse in electrical current, probably at the time of the lightning strikes. The consensus of the investigating teams was that the auto-feather feature must not have worked or had been turned off accidently by one of the pilots. The malfunction had caused the plane to suddenly spiral into a steep dive.

Great efforts were made by the crew to regain control of the plane. The rapid descent caused decompression in the cabin, probably rendering all aboard unconscious. It can be assumed that they remained unconscious until the moment of impact.

The only explanation for the lack of human remains was that the plane and its passengers were incinerated in an instant conflagration unlike any witnessed in a mountain impact.

Investigators went back and re-interviewed Billy's son. The boy agreed with them that the heat from the inferno was great but wasn't certain he'd seen a huge fireball.

Early reports of finding DNA imbedded in the granite rock turned out to be that of an animal, probably a coyote howling in the snow at the wrong time and place.

Airline representatives were almost certain the crash occurred due to pilot error. They continued to offer loved ones modest settlements. Counselors and legal department liaisons worked with the survivors in a manner obvious to many that seemed rushed and very well rehearsed. Some survivors were desperate emotionally and financially, wanting to resume their normal lives and needing the immediate cash for funerals expenses. Only half a dozen refused the out-of-court offers and instead hired personal tort attorneys. Those, the airline attorneys knew, would play out in settlement courts, eventually accepting what their lawyers would convince them were reasonable compensations. The airlines would never allow a case to go to a jury due to the damage that negative publicity would bring.

Boeing held no liability because there were no obvious mechanical problems with the plane. Golden Airways had already established through the Civil Aeronautics Board a maximum liability limit of $65,000 per claimant. Even in the worst case scenario, the airlines wouldn't go bankrupt.

A bronze memorial plaque paid for by the airlines was placed at the crash site. It was a copy of the larger main memorial at the airport in Denver.

As in most airplane disasters, the TV media used coverage of Golden 100 as fodder for audience attendance. Cable news ratings rose proportionally to live coverage, and it seemed to many veteran viewers they were bleeding the topic for every drop of advertising it would garnish. Entertainment news was something most people wanted these days.

In not but a few cases, according to news interviews, survivors used the settlement cash to donate to their loved ones' favorite charity or cause. They referred to the cash settlements as *blood money*.

One young woman who had lost her mother in the crash and who was the most vocal at survivor and news conferences refused the cash entirely, walking out of the settlement meetings with her partner and never returning. The airline made numerous efforts to contact her but was unsuccessful.

Unlike many aviation disasters where planes and victims were never located, most of them occurring in deep waters, the wreckage of flight Golden 100 had been identified in a relatively short period of time. While the grieving of survivors would linger for a lifetime, the newsworthy value of the accident diminished rapidly. Within five months reference to the disaster had dropped from the news media altogether.

◆

Laura Anderson, the pilot's wife, eventually moved their daughters to Kansas, moving into the old house and fifty acres north of Medicine Lodge. She had been living near San Francisco at the time of the accident and, unbeknown to her husband, had nourished an angst about Scott flying. He was a great pilot, but as he logged each hour of flight time she wondered if their kiss would be the last. The spouses of most pilots held similar anxieties, but to Laura, who was prone to bad dreams, the fear had almost turned into phobia.

Guilt riddled her for months. If she had only shared her concern with her husband, if only she had mentioned the recurring dream of a young girl aboard a doomed flight...

If only she had told Scott that she wanted him to retire early.

The girls took it hard. Clara, the youngest, ensconced herself in her bedroom for days. Eva, who was a senior in high school, stayed among her close friends and seemed cemented in denial.

One day when Laura was tending to the bougainvillea in her garden, Clara knelt down beside her and began gathering the clippings, an urgent need to talk etched on her face.

"Is Daddy in Heaven?" she asked.

"Of course. He's with God and looking down at us right now."

"Do you think he's happy?"

"If you're with God in Heaven, you have to be happy," Laura said carefully.

"Then he doesn't miss us?"

Laura took a deep breath. "Of course he misses us just as we miss him. But he's happy where he is, where all of us will join up one day and be a family again."

Tears flooded Clara's face. She rubbed at her nose. A brief, stoic look interrupted the tears. "I just miss him so much, Mom."

"I know, sweetheart, I know. I miss him so much too," Laura said, wrapping her arm around her daughter's back, feeling her frustration and pain.

Scott and Laura had purchased the property in Kansas five years ago. Scott loved to refurbish old houses when he had the time and planned to expand the large farmhouse when he retired. They'd visited several times, giving Scott the time to design floor plans and the large sunroom in the back. It was a granite structure and walls so thick it was hard to hear anything outside. The house had a stone basement, an area of it built as a safe house, a place to ride out heavy snowstorms and tornadoes. The house had been erected sometime at the turn of the century.

When they arrived in late April, snow still mantled the untended cornfields behind the house. Most of it had melted and run off the roof and window ledges. The old wooden swing on the stone porch was still in good shape, although the hanging chains were rusted and made Laura feel the swing was unsafe.

The girls went straight for it, using their legs to propel it almost to the railing of the porch. Laura looked on in dismay but was reminded how Scott used to do the same thing on their short visits. If Scott was with God, surely he was protecting his daughters from his lofty venue.

Although unable to attend the official graduation at high school, Eva had completed the required courses and was given her diploma in a small ceremony with her friends at school. She planned to go to college and had already been accepted by several universities and colleges, including the University of Kansas in Lawrence. She planned to accept admission to the latter school in order to be closer to her mother and sister.

Clara had another year before high school, and Laura had already had her records transferred to the middle school in Medicine Lodge.

It was obvious that there were anger issues with her youngest daughter. While she accepted that her father was in Heaven, Clara seemed to have unsettled issues with God. She had started counseling in California. Immediately upon arrival, Laura found a minister at the local Baptist church who had credentials and experience in counseling psychology. After a couple of sessions, Clara seemed comfortable with her counseling, although she communicated little about her sessions.

Kansas was a far cry from California, the former feeling very conservative and heavily influenced by Baptist beliefs. Although Laura at first felt stifled by the attitudes and the religious constraints of the community, she felt the place to be safe and family oriented.

One day in early May Laura received a letter from a woman who claimed she was a surviving loved one from flight 100. It said in handwritten script that the woman was contacting each family survivor personally to send her love and to offer whatever assistance she could provide. It left a telephone number at the bottom of the page.

At first Laura thought it was a cruel joke or perhaps someone with fraudulent intentions. She had spent the last months trying to clear her mind of the details of the accident and held no desire to revisit those feelings, even if the person was legitimate and was really trying to reach out to the many loves ones who had lost family members in the crash.

The letter sat in its envelope on the old roll top desk in the living room for a week. Its contents began to dwell on Laura's mind, soon kindling a curiosity that felt like a magnet. Every time she passed the desk, she paused and gazed at the letter.

Eventually, on a rainy Sunday afternoon Laura reopened the envelope and reread the letter. She called the number and let it ring three times, relieved in a way that no one had answered, but then heard the click and the voice.

"Who is this?" Laura said.

"Is this about my letter?" the woman said.

"Yes."

"Mrs. Anderson, I'm so glad you called."

"How did you know my name?" Laura said.

"Your husband was the pilot. I know your voice from one of the conferences held by the airlines. We actually spoke for a few minutes."

"I don't remember. In fact, I've forced myself to forget most of what went on back then. How did you find me?"

"Your forwarding address. I'm sorry if you feel I'm intruding because that is not my intention. My name is Macy Gibson and I lost my mother aboard flight 100."

"I'm sorry, Macy. Please call me Laura." She paused and then said, "How are you doing?"

"I've accepted and am trying to move on. You were the last on the list and I'm so glad you responded."

"List?"

"Passenger and crew member list. I've made contact with all the other survivors whose loved ones were aboard the flight, Laura. That is what I had to do. Instead of taking the settlement I decided that I would pay forward, that I would reach out to surviving members of each family. I've spent the better part of five months doing so."

"That's quite noble of you," Laura said and quickly realized that her comment might have sounded sarcastic. "I mean, of course, that is a wonderful token of compassion and love for people you don't know."

"Certainly you know that your husband wasn't to blame."

"No, he wasn't. My husband had 18,000 hours of flight time, nearly all of them as a captain. Flying was in his blood. He absolutely loved what he did for a living. Maybe I had my reservations, but Scott had a passion for flying jets, especially the 737."

"Please tell me more about him," Macy said.

Laura could hardly stop talking. She mentioned how they'd met on a beach in California, the courtship and finally their engagement in Hawaii when he was a first officer on TWA just before its demise. They married on Laguna Beach at sunset. They waited to have children so that she could fly with him and spend stopovers in cities all over the country. And then came the children.

"What are their names?" Macy said.

"Eva and Clara. God, they adored their father."

"Are they doing okay now?"

"It's going to take some time for the younger one. She's only twelve and struggling with pre-teen emotions. But she seems to be benefitting from counseling."

There was a pause in the conversation. Macy broke the silence by saying, "Do you mind my asking what were the last words you remember your husband telling you?"

The question was asked so ingenuously Laura had no reservations answering it. She thought for a moment and said, "It was during the early part of the flight, maybe half an hour after they departed San Francisco. Scott told me he loved me very much and to share that love with the girls. He said he'd call me after settling in to the motel in Denver. The very last word, our favorite expression we learned in Hawaii, was *ke'aloha*, which means *love is all around*."

"That's beautiful," Macy said.

Laura asked about Macy's mother. The young woman shared fond memories of their lives and how her mother hadn't had it easy in a bad marriage. She told Laura about the skiing accident and the long coma in the hospital and how her mother had fought her father and the courts to keep her alive.

Soon they began to share spiritual feelings and other personal thoughts Laura had only done so with her closest friend in San Francisco. She learned that Macy had a boyfriend and that she was about to attend the Iowa writing program.

The conversation went on until there was nothing more to be said. Laura looked at her watch and was astonished to see that an hour and a half had gone by. They both laughed about the time, and then Laura said, "Macy, thank you so much for contacting me. Somehow our talk has released so much for me. I feel like a great weight has been lifted, and I feel stronger now."

"Me too."

"I want us to keep in touch."

"We will. I promise," Macy said.

◆

One afternoon Laura and the girls were returning from Medicine Lodge after a day of shopping.

Clara was in the back seat of the old Bronco, her head twisted sideways as she looked up at the swirling sulfur-gray overcast.

"It doesn't look good, Mom," she said.

"Don't worry, honey. We'll make it."

Clara asked if she could sit next to her sister in the front. She was frightened being alone in the back.

All buckled in, they drove south along the gravel back road. Laura knew she was driving too fast. Rocks hit the underside of the SUV, clattering like a barrage of bullets. Larger ones spun into the wheel wells, ricocheting wildly like balls helter-skelter in a pinball machine.

"Slow down, Mom," Eva warned.

But Laura didn't because of what she was observing in the rearview mirror. A vortex bulged from the freakish dark anvil cloud and hovered over the vast plains behind them. A twister was forming.

They had experienced just one tornado before, during the first week after they'd moved. It was barely an F1 but managed to rip trees from the ground and tear down one door to the old barn. Surviving her first tornado, Laura formed a deep respect for the unpredictable and violent forces of nature.

Now she had no choice but to try and outrun the snaking cloud formation behind her.

Clara was crying, huddled against her big sister. Eva managed to turn around for a quick glimpse of the monster-size cloud.

Her attention fixed on the rearview mirror, Laura swerved on the road. It felt like the vehicle was balancing precariously on two wheels. It slammed down on all fours, jerking to the left and causing Clara to hit her head against the passenger window.

"Mom!" she cried. The voice didn't sound her own but rather like a creature in the face of sudden and primitive fright.

They were still a quarter of a mile from the farmhouse.

"We'll make it...we'll make it!" Laura tried to reassure the girls. And herself.

Right then, as Laura was rehearsing in her mind how they would scramble from the truck and run down into the cellar safe room, the Bronco hit a tree stump head-on, hurling them forward against the dashboard.

"Please God..." Laura cried out.

A quick glance in large fender mirror made her shudder with terror. The coppery taste of fear in her mouth made her gasp.

The sinister outcrop of the black cloud suddenly fell, snaking its way to the ground in a giant rotating puff. Instantly the base of the twister turned dark with the swirling and pounding intake of debris.

They weren't going to make it. Laura couldn't free her hands because of the steel grip she had on the steering wheel. The girls were screaming, Clara pulling frantically on her mother's arm to exit the truck.

Rain exploded, pelting the roof. And then a machinegun fire of ice pellets. Sudden gusts of wind shook the trees out the window.

What finally made Laura scramble out of the passenger door, towed by Clara's strong grip, was the strange, calming voice of her husband. It was almost as if all of his guidance and strength were inside Clara's body. Laura could feel his peace and confidence.

"Come on, Mom!" Clara cried out as they all started running down the road toward the house. It wasn't even in sight.

With ice pellets stinging her face and head, Laura held the girls close and ran down the roadway, occasionally slipping.

Eva lost her footing and landed in a swirling puddle on side of the road.

"My foot!" she cried out in pain.

Laura stopped and looked behind to see the swirling froth of the twister catching up to them. It was huge, its base now covering probably half a mile.

They wouldn't make it in time. In seconds they would be sucked up into the massive tongue of debris. Laura prayed to have God spare her children pain when it happened.

And then Scott's voice urging her to move on, to have faith in her strength.

With an iron grip on Clara's hand she followed Eva, now sprinting down the road despite her foot injury.

The twister had an evil sound to it, a locomotive run wild, and could be felt in the ground as it gouged out a direct path toward them. Debris, the smaller branches, corn stalks and rocks, began to whip against the backs of their legs and arms.

When she turned around for the last time, Laura saw only a huge black wall exploding the ground a few yards behind them. She didn't think she could run any longer and felt Clara slipping from her grip.

It was as if the edge of the twister scooped them up and dropped them in front of the door. Eva unlocked and opened it and screamed at her mom to run for the shelter.

When she looked back as she hit the stairs, Laura saw Eva bravely trying to close the door, her back pushing against the infallible power of the twister. She finally let go and was tossed down the stairs, as they all scrambled for the safe room.

They all sat huddled in the corner of the room.

The F3 tornado battered the old stone cottage. The wind roared. A window upstairs blew out. The sturdy walls shook.

And then, thirty seconds later, it stopped, an aftermath filled with a soundless and stunning stillness.

Chapter Twenty Seven

K athryn Lewis was sitting on the front porch of her cabin with her German shepherd Timber. It was a cool spring day with timid sunlight streaking through a tapestry of clouds. The overnight rain made the thick pines sparkle and the pinewood floor appear a darker shade than the inside of the cabin. The scent of pine hung in the air.

She had not attended any of the airline's meetings and conferences. Although Ethan's lover, she felt those assemblies were reserved for family members alone.

She had cried her heart out on many occasions as she followed the terrible news of the crash and the ensuing months of the investigation.

Kathryn had fallen in love with Ethan at a secular retreat in the mountains. They had dated several times since that meeting and she had allowed Ethan to spend the night at her cabin, where they had consummated their affair. It was the following morning when he confessed that he was an expatriating Catholic priest.

It was a whirlwind romance that seemed to be heading towards a nuptial conclusion. They had talked about getting married within the year but had kept the news quiet.

Kathryn was ten years Ethan's junior. She had spent most of her adult life working with relief agencies, including the Red Cross, UNICEF and eventually the Peace Corps. She was as much of an altruist as Ethan was and had never given herself time and permission to tend to her own needs through meaningful relationships. They just happened to meet at the right time, each having completed a lifetime of providing assistance to others, now ready to make a course change in their lives.

Even though she had been raised as a Catholic, Kathryn had over the years distanced herself from the church. The irony that she had fallen in love with an ex-priest felt at first strange but then seemed curiously destined. Ethan had come into her life for a reason.

On this May morning she was thinking of Ethan, but not in a sad way. She had received the news a month after the crash but had managed to keep it a secret from her close friends and the only neighbor a mile down the mountain.

In less than three months she was going to have Ethan's baby. If there was sadness it was only because Ethan never knew of the pregnancy and that soon he would be a *real* father. They had never talked that far into the future and, although Kathryn didn't know whether he'd ever entertained the thought about children of their own, she just knew he would be full of excitement and joy about the occasion.

She had already decided that she would have a home birth. When the time was right she would contact a midwife and eventually share her news with her best friend Nora, whom she had know for years from the early days in the Peace Corps.

Kathryn knew intuitively that she would deliver a boy and that she would name the child after his father.

It became such a certainty in her mind she had already ordered a blue bassinette, male infant clothing, blankets and other infant sundries.

He would be named Ethan Lydia Lewis, his middle name after Ethan's mother. He would be a handsome infant who would develop the same sturdy features of his father, as well as his kindness and his benevolent ways.

◆

The night was dark and very windy. Winds of this kind swept up from the valley in gusty escapes from the warmer temperatures below. They rose and swirled like miniature tornadoes, causing the taller pines to dance in eerie pirouettes. Sometimes they would continue most of the night and cause Kathryn sleepless hours, especially when the timber walls creaked.

She heard the banging at the door but chose to ignore it. Maybe it was a neighbor caught in the ditch needing to use the phone. A drifter perhaps. Or maybe just a heavy branch thumping against the door.

Timber, the old shepherd, lay on the floor beside the bed, now hardly moving as the sound grew louder and more persistent. She had given the dog an aspirin to ease the pain of his advancing arthritis.

Kathryn thought she heard a voice smothered by the wind.

The baby kicked as she swung her legs over the edge of the bed. At the window, she parted the curtains to see if she could make out someone outside. The door was hidden by the low-hanging eave.

Downstairs she went to the small foyer, flipped the porch light on and then peered through the small bathroom window off the entranceway. A man with a red baseball cap and a denim jacket was huddled at the door. He had stopped banging when the lights were turned on.

Timber had taken his time managing the stairs and now in the foyer just lay his head on the floor.

"Who is it?" Kathryn said loudly.

She could just make out the muffled voice on the other side. Something about his car and a dead battery. Could he use the phone to call for assistance?

Commonsense told her that something wasn't right. Wasn't that exactly what evil characters in a movie said when trying to gain entry to a house? Why would someone drive halfway up a private mountain road where there were only two cabins? Caution and instinct made her hesitate.

The man outside insisted that he only needed to use her phone.

"Just hand me your cellphone," he said during an abrupt lull in the wind. "It'll only take a minute. Please, Ma'am."

"I'll make the call for you," Kathryn said.

The visitor said nothing but just stood at the door.

"I'll be glad to call for a tow truck. Do you want me to look one up?"

Finally the man said, "Ma'am, I'm afraid I don't have the money to pay for the service. I just wanted to call my brother."

It seemed cruel to be denying assistance to someone who seemed down on their luck. She had devoted her entire adult life to helping others. That vein of commitment didn't exclude people in need of help. She could never live with herself if she didn't open the door.

She could hear the man shuffle his feet. "Ma'am, it's alright. I'll go back to my truck and wait it out until morning," he said, his voice trailing off as she saw the figure walking away.

When she pulled the door open, the man was already descending the porch steps.

"I'm sorry, Kathryn said, "please come in."

"Thank you, Ma'am," he said, turning around and then entering the cabin.

"May I use your bathroom?"

"You said you need to use the phone."

"Yes Ma'am. Let me do that first."

She showed him the old-fashioned phone on the wall and then watched as he dialed a number. He turned toward her, his palm on the lower part of the phone as he finished dialing and said, "My brother, Jake. He's not far from here."

The conversation sounded legitimate. The man even stopped and asked Kathryn for the name or number of the road. When he finished the call he told her that he would wait for his brother on the porch if that was okay with her.

"Listen, I'm sorry," Kathryn said. "It's just that it's late at night and I usually don't get visitors way up here. Would you like some tea? While I fix it you're welcome to use the half-bath off the foyer."

"Ma'am, I appreciate that. Name's Maynard...Maynard Phelps."

"Yes. My name is Kathryn."

She fixed two mugs of green tea and put one in the microwave. Half a minute later it dinged, and then she replaced it with the cold mug. She heard the bathroom flush and the sound of washing at the sink.

She didn't know how long he was standing at the kitchen doorway, but it startled her when she turned.

"I can see that you're with child. You must feel overjoyed."

Surprised that her baby bump showed through her house coat, she ran her hand over her stomach, carving the shape. She laughed.

"You have a sneaky eye, don't you?" she said to the stranger.

He smiled as he was led into the living room.

"I don't want to wake your husband."

"Oh no...," she began, stopping what she had intended to say. "Well, actually he's quite a hard sleeper. He's a logger down in the valley and works himself to exhaustion. I don't think if the cabin fell apart he would even notice."

The man smiled.

Timber lay at Kathryn's feet. He uttered a faint growl.

Panic crept up Kathryn's spine. She shivered. Something wasn't right.

She handed the man his tea, which he placed on the lamp table next to the armrest. She took a seat opposite him in a tattered velour arm chair.

"Have you a name for the child?"

"Yes, I do. Ethan, my husband's name."

"A junior in the family," the man said with faint smile.

"Do you have children?" Kathryn asked, realizing as she said it that she hoped he would say yes and introduce the name of his wife. She noticed that he didn't appear to have a wedding band on.

"No Ma'am. Me and my brother are bachelors."

"Oh," Kathryn said in a surprised sort of way. She added, "You just look like the married type, Mr. Phelps."

"How's that, Ma'am?"

"You have a kind face." Her statement was hardly true, as the man's hirsute face was unkempt and he possessed the dark probing eyes of a permanent stranger.

He smiled again.

The dog growled again.

"Your brother...did he say how long it would take for him to drive here?"

"He knows these parts like the back of his hand," the man said.

Silence passed between them. Kathryn took another sip of her tea and tried to relax in her chair, hoping he would not notice that her hands were trembling.

She felt now that she was being cornered, by time and by the uncommon presence of the stranger. Her mind was racing.

Timber raised himself with great effort and sat at Kathryn's feet.

"Ever thought about putting the mutt down? I'd say he's worn out his life."

"Timber's been with me for a lifetime. He'll tell me when it's time," Kathryn said, reaching down to scratch the dog's ears.

The man smiled again. "Yes, Ma'am," he said.

Kathryn felt the baby kick.

"Oh, it's nearly four o'clock," she said, rising from her chair. "It's time to wake my husband and get him off to work."

"Please sit down," the man said in a level voice. He crossed his legs, holding one ankle firmly on his knee.

Kathryn's mind darted again. She could feel her heart straining wildly in her chest. She felt stupid and duped and suddenly afraid for her unborn child.

Timber growled, this time showing his teeth.

"But you haven't touched your tea," she said.

"No Ma'am, I haven't." He smiled and stood up. "That's not exactly why I'm here."

Chapter Twenty Eight

Billy had just finished washing the dinner plates when his son approached him from behind. He sensed his presence and turned around.

"What is it, Son?" he asked.

Expecting the sign language they had always used to communicate since the crash, Billy was astonished when his son spoke out loud.

"I don't remember, Father," he said in soft but clear voice.

Billy took his son and both sat down in the main room in the cabin.

"Who has given you your voice back to you?"

The boy had the glossy black hair and high cheeks of the Cherokee line but his hands were small, with almost a feminine quality to them. That he was of mixed blood made him special in his father's eyes. Billy had found him abandoned on the side of a fire road when the boy was around five and had raised him as his own.

"A spirit," he answered his father.

Billy looked doubtful but nonetheless interested in his son's account. "Speak the name of this spirit."

"I'm sorry, Father, but I have no name for her."

"It is a *she* spirit?"

"I think she visited me on Uncompahgre Peak when I was able to remember." The boy dropped his head.

"When you were able to remember? What does that mean? You *did* see the crash?" Billy said.

"I don't remember."

"How could you forget, Son?"

"The great *She Spirit* made me forget. Maybe I only imagined it."

"What do you mean when you said the spirit *made you forget*? That doesn't make sense to me. So, you imagined the terrible crash...is that what you are trying to say?"

The boy said nothing.

Billy became impatient and irritated. "So I must tell everybody that what you saw was a dream, that you didn't witness the crash?

Son, this is talk of an evil spirit. What is real is real. You cannot undo what has come to pass. Only God can achieve this."

The boy looked up but didn't say anything. Billy stood up and towered over the seated boy.

"Son, is there something wrong with your mind? Are you making things up again?"

"I tell only the truth, Father. I cannot explain it. I just don't remember now. The *She Spirit* said that I am no longer a witness, that I must travel a new path now."

Fretted by what he had heard, Billy said, "We must seek a tribal counsel and ask for their advice. This nonsense must derive from an evil source, and we may need the advice and support from higher believers."

The boy looked up into the eyes of his father. "According to the *She Spirit*, I am a higher believer."

◆

The next day the council of the elders met and discussed the case with Billy. They were an anachronistic part of the modern-day reservation. They held no formal governing role and were there for the older tribesmen who still held to ancient tradition. Billy was one of them.

The boy waited outside of the small tavern, fearing that he would be punished for his words.

The highest elder, a man in his nineties, wore two thick braids of white hair and the weathered face of long wisdom. He was dressed in buffalo-skin jacket and pants, two long eagle feathers held firmly inside his beaded headband. Sitting cross-legged on a blanket on the floor, his arms poised at the end of his knees, he stared slightly upward as if listening to the Great Spirit.

Billy had recounted each detail of his son's confession. He did this with great uncertainty and was aware that he risked having his son banished from the tribe, if not the reservation.

The looks on the faces of the junior tribesmen did not portend a favorable outcome. They looked wary, many appearing as if they had already made up their minds.

"Billy Whitefeather," he spoke. "Do you believe your son is telling the truth?"

"Yes, his words are his own truth and I believe they come from his heart. How could I *not* believe my son?"

"Please allow the boy in," the great elder said with a sweep of his hand."

Billy went outside and whispered to the boy, "Tell what you know to be the truth."

The boy nodded and was then led inside the council quarters. He was told to sit down and he did so, assuming the same posture as that of the great elder. He looked about at the semicircle of elders, fearful of making eye contact with any of them. Then his eyes were drawn into those of the great elder.

"Are you the son of Billy Whitefeather?"

The boy nodded.

"Have you told your father a lie?"

"No, I have only told him the truth."

"But you told others who came to the mountain to ask questions that what you saw was the truth. How can that be, son?"

"I told them then what I thought to be the truth, what my eyes told my heart to believe. The *She Spirit* told me I must forget, that my memory would leave me. I must start another journey. I am part of the *Great Truth*."

The younger tribesmen were talking in hushed voices, some stifling laughter, others pointing to the boy and shaking their heads.

The great elder shifted in his seat and then clasped his hands together in his lap. Billy was looking at his son hoping the meeting would soon be over.

"And what *is* that *Great Truth*, son?"

"That most human truths are false, that we make them up for our own life journeys. The *Great Truth* says there is no death, no man-made spirits, no evil but which lives in the human heart. The Truth is transparent, so we cannot see it. You see, all life is just one life...here on earth and across the great white universe. We are all one, even though our thoughts don't allow us to comprehend that."

The other elders in the room were now mocking the boy.

"What he says is self-serving and evil; his tongue lies," one said.

"If what he says is truth then all tribes are one. And that cannot be," said another, rising from his seat.

The great elder motioned for the boy to come to his side. He grabbed the youngster's hand and then closed his eyes. He whispered an incantation and appeared to be waiting for the answer.

"This boy," he finally said, "is of another world. We should not mock what we cannot understand. I feel his truth but I am not one to understand it fully. Some of it comes from our great fathers, before the white man came, in the land of free spirits. It is not our role to test his truth. Is there anyone here who thinks he knows better than the boy?"

The silence in the room was full of anticipation.

"Do you have anything else to say to us?" the great elder said.

Billy Whitefeather's son, the unnamed member of the tribe, looked into the elder's eyes.

"I have told you all of the truth I know," he said.

◆

Several weeks later the boy grew gravely ill. He was not eating or sleeping. He lost weight and the boyish features of his face grew harder, as if he had suddenly aged.

The medicine man and several other healers came to assess the boy's condition. They talked about cancer and deadly infections, one older healer saying it was only in his head. They forced him to drink bitter healing potions and placed heated rocks around his body in hopes that the evil illness would be purged with the boy's sweat.

By the next day the young boy's condition had worsened. They could not get him to drink water. His lips were parched and cracked and his forehead was hot to the touch.

"I will take you to the white man's hospital so that they can give you medicine," Billy told his son.

The boy could not speak but stiffly shook his head. His body stiffened and his torso lifted from the bed with defiance. Tears filled his eyes.

"I will not lose you," Billy said.

As he watched his son's suffering body, a great silence came between them. The knowledge that transferred from son to father almost knocked the wind out of Billy. He stumbled backward as the clarity brightened, and then rushed to hold his son in his arms.

He knew.

Then his son drew his last breath.

A cold wind swept up from the *Great Basin*, animating the overhanging pines, whistling through the tender young spruce branches of early spring.

Many from the Ute village made the climb to the rocky ledge next to where Billy said his son wanted to be buried. The boy's body was lowered into the shallow grave within a grotto of pines, just a hundred yards from Uncompahgre Peak. Heavy rocks were rolled over the grave and piled there to protect the body and to make sure his spirit would not return.

At a time when he should have been wracked by grief and supported by others, Billy Whitefeather was off to the side, looking up through a narrow aperture in the trees at a glistening morning sun, prideful tears in his eyes.

Chapter Twenty Nine

She had been beaten and raped and left for dead. When she came to she was naked on the floor, badly bruised, her face a mass of blood and contusions. Her eyes had swollen so she could hardly open them.

The taste of blood made her nauseous as she drew up onto her elbows and tried to view her blurry surroundings.

She grabbed for her stomach and began weeping.

"Ethan!" she cried out, gently massaging her stomach, hoping to feel movement that would be a sign that her son was still alive. She felt nothing.

Kathryn only vaguely remembered the man who had done this to her, a recalcitrant memory that refused to surface to tell her it was all real and that there were horrible details to face.

She felt the tacky sensation of blood on her legs, and suddenly a great strength came to her. She grabbed for her housecoat and a pair of slippers and took to the stairs, slowly, carefully, inching her way down, full weight on the bannister.

She felt in her jacket for the keys to the old Toyota Cruiser. Not finding them, she opened the door and saw that her truck was missing.

She looked into the mirror in the bathroom and was horrified at what she saw. She cupped a handful of tap water to her lips and watched the pink saliva drool into the sink.

Putting on the jacket over her housecoat and slipping into a pair of boots, Kathryn then hobbled outside, feeling her way clumsily down the dirt road.

She saw her beloved Timber on his side at the edge of the road, motionless, a trail of blood coming from his mouth. Her instinct at that moment was to go to his side, but realized that she would have to save her energy to make it down the road.

She fell fifty yards ahead, picked herself up and fell again. At the curve in the road where there was a steep decline, she scuttled down on her backside until the road leveled out. Her legs were wobbly but

she forced herself into a hobbling gait, falling again and then groping until she found her legs.

She knew it was a long way but had to make it to her only neighbor at the bottom of road. She couldn't remember his name or what he looked like or where exactly the cabin was located. It was all an oblivious fog.

The next time she fell she could barely raise herself enough to lock her elbows. Drifts of unreal snow crowded her peripheral vision and motes of blurriness swarmed in her eyes. She dropped to the road and soon felt all senses slip away into an abyss of nothingness.

◆

He discovered her by accident while driving up to check the north markers of his acreage.

She was nonresponsive and looked to be dead. He gingerly felt for a pulse and found none. He recognized it be a crime scene and by habit backed away from the body and let his trained eye survey the area. The crime had not been committed there. Her body had been dragged down the road and dumped like a piece of garbage.

He shook his head and pulled out his cellphone. He punched the number for the Gilpin County's sheriff's office. Deputies and the coroner needed to be summoned as quickly as possible.

"It's Dan," he said and was instantly recognized as the retired sheriff of that county.

"How long to send a team to my place? There's a potential homicide to investigate."

Dan listened to the reply and then suddenly dropped the phone in his pocket. He couldn't believe his eyes.

The woman, whom he now recognized as his northern neighbor, was moving her head. He dropped to his knees and told her that he was getting help. He draped his jacket over her and held her hand.

Kathryn mouthed the words at first and then repeated them as the man put his ear near her lips. "I'm...I'm...having my baby. Please help me."

"Please, Ma'am, I need to check," Dan said, gently lifting her housecoat. He saw what he thought was a tiny head but couldn't be sure due to all the blood.

He assured her that everything was going to be okay, even though he knew for certain that neither the woman nor her baby would probably make it. She had lost a lot of blood.

He scooped her up as gently as he could and sat her sideways in his truck, carefully tightening the seatbelt around her chest.

The truck began rolling before he'd released the brakes. Dan knew he had fifteen minutes or less to get her to the hospital. The baby probably wouldn't survive the trip but now he felt there was hope for the woman.

At times he reached 60 mph on a mountain road that posted a maximum speed of thirty. He called the hospital using the police radio. Once on the hard surface of the highway he flipped on the blue light on his dashboard and let the siren wail. He was doing 90 mph when he reached the turnoff for the hospital.

◆

It may have been days or weeks when Kathryn finally opened her eyes and began to absorb her surroundings. Past recognition was there, somewhere couching amorphously in an untouchable hideout in her mind. She knew something had happened but that memory refused to present itself.

What she saw of the hospital room without moving her head was a static scenery of beige walls, a picture of foxhounds against a fawn landscape, two metal chairs at the foot of the bed, part of a corridor and, to her right, drapes drawn against the skeleton of the window.

She hurt but it was a muffled pain, clearly muted by strong pain medication. She saw the intravenous tube in her arm and another catheter taped to her right wrist.

A nurse came into view from the corridor and checked the IV lines, hovering for several seconds over Kathryn's waist. Her uniform smelled of faint antiseptic and starch.

"How are you feeling now?"

Surprised that she had even been noticed, Kathryn asked for a cup of water. She took two sips and said, "How long have I been here?"

"It's been four days. You've been under sedation, Kathryn. Do you remember anything?"

"No," she said, taking another sip of cool water. "Why am I in a hospital?"

"You were hurt, sweetheart. An assault. There are detectives from the Sheriff's Department who need to ask you some questions."

"But I don't remember..."

And then the damn broke and a barrage of awful, unspeakable memories swirled in her mind. She reached for the nurse's arm and grabbed forcefully. "My baby! For God sakes...my baby."

The nurse sat down on the edge of the bed. Kathryn released her iron grip and reached for her hand.

"You have no recollection of the assault?"

"No, goddamnit! I don't care what happened to me. Where is my baby? Where is Ethan?" Tears were searing her eyes.

By the time the neonatologist arrived probably less then a minute had passed, but to Kathryn it was an agonizing eternity. The room nurse stood up and the other woman approached.

"Kathryn," she said. "We are taking it hour by hour but as of now your baby boy is stable. He is inside an incubator and will probably remain there for another month or two, depending on how he progresses."

"Oh my God! Thank you," Kathryn gasped. Tears were flowing, her nose running. She grabbed several tissues from the box on the table and buried her face in the pile.

The nurse introduced herself as Robin, the senior neonatologist nurse on the unit. "Your doctors performed an emergency caesarean and then the baby was whisked into our unit. There was no heartbeat at first and then with a defibrillator and some medicine they were able to revive him. We don't know fully how his organs were affected or if there has been any brain damage. Only time will tell, Kathryn."

"Yes, I understand. When will I be able to see my son?"

"As soon as you are up and about," Robin said.

The other nurse came over and as she sat down on the edge of the bed, a searing pain ripped through Kathryn's stomach. "Because of the damage you are scheduled for at least a partial hysterectomy. I'm sorry. The assault was violent and caused damage to your uterus."

That memory abruptly flashed into focus. It angered her but more so caused conviction and strength to steel her body. Kathryn said she would not agree to the operation unless someone allowed her to visit her son first. She swung her legs over the bed and tried to stand, falling back, only to redouble her efforts and make it successfully to her feet.

The nurse tried to force her to sit but Kathryn threatened to rip out her IV. She was holding the tubing so tightly any effort to make her release her grip seemed fruitless.

Finally Robin said, "Okay, Kathryn. We'll get you into a wheelchair and I'll take you upstairs."

"When?!"

"Just give me fifteen minutes. We won't tell your doctors."

Kathryn finally let go and sat down on the bed. The pain returned and she doubled over. She didn't care if the pain worsened or if she bled to death. She *was* going to see little Ethan.

They wheeled her to a narrow viewing area in the neonatology unit. Preemies in small incubators were lined up against one side, only the Plexiglas containers visible, some with numbers and surnames taped on the tops.

A nurse on the other side of the partition was moving the incubators aside.

Kathryn stood up in her wheelchair with the help of her nurse and tried to get a view of the incubator Robin was now turning around. She held her hand to her mouth, afraid that she might scream.

There he was, a wrinkled purplish form maybe only six inches long, his face and mouth buried in tubes, one miniature hand curled into a fist that seemed so minute it would probably disappear in a thimble. His eyes were taped shut. He wore a tiny blue skull cap and matching socks on his tiny feet.

Kathryn saw his leg move and then an arm, and she fell back into her chair, tears of anguish and joy blurring her vision. She tried frantically to wipe them away and, with the help of more tissues, finally recognized the index card taped to Plexiglas top.

It read, ~~Baby Lewis~~ and beneath it, in bold blue letters, ***Ethan Lydia Lewis. The miracle boy.***

PART FOUR

"We can't have full knowledge all at once. We must start by believing; then afterwards we may be led on to master the evidence for ourselves."

−Thomas Aquinas

Chapter Thirty

The ground thaw was late that May in Watertown, as was the ice melt on the two great lakes to the west of the city. The larger Lake Kampesca was largely free due to the spring boaters that sped through the waters. Its western position received more sunlight than the smaller more narrow Lake Pelican, situated southwest of the city.

Lydia had kept herself busy since the crash by spending more time at the newspaper. She decided to write a personal article about Flight 100, from a survivor's point of view. She had spent weeks researching all she could find about the flight and the crash, dipping into FAA and Civil Aeronautics Authority records, as well as documents released by Golden Airways and private satellite tracking companies.

She wasn't trying to find a reason for the crash as much as she was attempting to connect with the loved ones left behind. Their answers would never be answered, nor the pain in their hearts quelled.

The article was clear, sensitive and written with a subtle spiritual tone in its words. Other editors at the paper thought it beautifully written. It was picked up by Reuters and eventually landed on the third page of the Sunday *Washington Post*. She was honored by the email and correspondence it generated, many of them long-term survivors of disasters and accidents. Most poignant was a letter written by a mother whose son was aboard the United Airlines flight 93 during the 911 attacks. She thanked Lydia for presenting such a sensitive and articulate account of the disaster and for sharing such personal notes about her own son killed in the crash.

Lydia also wrote a short piece about her daughter Emma and the profound spirituality that had been part of her brief life. She posted it in the obit section of the paper, along with a picture of a bonneted Em standing in a meadow of blue cornflowers when she was five.

On sleepless nights Lydia would *communicate* with both Emma and Ethan, although she felt more receptive to her daughter's energy, which came to her in bursts of vivid presence. Ethan, on the other hand, seemed more dead, more removed from the life he'd once led.

It was an inexplicable distinction, just a feeling that her son had more fully passed on. She loved and missed them equally but Emma just seemed to be more alive on the other side. Maybe some souls, especially young ones, remained for a reason before passing to the other side.

Lydia came to terms with Emma's death in other ways. When she found the courage to enter her daughter's bedroom for the second time after Ethan's death, she sat down on the corner of the bed and looked about the room. She found Emma's favorite pair of jeans, socks and sweatshirt hanging on the backside of the closet door. It was what she had worn the day before she died. There were copies of spiritual readings by Chopra, Teilhard de Chardin, Tolle, the Dalai Lama and Neal Donald Walsch. Thumbing through some of the books, Lydia found margin notes written by Emma in the form of comments and explanations. There were also copies of the New Testament, the Hebrew Bible and the Koran.

She spent most of the morning in the room, reading, touching and smelling Emma's possessions. The sterling silver mirror that had once belonged to her own mother and given to Emma on her seventh birthday held strands of thin blonde hair. Lydia pulled them out and coiled the hair in her palm, raising it to her nose, a strong aching in her heart as she did so. This was all she had left of her living daughter.

She found the diary again and thumbed through its pages. The earliest entry was about a year ago, the last the morning of the day she died. How could she have missed it? Lydia wiped at her eyes and began reading the last entry.

Mom, I know that you are reading this and I am so glad you found it.

My little journeys began when I was just a young girl. I remember the first when you and Dad took me home from the circus in town. I don't know how old I was, but that night I floated out of my body and went on my first mission. It just happened. I don't think either of you noticed the next morning. I can only remember it as being in another world. I wasn't afraid and knew that there were to be more journeys ahead. And there were.

Please don't be alarmed when I tell you that I have traveled to many foreign places and times, some in this world, others in realms I don't really understand. They occur when terrible things are about to happen, like a car accident, someone about to be killed in a war, or a disaster like the plane crash Ethan died in. I have to be there as a witness and to give guidance to souls, especially those who are facing death for the first time.

I have been present at many disasters where souls must pass on. I'm not really sure but I think my purpose comes from a higher power, a whiter realm of light more soft and pure than the newly fallen snow I recall from my childhood.

Sometimes I seem to travel in time, awakening in future moments or those in the long-forgotten past. There is no distance between the past and the future because, I think, they occur at the same time but in different realms of awareness. (I know I'm freaking you out, Mom, but I don't mean to.)

We are all connected. We are the source and the continuance of our being. Death as we are taught does not exist. In one sense, death is birth. It's all about transference, love and connection.

With me it began with awareness. I learned to meditate to open up that awareness and then became my own awareness, seeking nothing but unknowingly aware of everything. It's like a very peaceful state of higher, pure consciousness.

I know you are missing me terribly, Mom. Soon Ethan and I will be together. Please believe that I am not far away. I fact, I am a part of you and you a part of me. I am always listening. Every time you breathe I can hear your heart. It beats still within me and also echoes throughout the universe. Ethan can hear it too.

Lydia put the diary down on her lap. She was trying to absorb what her daughter was telling her. She took a breath and imagined her heartbeat bouncing back to Emma and Ethan and beyond. She so strongly felt her daughter's presence she feared that all of it might disappear if she went back to reading. She waited for a few moments and then reopened the book.

I know you just paused, Mom. This a lot to wrap your head around. The thing is that you don't really have to understand what I am sharing with you. Just let your awareness handle it. Let its truth seek its place in your heart.

Thank you for following my wishes and having my body cremated. I don't know whether you and Dad have sprinkled my ashes on the lake yet but when you do please allow joy, love and celebration to be part of giving me away.

And, of course, let me go!

Love always amidst us,

Your daughter, Em.

Lydia put the diary down and took a deep breath. Tears were tilting from her eyes, and she blinked in an unsuccessful attempt to hold them back. She lay down on the bed and let the calming clarity of awareness fill her mind.

Memories of Emma came alive almost as if Lydia was watching a video. Bill was blowing up balloons for Em's birthday party. Children were playing in the small garden looking, from Lydia's viewpoint, like cherubim frolicking among the cornflowers, tossing ribbons and confetti in the air. Emma was sitting in a small rocking chair in the garden, her face adorned with painted colors and her hair filled with tiny tinsel-tied flowers. Lydia saw herself approach with the cake and five lit candles. She lowered it so that Em could blow them out.

With that one successful breath, the recollection ended.

Chapter Thirty One

Macy, Greg and Hattie were on the way to Watertown, South Dakota to be with Lydia and Bill for the spreading of Emma's ashes on the lake.

They had spent the night in a motel in Valentine, Nebraska, just south of the South Dakota border. Greg was the designated driver for the trip, which left the women time to read and play pinochle in the back seat.

Macy had taken her mom's car, a cream Infinity SUV, which she had retrieved from the parking area at the airport a month after the accident. It was much more comfortable than Greg's car and with more than ample space in the back for extra seating and luggage. Greg had taken fancy to the navigation system, which effortlessly directed him along their chosen route.

"I think you'd make a wonderful professional chauffeur, Macy said, leaning forward between the front seats. She kissed Greg on the cheek.

"Not my life's ambition. But no doubt you'd make a great *Miss Daisy*."

In three weeks Macy was scheduled to begin the full course at the Iowa workshop. She had completed her novel last month and had a tentative publisher recommended by one of her professors at Wellesley. She had held off pursuing that effort because she wasn't sure whether she would rather present the manuscript at the upcoming workshop.

Greg had decided to extend his studies at BU and pursue a Master's degree there. He had recently become interested in broadcast journalism, which Macy had assured him that he was exceedingly qualified for because of his intelligence and good looks.

Their relationship had deepened since the accident, Greg flying down from Boston every weekend or meeting up for secret trysts at getaway spots along the coasts in Massachusetts. During spring break they had spent the whole time in Macy's house, making love at all hours of the day, talking, sharing ideas about their futures and the possibility of combining those futures.

They had talked about marriage, at first in a youthful promissory way and then more seriously during the months following the accident. Although her mother had never met Greg, Macy felt her approbation in subtle and affirming ways.

A week before they left for South Dakota, Greg formally asked Macy for her hand in marriage, presenting her with a gold two-karat diamond. Jokingly, she had said, "Did you keep the receipt?" And then she'd kissed him, tears flowing, and watched as he slipped the ring on her finger.

Greg was brought up in a Catholic family and was surprised when Macy agreed to a mass and wedding at his family's church in Boston. They hadn't settled on a date, though Macy thought September would be a perfect month. Hattie had agreed to be her bridesmaid. Greg was still searching for a suitable best man.

With their educations on track, well in pursuit of their careers, and their nuptials around the corner, both felt challenged and excited by a sense that they were embarking upon a journey of discovery and long lasting happiness.

Hattie had played the role as Macy's surrogate mother and had spoken to both of them, reminding them of responsibilities, obligations and the realities they would encounter in their married lives. Then she had blessed them with her excited approval.

When they reached Chamberlain, just across the Missouri River, Macy called Lydia to report they had just three more hours of driving and would probably arrive in Watertown before six. Lydia was excited and told Macy that she had so much to share with her.

She said that the weather was going to be beautiful tomorrow. Bill had rented a boat and had purchased a plaque he had received permission to affix to one of the park benches around the lake. "Everyone will know Emma is in her final resting place," she said.

"We're so glad we'll be there," Macy said. "It's such an honor."

◆

The object came hurling toward them and in Greg's mind looked like some sort of a red missile, spinning, tumbling. He swerved hard to his right and onto the shoulder.

He missed the runaway bicycle but only by feet and quickly realized it must have fallen off the bike rack on the ladder of the old motorhome ahead of them.

Both Macy and Hattie were thrown hard in their seatbelts to the left side of the backseat.

"Goddammit!" Macy said.

Greg was intently watching in his rearview mirror to see if anyone behind had collided with the bike. It appeared that someone had about six cars behind them. The vehicle had run up onto the grassy median. Greg slowed down and was deciding whether to pull over and backtrack by foot to see if he could help. A big eighteen wheeler came up on his rear, blasting its horn, forcing Greg to accelerate.

"Are you trying to us get killed?" Macy cried out.

Greg explained what had happened and eventually calmed Macy down. Hattie had apparently seen the near-accident and explained what she saw to Macy.

"I'm sorry, honey," Macy said. "I didn't mean to sound like it was your fault."

"Mighty good reflexes, I'd say," Hattie chimed in.

The near-collision had released a surge of adrenalin in Greg's body. His heart was still pounding, his neck stiff, a slight feeling of nausea in his stomach. It was the first time in his young life that he had come so close to danger. He realized that if he'd run over the bike, the SUV might have overturned, injuring Macy and Hattie...or worse. Had he been looking at the navigation screen or turning the knob on the radio he might not have seen the bike tumbling towards him.

Sobered by his adventitious escape from disaster, Greg gripped the wheel firmly in both hands and drove on. He thought about this for the rest of the trip, weighing in his mind whether plain luck or some higher intervention had influenced the near-miss.

And what about other near-misses in life? Or those events that end in disaster...plane crashes, train wrecks, people standing on a balcony when it suddenly collapses?

Are they just random events or are they influenced by known factors? Is there a connection, a fundamental causation?

Or is it all just a matter of luck?

Hours later Greg's thoughts were still spinning and he was in such a daze, he missed the Watertown exit.

Chapter Thirty Two

Gars Strohm sat in the large conference room selected for a presentation of the executive summary of the National Transportation and Safety Board regarding the crash of Golden Airways flight 100.

He was the first to arrive and took his seat at the end of the conference table on which a dozen or so printed reports were arranged.

He opened the thick report to the first page.

NATIONAL TRANSPORTATION SAFETY BOARD
Public Meeting of May 18, 2015 (Information subject to editing)
Fatal Crash of Golden Airways Flight 100

This is a synopsis from the NTSB's report and does not include the Board's reasons for the conclusions, probable cause, and safety recommendations. The final report and pertinent safety recommendation letters will be distributed to the appropriate recipients as soon as possible. The attached information is subject to further review and editing.

Executive Summary

On December 11, 2014, at 1100:15 Mountain daylight time, Salt Lake ATCT lost voice contract with the aircraft, a Boeing 737-300, flying from San Francisco to Denver.

Last transponder contact with the plane was at 1130:37 Mountain daylight time by Montrose, Colorado ATC. This is assumed to be the moment of impact, which occurred at latitude 38.08539186, longitude -107.45470047 at an elevation of 3864 meters or approximately 12,677 feet. Data recorder information confirms the time and position upon the impact.

One hundred passengers and five crew members perished in the crash. There were no fatalities on the ground.

Strohm flipped through the report until he located what he was looking for.

Findings

1. The pilot and copilot were properly certificated and qualified. Fatigue and medical and pathological issues were not factors in this accident.

2. Both pilots initiated the standard procedure for onboard combustion, a condition not confirmed by inboard data but reported to the Salt Lake City ATCT. Their efforts to drop to a lower altitude is consistent with flight manual procedures for this situation.

3. Flameout on number 2 engine is confirmed by the onboard data recorder.

4. The pilot, not the copilot, was in control at the time of engine failure.

5. Lightning strikes did not factor in the downing of the plane.

6. Flight Data Recorder data indicates that one of the pilots incorrectly turned off the auto-feather control following flameout. Air drag on the starboard engine caused loss of stability, eventually pitching the aircraft into an unrecoverable stall and causing the final descent to its impact point.

7. It is the conclusion of this investigation that this error occurred inadvertently, not due to mechanical failure or pilot intention.

8. Findings of this panel do not suggest or infer liability by the airlines, the crew or the manufacturer of the aircraft.

There were fifteen more items on the list. Strohm looked up, the relief he felt not visible on the face, which bore an expression of a man who had repeatedly failed and had suffered great punitive consequences.

It wasn't the matter of liability, nor was it the fact of pilot error that added to Strohm's beaten look. He had still not come to terms with the fact that his airline had caused the deaths of so many people along with the emotional suffering of hundreds of survivors.

The relief he was trying to embrace was that there had been no intentional behavior by either pilot to indicate a suicide or terrorist motive.

Human error. An inadvertent action during a time of heightened stress was in Strohm's mind forgivable.

There had been thorough investigations into the personal lives of the pilots. Pilot Anderson's professional background review pointed to an exceptional flying record and no indicators to suggest anything but a normal, healthy personal life.

A check of the copilot's background, including his military experience, indicated a substance abuse problem involving alcohol consumption. Air Force records revealed an official reprimand for reporting to duty while under the influence. Texas motor vehicle records revealed a conviction for DWI. Both of these infractions occurred when the Granger was twenty-four years old, almost five years ago.

Due to the lack of human remains, tissue and blood testing could not be performed and, therefore, no conclusion could be drawn as to the copilot's condition during the flight. He had an uneventful flying record with Golden Airways.

Could Granger have been impaired during the flight? Strohm thought not. Captain Anderson was operating the plane during that critical period leading up to the crash. Everything but the evidence of an inboard fire was consistent with data from the flight recorder.

Golden Airways had paid out over twenty million dollars to survivors, including monies set aside for an education fund for the children of the passengers and crew.

The beleaguered CEO was determined to keep his company afloat. He, his accountants and lawyers had projected that full financial recovery could be achieved within eight years at the current rate of revenue. He would not consider employee layoffs or raising the cost of tickets. He did, though, sell off some his stock and cut his own salary nearly in half.

Gars Strohm got up from the conference table and went to one of the windows in the room. He pulled a section of the curtain aside and stared out into the morning drizzle. Dark clouds had rolled in from the west, a few causing the roll of thunder and intermittent lightning flashes. The inclement weather was just temporary, for the weather forecast promised partially sunny skies by the afternoon.

They needed the rain to wash away the lingering evidence of the long winter months. Stubborn mounds of what amounted to dirty granular ice could still be seen in the large parking area, hugging the base of lampposts and strewn along sections of curb.

For a few moments, along a margin of higher bright clouds, sunlight strained to make an appearance, piercing through its cloudy barricade in stunning luminous streaks.

Always a silver lining Strohm thought as he turned around and watched members of the NTSB begin to enter the room.

Chapter Thirty-Three

I watch them carry my urn to Pelican Lake. It is a brilliant Sunday afternoon in May with a cloudless sky. The surface of the water glimmers in trinkets of gold and silver, jewels of such brilliance that cause my mother to squint. There is a cool breeze that occasionally skims across the surface of the lake, leaving a quivering glimpse of presence in its wake.

My mother and father are handling their grief well as they boat out of the marina and head to the center of the lake.

Macy and Greg are there. Their presence gives my parents comfort and faith in love, the bond that can heal those with false choice in their hearts. It is from love of self that faith flows and connects us all by one infinite thread of meaning.

Some have asked about alternate realities, whether they exist or not. They do to those whose awareness allows those realities. If it is real to you then that's all that counts. What is real is only true after you have made the choice to make it real.

All life forms make choices. Some humans are aware of their choice, others not. Remember that the tree, the growing blade of grass, the stone in a gurgling brook and all inanimate matter have choices to exist or not.

There are many, many levels of existence, more than one human mind could possibly comprehend. To help you understand this, remember that all life continues, some experiences occurring simultaneously, others on different levels and plains of consciousness. Cessation cannot occur in the real realm and only exists as a concept for human need and comfort.

Life is boundless. It has no beginning or end. Imagine it as rainfall, a trickle of water, a brook, a river, an estuary and an ocean, where it rises again, an endless continuance.

Who am I? Just an observer who exists to help others in achieving awareness. I have no power, no energy beyond what love and choice have afforded me. I exist because many of you want me to. I cannot intervene but I can guide and provide comfort during difficult transitions.

Lastly and most importantly, I may not exist to those who are committed to absolute faith, be it a religion or a way of living that does not encourage the awareness of personal choice. Each of us exists at varying levels of consciousness and awareness, and a choice to trust in the wonder of blind faith is a privilege with many benefits and rewards.

Remember that there is no right or wrong way.

I have shared with Macy that her mother returned and joined Ethan on the other side. One is waiting to be born.

Soon my mother will not feel my presence as strongly as she does now. We all linger after we die. While she will always miss me, she will eventually let me go in small measures of acceptance and comfort.

And I shall let her go, too.

My Dad is carrying the small urn, his hands holding it as if it were a precious gold ornament or a lifetime of good memories. Greg is steering the outboard, Macy in the seat in front of him. The breeze ruffles his thick brown hair, rich with youth and the luster of promise.

They stop in the middle of Pelican Lake, the lake I would always see through the window above my bed, a distant magical reflection that I used to concentrate when I was meditating.

It is a perfect spot for my earthly remains, and I am so happy they are honoring my wishes.

Only Hattie is truly aware of my presence. We go back a long way. Some of you may have realized that I was once her daughter too. And she was my mother in a long ago present. Believe me, there's no coincidence to consider for all life is unbroken and all-connected. Everything happens for a purpose, a reason that may not be real to some, but exists as truth to those of higher awareness.

My mother and father are holding the urn together, my mother's hands more delicate and attractive than I ever remember. They remove the top. They are saying a prayer together. After they finish they swing the urn over the side, spilling my ashes and causing a small cloud of swirling dust as the breeze lifts it and I relish in the vision of myself settling peacefully over the surface of these quiet waters.

My mother's heart seems to lift as she watches the last traces of my bodily experience settle forever over my temporary home. Sunlight is spilling over me on the water's surface.

Of course I will rise up again, lifted by the radiance of sunlight, and the breeze will carry me up to where I existed, a droplet of moisture, where I will gather and fall upon other waters, meadows and the invisible footprints of other travelers to come.

The story goes on and on.

Oh but I wish you were here, in this endless moment, just to be, to breathe in the purity of absolute love and unbroken awareness.

You would understand that death is not what you have always thought it to be, not an ending but part of an incredible, profound continuance.

There is nothing to fear.

You would see that wars and hatred are the result of fear and unawareness. They exist for many reasons, some of them necessary, for they are part of the cohesive tension of human experience. But there are visionaries, beings of boundless awareness who are here now, growing and leading in quiet ways.

The presence of future and past are now, in this moment. You are not separated from youth, nor from old age, for they are one. All existence is one.

One day this will be the only truth you know.

One day.

A cormorant is skimming across the surface of the lake, cumbersome, the tips of its wings trailing in the calm, shimmering waters. It looks like it cannot achieve flight. And then suddenly it lifts, inches above the surface and then powerfully rises, banking to its right over the southern shoreline.

My mother is following the majestic bird and is smiling. She knows. She is finally aware.

I will always be there for her as I am for you, a shimmering presence striving for your awareness.

Always there.

Knowing in our hearts that all our paths will meet on the other side.

Again.

Epilogue

I t hadn't happened yet. But the fierce joy of its journey propelled it fast through pungent waters, past the others, upward, thriving within a nebula of warm, nourishing fluid, forward towards its other self and the esoteric lode of its creation.

At last joined, it was aware at an instinctive level that now its journey was out of its hands, beyond that solitary joy for survival. It tried to comprehend its burgeoning self, its globule of undifferentiated senses, its tiny storm of electrical pulses, the coursing and gushing of private nutrients, the slow, methodical acceleration of itself toward a magnificent expulsion.

Just before it was born, as its lungs slowly emptied, prepared for that brash and urgent first breath, an instant cognizance of its place in the universe exploded within its brain, in a region it would not use again until its death, an awakening so astonishing and instant it would result in a cry of rage and joy so profound its echo would serve as a clarion call to all those left behind.

You could see it in the infant's eyes, an evolutionary wink of wisdom fading against the unrelenting manipulation of human contact and love.

A soul, a physicality, a presence born into a time of its choosing.

Sensing the fuzzy image of its mother, reacting to the pheromone blooming in its senses, the infant opened wide its eyes.

And then it smiled.

Pure, naked joy.

Birth just like death, neither beginning or ending.